"I'd love to hear about life—" His phone buzz and he paused midsentence.

Caroline took advantage of his distraction and pushed away from the table. It was one thing to be cordial. It was something else to try to resume a relationship. The chair legs scraped against the rustic wooden floorboards.

"Unfortunately, I've got to return to work. I'm teaching a yoga class in twenty minutes. But it's been nice to see you and to meet Becca. And I do appreciate the apology."

She waved to them both and grabbed her cup to throw away.

"Caroline, wait!" Jared half rose from the table. "Please. I'd like to catch up on your life."

"Jared, what's the point? Our lives are different. You're in LA, I'm here. You're busy. Don't you think it's better if we leave the past in the past?"

"Come on. One dinner before Pesach. Please? It's my chance to hang out with an adult. You won't deny me that pleasure, will you?"

She groaned and gripped the back of the walnut chair. "Don't give me the puppy dog eyes." He didn't think she'd fall for that, did he? As if his deep blue eyes could erase their past...and then he grinned.

How did anyone resist him?

Dear Reader,

We all have responsibilities—to our parents, children, spouses, partners or friends. Some of those responsibilities we take on willingly and happily; others are thrust upon us. Either way, we carry them out because we know that the only way life works is when we all pitch in together.

As we handle those obligations, our lives and our plans change. Sometimes we set aside our dreams for something more practical. Our lives go in a completely different direction than we imagined. And along the way, we discover something even more magical than we thought possible.

That's just what happens to Caroline Weiss and Jared Leiman. Their dreams didn't quite work out as they planned. From the height of popularity and success to the depths of suffering and betrayal, these two people must learn to forgive themselves before they can hope to find a new happily-ever-after. And just maybe an adorable toddler can help them discover each other again.

Get ready to celebrate Passover as you dive into this second chance romance. You never know what you might discover as you join the hottest fundraiser of the season. I hope you enjoy Caroline and Jared's story!

Jennifer Wilck

MATZAH BALL BLUES

JENNIFER WILCK

HARLEQUIN
SPECIAL
EDITION

Recycling programs for this product may not exist in your area.

ISBN-13: 978-1-335-59461-7

Matzah Ball Blues

Harlequin Enterprises ULC
22 Adelaide St. West, 41st Floor
Toronto, Ontario M5H 4E3, Canada
www.Harlequin.com

Printed in Lithuania

MIX
Paper | Supporting responsible forestry
FSC® C021394

Jennifer Wilck is an award-winning contemporary romance author for readers who are passionate about love, laughter and happily-ever-after. Known for writing both Jewish and non-Jewish romances, she features damaged heroes, sassy and independent heroines, witty banter, yummy food and hot chemistry in her books. She believes humor is the only way to get through the day and does not believe in sharing her chocolate. You can find her at www.jenniferwilck.com.

Books by Jennifer Wilck

Harlequin Special Edition

Holidays, Heart and Chutzpah

Home for the Challah Days
Matzah Ball Blues

Visit the Author Profile page at Harlequin.com.

To Michael—no matter how our lives have changed,
I'd choose you over and over again.

Chapter One

"Caroline, this will be the trip of a lifetime."

The owner of The Flighty Mermaid Travel Agency handed Caroline Weiss brochures with beautiful color photos of Croatia, Bosnia and Herzegovina, and Greece. Deep blue ocean water, blinding white buildings, Moorish Revival architecture, arched bridges, and craggy mountains beckoned. Caroline's heartbeat quickened. She'd waited eight years for this trip. It was supposed to be her college graduation gift, when her life plans included an athletic scholarship to a Big Ten university. Instead, she'd taken classes from home as a part-time student, while taking care of her mother, who died of cancer three years ago. Now that she'd finally paid off the last of the medical bills, her trip was in reach. The next few months, until May and the day of her departure, couldn't come fast enough.

"Thank you, Georgia," she said. Her voice shook with giddiness. "I can't believe I've organized this trip. Part of me keeps waiting for the other shoe to drop."

The purple-haired woman gave her a motherly hug around the shoulders as she accompanied her to the front door of her office. Georgia's bangle bracelets jingled and her colorful boho skirt swayed with every movement. "I know, honey. But your airline tickets and hotels are booked, your transportation in-country is reserved, your tours and tickets are set, and nothing will get in the way of your dream. Trust me."

Caroline waved goodbye and strode down the street of

Browerville, NJ, on her way to work at the Jewish Community Center and nodded at the people she passed on Main Street. Midmorning on a weekday, young parents pushed strollers on the sidewalks and retirees enjoyed the brisk spring sunshine. Some paused to gaze in shop windows or entered or exited various shops and offices. The town Caroline had spent her entire life in was pretty, if predictable. Rose-colored buds covered the trees, ready to sprout into new green leaves. She inhaled. The first hints of spring tickled her nose and teased her with the new growth to come, as if imitating the approach of her new life as well. Her feet flew over the pavement in her excitement. She couldn't wait to explore the new cities she'd visit this summer.

But first, she needed a quick stop at the grocery store. The JCC's little juice bar with refrigerated energy drinks was running low, and she liked to keep it stocked in case any of the seniors needed an energy boost during class. She made a beeline to the health food aisle. Music played over the loudspeaker, something from Mamma Mia. Didn't that take place in the Greek Isles? What were the odds?

As she sang under her breath, she passed a man pushing a grocery cart. The little legs of a toddler swung into her view. Something about men with babies or little children warmed her heart. She turned down the correct aisle and filled her cart with some of the more popular drinks before she maneuvered her way toward the cashiers. The store was filled with morning shoppers, and she cut through the diaper aisle to skirt traffic. Ahead of her, another cart entered the aisle from the opposite direction.

The man with the toddler.

A few more steps, and she froze.

Jared Leiman.

An older, taller, broader, and harder version of the boy she'd dated in high school. She hadn't seen him since he broke her heart the summer after their sophomore year of college. Her mouth dried, and she shut it. Mouth breathers were unattractive. Jared, however, wasn't. He was gorgeous.

And he has a kid.

Chocolate-brown hair brushed away from his forehead. When she dated him, it had been unruly, always falling across his forehead. Deep blue eyes. They turned gray when he was angry and more midnight blue when passionate. Square jaw. It was less defined when he was younger. Broad shoulders, broader now and which her five-foot-five frame reached, as opposed to in high school, when she'd come up to his ear. He'd had a growth spurt. Large square hands gripped the cart as he stopped at the last second before he crashed into her.

"Sorry." He winced. "I was looking at the diapers. Didn't see you."

"Clearly."

He cocked his head to the side before his expression brightened in recognition. "Caroline Weiss. Wow."

Those three words oozed arrogance and sex appeal, made her knees tremble, and irritated her to no end. You know what else irritated her? His daughter. Not her, specifically, but her existence. Despite all rational thought that told her otherwise, the only thing she could think of at this moment was that he'd chosen to settle down and have a family with someone other than her. Guess his claims that he didn't want to be tied down with responsibility meant he didn't want to be tied to *her*.

"How are you, Jared?" A sliver of pleasure that she could still maintain her composure when her ex-boyfriend confronted her slithered along her spine.

"Out of my depth. I don't suppose you know anything about diapers?" he asked, a helpless look on his face.

"Sorry, no."

"How have you been?" he asked. "I cannot believe—"

His daughter fussed at the same time his phone buzzed. His eyebrows gathered in. "I'm sorry, I'd love to catch up, but…"

Caroline shook her head. "I've got to get to work anyway. Good luck."

Before he could say anything else, she made her escape. Of all the people to run into, it had to be him. Thoughts of Jared dulled Caroline's earlier excitement about her vacation as she arrived at the JCC. She entered the staff locker room and stripped down to her workout clothes—pink-and-black-striped leggings and a matching bright pink tank top—and twisted her light brown hair into a ponytail. She checked herself in the mirror and wondered what Jared saw when he looked at her. The lines of sadness—caused by her mom's illness—had faded. For the first time in ages, she looked happier. Not that Jared would notice. She doubted he'd noticed much about her.

With a quiet groan, she made her way into the bright workout room and put on some upbeat music as her clients entered. If anything could get her mind off Jared, it was this class. Most of her clients were in their seventies or older, looking to improve their health with moderate activity. They attended her workout classes every week, as much for the socializing as for the exercise.

"Hi, Hildie. Hey there, Artie." She greeted them by name as they entered, made sure they brought filled water bottles, and asked about their day.

"Caroline, doll, you look beautiful today," Martina said as she entered.

"Thank you. You do as well."

"Eh, I always do." She winked. "Got a new man?"

Caroline paused. "I've sworn off men."

"Ladies never swear, dear."

Caroline turned to an older gentleman. "Bob, how's the back?" she asked.

"A little sore, but much better."

"Please be careful and modify anything you need. Exercise is good, but I don't want you to get hurt."

She started her class with light warm-ups before she moved into the regular exercise program. When the routine ended, everyone hung around to schmooze before they returned to their homes. Once it cleared out, Caroline sank to the floor and leaned against the cinder block wall. Jared Leiman. In high school, she'd been head over heels in love with the guy. They'd discussed marriage, but that was before he'd shown his true colors. After two years at his fancy college, he'd changed his mind, telling her his dreams were too big to waste on Browerville and he didn't want to settle down. She could have understood that if he'd kept his promise of staying in touch and maintaining their friendship. But he'd ghosted her, never asking how she was or if he could help during those darkest days when her mom was sick.

Although the hurt had faded, and only a trace of its bitter aftertaste remained, her curiosity returned in full force. Jared had a baby! There was so much more she wanted to know.

What kind of guardian forgets diapers?

Berating himself for his lack of preparation, Jared Leiman pushed the shopping cart with his two-year-old niece along the diaper aisle and pocketed his phone. He scanned the brands. Although the store offered several choices, it didn't carry what his former nanny favored—some organic, biodegradable, granola brand, exclusive to California—and he was at a loss as to which replacement to get. Caroline wasn't any help, not that he'd expected it of her.

He groaned in exasperation. What kind of person didn't recognize his high school girlfriend? He shouldn't have been surprised to run into her, yet the sight of her threw him. The last time he'd seen her, his sophomore year of college, he hadn't treated her well. She'd grown more beautiful. He was used to his actress clients whose entire lives revolved around their careers and their artificial looks. Somehow, Caroline's appearance was fresher, more natural.

He pulled out his phone once again, ready to dial the nanny for advice, but paused. She'd quit and wouldn't be any help. Besides, he'd graduated top of his Ivy League university, number one in his law school, and was the most sought-after entertainment lawyer in LA. One small human's diaper needs weren't beyond him, were they?

His niece grabbed his hand and squeezed his finger. He looked at her, and she gave him a smile.

His heart pounded in panic. "What do you need, little one?"

Although he'd been her guardian since his brother and sister-in-law's deaths a year ago, this was his first trip alone with her. He'd left most of her care to the nanny he'd hired, and he was clueless. He scanned the aisle for someone to help him out, but no one was around. What kind of town had an empty diaper aisle in the middle of the morning? Did no one run out of diapers?

If his colleagues could see him now.

If his colleagues saw him now, they'd steal his clients away from him, confident he'd lost his edge. He shuddered at the thought. He hadn't lost his edge, he'd just... He didn't know what. But sometime between his brother's death, his niece coming to live with him, and his nanny quitting, he'd lost his ability to juggle responsibilities. He couldn't focus on work, didn't understand how to be a father-uncle, and for the first time in his life, he'd panicked. So, he'd taken an extended time off and come home to regroup, even if he didn't tell anyone else his reasons. Let his parents think he was here for a much-needed visit. Let his office think it was a long-overdue vacation. He'd spend time with his family for Passover, figure himself out, and return to LA better than ever. Or he hoped.

Speaking of LA, someone in his extensive client list must have children. He scrolled through his contacts. Angelina Jolie had six, she'd know what diaper brand to buy. No, her kids were too old. Alec Baldwin had a boatload of little ones. He scrolled, ready to hit dial when a woman with a baby came down the aisle.

Thank God.

"Excuse me," he said.

She looked up, a wary look on her bare face until she noticed Becca. "Yes?"

"I need diapers, and well…" he shrugged.

She nodded in sympathy, her messy bun bobbing. "It can be overwhelming, I know. Your wife didn't tell you what brand to buy?"

He was about to explain he didn't have a wife, but then he'd have to explain about his brother and sister-in-law. His chest tightened. It never occurred to them to fill him in on their diaper preferences.

"No, unfortunately."

"Hmm." She glanced at Becca, asked her age and weight, and reached for a box. "Why don't you try these? We like them."

"Thanks, I will."

With a sigh of relief, he paid for the small package and returned to his car. This time, it took him three tries to strap Becca into her car seat, plus the four extra checks he made to ensure she was protected. At the airport rental-car office, it had taken him a half an hour. Progress.

As he drove the tree-lined streets to his childhood home, he thought once again about Caroline. Babbling from the back of the car made him glance in the rearview mirror. Becca's blue eyes met his.

Caroline's eyes were also blue, but they were lighter than Becca's dark blue ones, and there was depth to them, as if he could see into her soul if he looked hard enough. He'd ended things during college. At the time, he wasn't ready for a long-distance commitment, especially when the trajectory of their lives was different. The amount of responsibility she had for her mother scared him. He hadn't been ready, and the more he'd talked to Caroline, the more afraid he'd become of losing his career goals. Now older and more mature, he realized what a selfish jerk he'd been. He'd failed her when she needed him most. Although she probably couldn't care less about him, he wished he'd talked to her longer today, if for no other reason than to apologize.

He pulled into the driveway of his parents' two-story colonial house and sighed with relief to have reached his destination. He left his luggage in the car, unstrapped Becca, and took her out of the car.

"Let's go see Grandma and Grandpa."

The house sat at the end of a quiet cul-de-sac. Budding, mature oak and maple trees surrounded it. The grass was still dormant from winter, and there were small piles of snow which had yet to melt. The brisk air made him wish he'd brought a heavier jacket, and he added it to the list of things he'd have to buy for Becca. Although she was wrapped in four blankets, he didn't want her to catch cold.

She strained against him. "Down, down!"

If he put her down, she'd be cold. With that in mind, he strode up the porch steps, eager to get inside where it was warm. "Knock, knock," he yelled as he opened the door.

Jared's mother, gray hair pulled into a ponytail, rushed into the foyer. "Oh my goodness, what a *punim*!" She stroked Becca's cheek as he held her, reverting to Yiddish as she did whenever she grew emotional.

Her gaze pierced Jared and her green eyes misted. "She's the spitting image of Noah."

Grief stabbed him, as it often did when he looked at the mirror image of his brother. Usually, he avoided thinking about what he'd lost by turning Becca over to the nanny and burying himself in work. But not this time. His throat clogged.

"Yeah." He forced out the single syllable.

Becca stared wide-eyed at her grandmother before she grabbed a stray lock of her gray hair. Jared jumped, ready to pull her hand away before she could tug, but his mother waved him away. She took her granddaughter in her arms and loosened the toddler's grip.

"It's soft, isn't it?" she asked Becca, her voice gentle.

"Soff," Becca echoed.

She stroked Becca's hair and ran her perfectly manicured hands through her brown curls. "Like yours."

As if she understood, Becca touched her grandmother's hair and then her own hair before she rested her head on her grandmother's shoulder.

Jared stared. "Smart like Noah, too," he whispered.

The smile on his mother's face took the edge off the pain when he thought about his brother. It had been too long since he'd seen it. They all still grieved.

"Come sit," his mother said. "How was your trip? Dad ran out to buy a few things I said we needed, but he'll be home soon. In the meantime, let's get this one settled."

Leading the way into the living room, she sat on the sofa. The gray-painted room with white curtains and deep blue furnishings was homey. Soft throw blankets rested on each armrest, family photos decorated the walls, and favorite biographies and historical fiction filled the shelves. The brick fireplace was unlit, but logs were arranged inside, as if waiting for a match. Jared remembered family game nights in front of that fire, where he battled with his brother for dominance. His chest tightened. No matter how often they'd argued, he'd never wanted to be an only child.

"Uneventful, considering I traveled with a toddler." His phone buzzed with a text, and he frowned before he put it aside.

His mother clucked in sympathy. "I'll bet it wasn't what you're used to."

He thought about the private jets he flew, owned by either his law firm or his clients, and marveled how much his situation had changed since he left home. Even first class on a commercial flight was a new experience.

"I'm glad you're here." His mother held Becca on her lap on the sofa.

She didn't squirm like usual. His niece was content, and the part of him that was hyperalert to her every breath relaxed.

He eased into the upholstered chair next to them. "Me too. I'm sorry it's been so long."

His mother grasped his arm. "Since the funeral." She looked away and swallowed. "You don't have to apologize. I know how busy you've been. But it's nice to see you two. Spending Passover together, well…"

He reached over and squeezed her hand. His brother and sister-in-law died a year ago, but he hadn't returned for any of the holidays. Instead, his parents flew out to him. Guilt wracked him. He'd avoided long trips home as much as possible, forgetting about how his parents might have needed him here.

"I'm sorry," he said, again. It wasn't enough, but it was all he could manage right now.

His mother nodded. She jiggled her knee and made Becca giggle. "This little one is the cutest!" She kissed her granddaughter's neck.

Jared marveled at Becca's reaction to the grandmother she hadn't seen in months. She was more at ease with his mother than she was with him.

His phone buzzed again, and he glanced at it before he returned his attention to his mother.

"I thought we could go to the playground later today," she said. "And they have toddler programs at the JCC we can check out while you're here. Dad and I have memberships there. It's not a problem."

"Sure. Lucinda takes her to the playground near our home all the time."

His mother raised an eyebrow. Uh-oh. He remembered that look from when he was a kid. It was directed at either him or Noah, rarely their dad. Probably because his dad was too smart to become the object of her disappointment. He and his brother got the look whenever they fought about something stupid—like something being "unfair"—and a lecture always followed. What had he done now?

"Lucinda? Your nanny? What about you? Don't you take her to the park?"

"I work, Mom. My clients expect me to be on call for them whenever they need me." He glanced at his watch.

"So does Becca."

His hackles rose. "You think I'm a bad guardian?"

His mother bit her lip. "How are the adoption papers coming?"

He swallowed. They were at home on his desk. "They're coming."

This time, his mother raised her other eyebrow.

"Priorities are like a deck of cards, Jared. Sometimes you have to shuffle the deck to play the hand you're meant to have."

He reached for Becca's legs and squeezed her chubby thighs, eliciting another squeal from her.

What if the deck was stacked against you?

Later that evening, Caroline let herself into her house, toed off her sneakers, and shuffled through the mail. Although she'd paid off all her mother's medical debts, she still held her breath every time she made her initial scan of the postal delivery. Some habits would never disappear.

Her phone rang as she cooked dinner.

"Hey, Sarah, how did you know I needed to talk to you?"

Sarah Abrams was a high school friend who returned to

Browerville after ten years away. Now their relationship was stronger than ever, and Caroline considered her one of her best friends.

"Psychic, I guess. Or Aaron mentioned he'd seen you in town. Nothing's wrong, is there?"

Aaron, her boyfriend, owned the most popular deli in town.

"Not in the way you mean, no. But life is crazy. My trip, running into Jared Leiman, planning programs for the dementia patients—"

"Wait, you ran into Jared? Tell me what happened!"

Caroline grabbed a package of frozen wontons and poured oil in a small pan.

"There's not much to tell—" okay, she was a liar "—I want to hear about your conference."

"Fascinating, exhausting. But I won't let you change the subject on me. Where did you see him?"

"I don't want to change the subject, either. Did you learn anything related to the JCC?" Sarah worked for the Jewish Federation, which oversaw the JCC.

"Ugh, you're driving me nuts. Clearly, we have to get together to discuss everything, which is tricky because with budget season, my hours are ridiculous."

With the oil heated, Caroline added the wontons to the pan and covered it. "That reminds me, I need to turn in my list of equipment for the gym before the budget is finalized, as well as whatever else I need for next year's senior programs."

Sarah cleared her throat.

"Uh-oh," Caroline said. "Did you hear something about funding?"

"Rumblings," Sarah said. "You know how it is at this time of year."

"I hate this part of the job."

"You and me both. Let's put something on the calendar

before my schedule blows up. Do you want to come over and order takeout?"

Sarah was notorious for her inability to cook. "Oh, different takeout menus from mine. That'll be a treat."

Sarah laughed. "Come over around six thirty."

When they finished, Caroline's wontons were ready.

She turned on the TV as she sat to eat. Scanning the channels, she paused on a dance competition reality show before she continued. A crime drama enticed her, but then she discovered a documentary on Greece.

"Perfect timing," she muttered. Reaching for her laptop, she pulled up her notes on her vacation and settled in to watch.

The host of the show interviewed the owner of a small hotel, and Caroline stared. She couldn't decide which was more beautiful—the immaculate hotel, steps away from the Acropolis, or the dark-haired man who owned the place. He laughed at something the documentary host said, and Caroline's memory flashed to Jared.

The Greek hotel owner was shorter and stockier than her ex, with jet-black hair and gleaming white teeth. Jared was taller, with broad shoulders and wavy dark hair. But the cut of their jaws and their bearings were similar.

"Ugh!"

Why did thoughts of Jared pop into her mind now? She shouldn't waste any more time on him. If she'd learned anything over the last ten years, it was he didn't care about her in the same way she'd cared about him. On the nights when she was scared and alone, he'd been out with friends, or doing whatever one did in college. He'd called a few times, but never caught up with her in person, although he'd said he would. She'd nursed her mom, dealt with insurance and unpaid bills, and mourned her mom's death while he'd studied, partied, and built his future. Without her.

She mentally poked the wound and found it didn't hurt the

way it used to. If she hadn't run into him today, she wouldn't have thought about him at all. Returning her attention to the TV, she listened to the tour guide describe an olive farm. She'd waited for so long for this trip. At times, it had been the one thing keeping her going as she dealt with the responsibility of caring for her mom. A twinge of guilt hit her. She loved her mom and cherished the time they'd spent together. But as her sole caretaker, with no one else to help her, she'd sometimes wished it wasn't just the two of them. Was that wrong?

"I'm sorry, Mom," she whispered. "I love you."

She straightened her spine. No more guilt about her mom, and no more thoughts of Jared.

For once, she was going to focus on herself.

Chapter Two

He'd planned for everything except for how many diapers one toddler went through in a day, Jared thought to himself that evening as he made his second trip to the grocery store. While the woman who helped him choose out the correct size was a godsend, she hadn't mentioned more was better when he'd selected the one small package of diapers.

His mom took one look at what he'd purchased and did a double take. So back to the store he went. As nice as it was to see his mom, he was a little bit grateful for the break away, however brief. She'd always been one to speak her mind. In fact, both of his parents were quick to give their thoughts on anything and everything. He suspected his confidence came from them. Still, listening to her opinions on priorities the second he'd walked in the door was a little more than he could handle. Especially since he didn't know what his priorities were. Here he was, in aisle seven, for the second time that day, a little too relieved.

"Jared?"

The sound of his name pulled him out of his self-reflection, and he turned. "Eli?"

The short man's round face broadened into a grin. "Son of a gun, I thought it was you."

The two men gave a one-armed hug, stepped back, and examined each other. "It's been ages," Jared said. He and Eli were on the debate club in high school together. Eli was the

VP; Jared was President. "But I'd recognize you and your voice anywhere."

"What are you doing here?" Jared asked. "Last I heard you got your master's?" He couldn't remember in what, though. They'd been friends in high school but lost touch.

"Architecture. I work in sustainability, with offices in New York and Browerville." He handed him a business card, and Jared whistled.

"Nice. So, you live…?"

"My husband and I split our time between Manhattan and here. What about you? I thought you were in LA."

Jared nodded. "Home, visiting my family." His phone buzzed, but he ignored it.

Eli sobered. "Hey, I was sorry to hear about your brother."

Jared swallowed. "Thanks, it's been tough. I'm guardian of my niece now."

A flash of respect crossed Eli's face. "Wow, big lifestyle change. Good for you for stepping up. You'll be a great dad."

Jared's body jolted. A dad? He still couldn't wrap his brain around it. When he'd pictured himself as a father, it was always sometime in the future, with a wife and a plan. Not thrust into the role of a single parent. But his friend looked at him with such confidence, he didn't think he could confess his fears. Not in the middle of the diaper aisle.

"Hey, we should get together before you leave," Eli said. "I play racquetball at the JCC in the mornings when I'm here. Want to join me tomorrow? I've got a court reserved for seven."

Becca was an early riser. By seven in the morning, the nanny always ensured she was dressed and fed. He wasn't as adept at morning schedules, but he'd bet his mother would love the chance. *Let me ask my mother.* He groaned to himself. Did everyone turn into a teenager when they returned to their hometown?

"Sounds good. I could use the chance to burn off some energy." He exchanged numbers with Eli, paid for the diapers, and returned to his car, where he answered the client texts that'd arrived while he shopped. Then he returned home.

When he walked in the house, little-girl giggles greeted him. He couldn't help but smile at his mother on the floor, playing with Becca.

"Hey there." He knelt on the Berber carpet next to his niece. He chucked her under the chin, perpetually surprised how soft her skin was. She babbled at him, inserting actual words here and there, and handing him a wooden block.

"Bock," she said.

Tousling her hair, he thanked her before he returned the block to her and addressed his mother.

"Would you mind handling her tomorrow morning? I ran into Eli Jacobs at the store, and he invited me to play racquetball with him at seven."

The grin his mother gave him put him at ease. "Of course! I'd love to take care of her." She stood and gave him a hug. "I'm glad you're reconnecting with people."

She didn't say anything else, but Jared saw the unspoken thoughts in her posture. His mother would like nothing better than for Becca and him to move back home. But the idea was a fantasy. His career was in LA. While he could promise to visit more often, he would never upend his life and return here.

Caroline blocked the sun with her arm, squeezed her eyelids closed, and rolled over in her queen-size bed. It was awfully bright this early in the morning.

With a start, she jumped out of bed and reached for her phone.

"No, no, no," she cried as it flashed 7:22 a.m.

She scrolled to the alarm app, and saw she'd never set it before bed.

She'd spent last night immersed in the Greek leg of her vacation, thanks to that documentary she'd watched, and must have forgotten to set her alarm. Now she had twenty minutes before her first class. She raced around her room, yanked off her pajamas, and grabbed leggings and a top for her first class of the morning—seniors with mobility issues.

So much for running, breakfast, or easing into the day. She brushed her teeth and rushed out the door as she finger-combed her hair. No matter how excited she might be for her vacation, she needed to keep her job to afford it.

Halfway to work, she remembered she had scheduled a meeting with her boss to discuss her budget. *Crap!* She didn't have time to return home and put together a more professional outfit, and she said a silent prayer and hoped she had left a spare one to use at the office.

Rounding the corner in the hallway of the JCC, she gasped and dodged to avoid two guys in athletic gear.

"Sorry!" Her stomach dropped. Jared and another guy who looked familiar stood there, sweat dripping down their faces.

"It feels like you're stalking me," she said.

Concern marred the other guy's face, while Jared looked amused. "What are the odds we'd both exercise here?"

Caroline was about to correct his assumption but stopped. She didn't have time to have the what-are-you-doing-now conversation.

"Well, this is the only JCC in town," she said. "I'm late for class, but one of these days we'll have to catch up." The words popped out without any forethought. She cringed inwardly and hoped he'd take it as an off-the-cuff remark. She turned to leave.

Jared's voice stopped her. "What about now? Feel like play-ing hooky and grabbing a cup of coffee?" He glanced at his watch.

She spun around, her face warm. In high school, they'd snuck off to spend time together—or kiss—when they should have been in class. Did he remember those times, too? She looked for a sign that he remembered—a glimmer of wicked-ness, a quirk of a brow, something. But she couldn't read him.

"I'm the instructor. I can't miss it." Before she said any-thing else she might regret, she waved and rushed to class.

Although her body performed all the requisite moves in the exercise class, and her mouth uttered words of encouragement to her clients, her mind was elsewhere.

This was twice she'd bumped into Jared. Although her stalker comment was a joke, she wondered. Were the fates against her? Part of her objected to his assumption she was taking an exercise class rather than leading it. Her rational side, however, reminded herself it was an honest mistake. He knew nothing about her life. He was a high-powered attorney. Now that she'd told him she was an exercise instructor—even though she was more than that—he'd probably want nothing to do with her. She scoffed in disgust. She shouldn't let him occupy her headspace rent-free, no matter how curious she was about his life.

When class ended, she went to her office and relief flooded through her when she found a spare set of clothes in her locker. She changed into them, fixed her hair, applied makeup, and walked to her boss's office.

"Doug?" She knocked on the door frame and waited until he motioned her inside.

"Come on in, Caroline. Sit. Gimme a second to finish some-thing. Sorry, the day's been crazy."

She sat across from the forty-something-year-old man. He was an easy guy to work for and had noticed her drive and determination from the moment he hired her. He'd taken her under his wing and gotten her involved in other areas of the JCC, not just the athletic department. She owed her career and her promised promotion to assistant program director to him.

"No problem."

After a few minutes, he shut his laptop and faced her. "Okay, I'm all yours."

She pulled a sheet of paper out of her folder. "I wanted to discuss equipment and supply needs before you finalize the budget. Here's my itemized list for athletics and senior programming, with estimated costs, as well as projected ROI."

Handing him the paper, she glanced around the Spartan office. In all the years she'd known her boss, he'd never decorated, other than a photo or two of his wife and kids. Someday, when she had an office, she'd fill it with photos of all the places she planned to travel.

Doug cleared his throat, and Caroline returned her attention to him. He didn't look at the list.

He folded his arms on his desk and leaned forward. "I'm afraid I have some bad news, Caroline. I was going to call you in later to discuss it, but since you're here, we might as well get it over with."

Caroline's throat tightened.

"We can't increase our budget allowance this year," he said. "In fact, we have to make cuts. We're facing a severe shortfall in funds. I'm not sure in this next fiscal year I can give you either your budget and supply needs, or that promotion I promised you. I had to fight to keep you on."

Shock and disappointment flooded through her. As much as she loved her athletics instruction, she'd found her calling in the programs she planned for seniors and her anticipated expanded role there. She fisted her hands in her lap. "What happened? I thought you said we were having a good financial year."

He frowned. "All I know is I was told yesterday we're several hundred thousand dollars short."

Dreams of a raise fizzled. "How is that possible?" Caroline's voice rose in pitch, and she took a moment to try to calm herself. "Thanks to the outside community, donations poured in after the anti-Semitic attacks a few months ago, not to mention those from our regular donors."

In fact, her friend Sarah had helped energize the community, and they'd talked about the great response together.

"I have no idea," Doug said. "I asked the same question. No one has a good answer. And they don't want to announce it for fear of turning people off future donations. All I can tell you is that this year, we have to tighten our belts."

He handed her the list.

"I'm sorry," he added. "I know how disappointed you are."

Numb, she rose in silence and returned to the locker room. She changed into workout clothes, a bitter taste in her mouth. The more she thought about it, the angrier she became. She'd completed her degree and had counted on moving into the programming department. Doug might accept the word from higher-ups without question, but she was going to find out what happened.

"Why did she look familiar to me?" Eli asked Jared.

Jared turned away from the empty hallway, down which Caroline had fled, and refocused on Eli. "Because she was my high school girlfriend."

"Right!" Eli frowned. "I can't believe I didn't recognize her. When's the last time you talked to her?"

You mean other than banging into each other? He needed to stop...or get his vision checked. "College." He vaguely recollected a few stilted conversations, and afterward, nothing. "We're on different life tracks." Especially now that he was responsible for his niece.

"Wait, is she the one...?" Eli grabbed a flier off the bulletin board and pointed to her last name. "Yup, she's the one whose mom had cancer. She gave up her track scholarship, stayed home to care for her, and got buried under a boatload of medical bills. Her mom died a few years ago, and rumor has it she just finished paying the last of the bills."

Jared's body jolted. Caroline had to stay home to care for her mom. At the time, he hadn't realized how serious it was. Or maybe he'd been too caught up with his own life to care. How could he have ignored her? He'd been a selfish jerk who wanted nothing but a successful career, that's how. His face heated in shame. He'd never contacted her after her mom died. And today, he'd made some comment about her taking an exercise class, without considering she could run it.

Memories of her athletic talents flooded him. She'd been a track star, setting state and national records. She could have gone to college anywhere she wanted, but she'd remained here and attended community college instead. He was quiet in the locker room as they showered and dressed for the day. She'd been thrown into a horrible situation, and she'd borne the brunt of it alone. While they didn't have to maintain a romantic relationship, he could have kept up the friendship if he'd made a halfway decent effort. He'd been a jerk and he owed her an apology. His phone buzzed with a text from his mom.

Going to the park. Meet us there?

He read the message and squeezed the phone. What he wanted to do was find Caroline and apologize. But then he'd make the same mistake with Becca as he'd made all those years ago with Caroline—putting his own desires first. As much as Caroline deserved an apology, Becca needed him right now.

He texted his assent and turned to Eli. "Great workout."

Eli nodded. "We should do it again, soon."

"Next time you're in town, we'll grab a beer."

"I don't drink anymore. But the Gold Bar makes a mean Pepsi. I'll make sure to call you."

Jeez, he couldn't stop putting his foot in his mouth. "Sounds good. Thanks, Eli."

Ten minutes later, he arrived at the park on the other end of town. He looked at his watch as he walked to the playground filled with adults supervising little ones on this beautiful day. His mother and niece were at the swings.

"Hi, Mom. Thanks for the text." He looked at his watch. "Hey, sweetheart."

He chucked Becca under the chin, and she shrieked. Her little legs were splayed through the leg holes of the toddler swing, her fingers grasped the bucket seat, and she bounced up and down.

"Push, push!" she cried.

His mother pushed from behind, and he pushed from the front. They both smiled at Becca's joy.

"Good to see your friend?" his mother asked.

Jared nodded and looked at his watch. "Yeah, time melted away." He rubbed his shoulder. "And I got a helluva workout."

"Don't you work out in LA?"

"Yeah, but racquetball is different."

His mother nodded. "I know. And telling a mother not to worry is like telling a Shabbat candle not to flicker. Useless."

He looked at his watch.

"Got somewhere to be?" His mother gave him a questioning look.

"No, why?"

"Because you haven't stopped looking at your watch."

Jared frowned. *Huh.* He hadn't realized he did that. "Sorry, it's a habit from keeping track of billable hours."

Her gaze softened. "You *do* need a vacation. Here, give me your watch."

Jared retreated a step in horror. "What? No."

"If you don't wear your watch, you won't worry about the time, and you'll relax more."

Lifting Becca out of the swing, he gave her a hug and put her down on the rubber pieces that softened the ground. She toddled along, and they followed her zigzag movement.

"If I don't wear my watch, I won't get text alerts, won't track my steps, and will stress over everything I miss."

His mother lifted Becca onto an elephant attached to a spring that made it rock. "Somehow, I don't think the answer to what you lack is found in a smartwatch app but suit yourself."

The annoying thing about mothers is they were often right. But Jared would have swallowed the bouncy elephant whole before he'd admit it to her. Instead, he remained silent, took a deep breath, and enjoyed the time with his mother and niece. It took all his willpower, but he didn't look once at his watch for the remainder of the morning.

"I ran into Caroline Weiss today," he said. He refrained from including the word *literally*, as he suspected that would create a different conversation.

"She sent us a sympathy card and donated to the temple in Noah and Rachel's honor."

Shards of guilt pierced him. He'd never acknowledged the death of her mother. God, he was an awful human. He made a silent vow to leave Browerville a better person than who he was on arrival.

"She was always sweet. I might see if she wants to catch up."

His mother spun around and pierced him with a sharp gaze. "Do not do anything to hurt that woman. She has been through hell, and she's finally getting her life together. The last thing she needs is you upending it. Again."

His jaw dropped. He'd assumed his mother would be happy to see them together. She'd always had a soft spot for Caroline and was disappointed when they broke up. She was acting like a mama bear, only for the wrong cub.

"I won't upend anything, I promise. I want to apologize for my bad behavior. That's it."

His mother was silent for several moments. She cleared her throat before she spoke. "Be careful about the promises you make."

Chapter Three

Caroline's heart pounded against her rib cage as she knocked on Sarah's, door that night.

"Caro, what's wrong?" Sarah frowned.

Caroline fisted her hands at her sides. Her anger had grown stronger as the day progressed, and now, she was irate. "My budget requests were denied, and my promotion Doug promised is off the table." She yanked off her coat and threw it over the back of a chair.

Sarah shut the door and gave Caroline a hug. "I'm sorry. I was afraid that would happen."

Caroline pulled away from the embrace in alarm. "What?"

Sarah held up her hands. "Not the promotion part. I knew nothing about that. But like I told you on the phone, I heard rumors about a budget crisis at the conference."

Caroline wore a tread into the burgundy-colored living-room carpet as she paced. A million questions tumbled through her mind. Her gaze skittered across the cream-painted walls, the cream-beige-and-burgundy-plaid sofa, and the cityscape posters on the walls.

Sarah picked up a menu. "Let's figure out what to order, and then we can talk about it."

"I'm too upset to eat," Caroline said. "What did you hear? Because Doug said he knew nothing about it until the financial restrictions were conveyed to him."

"At the Federation conference, there were rumors about

missing funds," Sarah said, "but I couldn't ask too many questions. I'm still new. I don't know a lot of people, and the last thing I want anyone to think is I like drama or gossip. I know our advocacy training budget also faces cuts, but my boss is trying to keep them to a minimum, based on the current climate, with anti-Semitism on the rise."

Caroline sank onto the plaid couch and faced her friend. "It makes sense, I guess. Sorry, I don't mean to begrudge your department anything." She looked around the modern, airy apartment. "Where's Emily?"

"Vacation. I have the place to myself for a few days."

No matter how much Caroline wanted to talk about other things, she couldn't focus on anything but her budget predicament. "And they had no idea what caused the shortfall? Your advocacy work was so successful, I thought the donations were pouring in."

Her friend blushed. "It was a team effort, and caused, I think, by people's horror at the rise in anti-Semitism. That's what frustrates me, to be honest. We had the money, and now, poof, it's gone." Sarah reached over and squeezed Caroline's hand. "I want to know what happened as much as you do. If people think funds were mismanaged or worse, they won't donate."

"You think someone stole the money?" Caroline had worked for the JCC since college, and while she wasn't privy to everything, she would have heard about someone breaking the law. Wouldn't she?

Sarah shrugged. "I don't know, but I hope not."

"If you hear anything else, will you let me know?" Caroline asked. "I'll see if I can sniff out information from anyone else."

Sarah nodded. "Of course. But be careful." Her stomach growled, and she placed a hand over it. "Now, can we please order dinner? I'm starved."

Caroline nodded. "Show me what menus you've got."

They settled on Thai food, and while they waited for the delivery, Sarah told Caroline more about her conference. Caroline discussed her vacation plans, pulling out her phone to show photos of the hotels and some of the attractions she planned to visit. The food arrived, and they sat at the granite island separating the kitchen from the living room.

"Your vacation sounds amazing! I'm excited you finally get to go," Sarah said.

Caroline swallowed a bite of her *pad Thai*. "I still can't believe it. I keep expecting a snafu to change my plans. Plus, I feel guilty."

"Why?"

"It feels like I'm disloyal to my mom, begrudging the time I cared for her by my excitement for this trip."

Sarah slapped the table. "Your mom would be the first to tell you to go and enjoy yourself. You have to know that, right?"

Caroline smiled. "She'd be pretty excited for me."

Sarah reached over and squeezed Caroline's shoulder. "You've had a rough stretch, but nothing will waylay you this time. Trust me, I'll beat up anyone who gets in your way."

Caroline raised an eyebrow. "I love you, Sarah, but you're not a threat."

"Oh? You should see what I can do with one of Aaron's stale challahs."

"I didn't think he *had* any stale challahs! Does his mother know?"

Isaacson's Deli was Aaron's family-run business, and both his parents took the deli's reputation seriously.

Sarah leaned forward, eyes dancing, finger to her lips. "Shh, don't tell anyone. Now tell me, what's this about you and Jared Leiman?"

Caroline wiped her mouth sipped her wine. "There's not much to tell. I ran into him twice. We spoke maybe three sentences."

Sarah angled herself to meet Caroline's gaze. "But how do you feel? You were devastated when he left."

"I was, but that was ten years ago. I think it was the abandonment that made it much harder. Now? I'm curious about his life, especially now that he's married with a child."

Sarah shook her head. "Unless something happened that Aaron's grandma doesn't know about—which is unlikely—he's still single. But when his brother and sister-in-law were killed in that car crash a year ago, he became his niece's guardian."

Caroline remembered the accident. She'd sent his parents a sympathy card. But she thought it was temporary and hadn't made the connection when she saw him with the baby.

"The wife's relatives didn't step in?" she asked.

Sarah shrugged. "I think I remember Aaron's grandma saying something like his wife was an only child, and her parents are much older. I guess it made more sense to appoint Jared guardian."

So, he was a single dad. She hadn't noticed a wedding ring when she'd seen his hands on the shopping cart. Not that every married man wore one, but still. She pictured his hands—long fingers, firm grasp…and cleared her throat.

Nope, not going there.

"So, you're over him?" Sarah asked. "Seeing him didn't stir up any old feelings?"

Caroline thought about it for a few moments. "I don't know. I think I'm more curious than anything. I mean, he didn't want to deal with my responsibilities, but here he is parenting his niece."

Sarah reached over to her, but Caroline held up a hand. "No, wait, I know that's not fair. It's been ten years, and I'm sure he's more mature. I think it was the surprise of seeing him with a toddler. But as for old feelings, no, I turned down coffee with him."

"Wait, he asked you out?"

"No. He wanted to catch up after I mentioned something by accident. He was being polite."

Sarah shook her head. "I can't believe you said no."

Caroline fidgeted in her chair. She could either live in the past or embrace the present. "The past is over, and nothing I do now will change it."

Besides, if she could change the past, she'd make her mom healthy. The guilt returned. Her eyes misted, and she blinked.

Sarah raised her glass in a toast to Caroline. "I'm impressed. I wasn't as coolheaded as you are when I ran into Aaron."

"That's because *you* never lost your feelings for him," Caroline said. "*I'm* fine."

It will be fine, Jared whispered to himself the next morning. He grabbed his cell phone, glanced at a napping Becca, and tiptoed out of the room. He'd asked plenty of women out for coffee, yet nerves hadn't caused him this much anxiety since college. His mother was getting to him. With a huge sigh to dislodge whatever leftover remnants of nerves there might be, he jogged down the stairs.

His father stopped him. "I'm going to the grocery store with your mother for our first, and hopefully only, Passover trip," he said. "Anything in particular you want us to pick up for you?"

"*Only* Passover trip," Jared quipped. "You're funny."

"I'm an optimist."

More like delusional, but Jared would never say it out loud. There had never been a Passover in the entire Leiman history of Passovers that required only one shopping trip. As it was, they started weeks early and made sure to grab as many non-perishables as they thought they needed. And no matter how many lists his mother made—for the seder as well as for all the meals and snacks during the entire seven-day holiday—there was always something they realized they wanted "just in case."

"Thanks," he said, "but I haven't thought that far ahead." Something else he had to figure out. "Don't worry about me. I can always shop for myself later."

"Text me if you think of anything while we're gone." His father waved and left.

"I'll see what I can get for you and Becca, since I'd hate for them to run out before you get around to it." His mother followed his father out the door.

Alone, Jared paced the living room. All he had to do was call Caroline, invite her for coffee, for real this time, and apologize for being an idiot in college. No big deal. He brokered multimillion dollar deals with A-list celebrities and never broke a sweat.

He could do this.

He *had* to do this to prove to himself that he wasn't that asshole anymore.

Ignoring the texts that already came in from clients, he looked up the JCC and tapped the number. "Caroline Weiss, please." He waited several seconds.

"Hello, this is Caroline Weiss."

"Caroline, it's Jared Leiman. I wondered if you'd like to meet for coffee."

Silence stretched over the line. Was he too abrupt? In his profession, it was best to get right to the point, although in some contexts, easing into a situation was a better strategy. Was this one of those times?

"You won't spill it on me, will you?"

He frowned. Out of all her responses, he never anticipated this one. "What?"

"We keep bumping into each other. Literally. If this is the next step, I don't want to get coffee all over myself."

His breath tripped as a laugh bubbled in his chest, but he stopped. He couldn't be sure she was teasing, and he didn't want to make it worse if she was serious.

"I promise not to spill it on you. Can't guarantee I won't spill it on myself."

She sighed. "Are you asking me for coffee because of what I said to you at the JCC?"

He tried to remember what she'd said but came up empty. Time to be honest. "No. I'm asking you because I owe you an apology."

"Now I'm intrigued," she said.

The back of his neck was damp, and he rubbed it. Was she always this opaque? "Intrigued enough to accept my offer?"

"I guess it depends on when." Her voice was lighter, and he dared to take a deep breath. "I'm working."

He wouldn't make the same mistake again and assume things he shouldn't. "Are you free this afternoon?"

She paused. He wondered if she was checking her calendar or making him wait. If her current job didn't work out, he'd hire her. She'd be a great negotiator. Finally, she replied, "I have an hour between three and four. I can meet you at the Caffeine Drip."

Browerville had changed since he'd last lived here, and he had no idea where that was, but he wasn't about to admit it to her. "I look forward to it."

Caroline paused outside the Caffeine Drip. The only reason she'd agreed to meet Jared was he sounded different on the phone. A little less cocky, a little more sincere. And no one ever turned down an apology from an ex. Maybe she'd learn something to satisfy her curiosity. Squaring her shoulders, she stepped into the coffeehouse and scanned the seating area, designed with brick walls and bronze accent lighting, for Jared. There were few scuffed tables occupied at this time of day during the week, and since he wasn't seated, she walked over to the counter to order. Her time was limited, and the sooner she ordered, the better.

"Latte with almond milk, please," she said to the barista behind the counter.

"Put it on my bill, along with a large black coffee with milk and two sugars."

Jared's urbane voice from behind startled her, and she turned. He stood three feet away, an uncertain look at odds with how she remembered him.

"Hi," he said. "I hope you don't mind, but I brought Becca."

Babbling drew her gaze to the stroller next to him. Unlike at the grocery store, where she'd gotten a passing glance at the child, this time, she took in all the details. Becca kicked her legs and spoke toddler gibberish. She was the cutest little girl she'd ever seen. Her head was a mass of curls that made Caroline jealous, and she wore a crooked pink bow perched above her ear. Caroline's heart melted.

"She's adorable."

She knelt and touched the back of Becca's hand with one finger. The toddler's skin was soft. "Hello, Becca. I'm Caroline."

"Cawo," Becca said. "Moke." She held out her sippy cup.

"You want milk?" She started to reach for the cup, but Becca pulled it away and drank from it. Caroline rose and addressed Jared. "Thanks for the coffee, by the way."

"I'm glad I got here in time. Toddler hours are a little different than lawyer hours."

She took both cups while he paid and led them to a table next to the window overlooking a side street. Gesturing to Becca, she asked, "Does she need anything?"

With a triumphant grin, he pulled out a bag of crackers. "Ta-da! We'll be good for a while." His phone buzzed, and after he glanced at it, he turned it face down on the table.

After she took a sip of her latte, she wiped her mouth. "I was sorry to hear about your brother and sister-in-law. You seem to handle Becca well, though."

A muscle in Jared's jaw twitched. "I have no idea what I'm doing. But I'm the one who owes you an apology."

"You mentioned that on the phone." Was it awful if she let him do all the heavy lifting?

"I was a complete jerk when we broke up. Hell, for breaking up with you in the first place. And then I compounded it by not keeping in touch, even when your mom died."

The look he gave her was so intense, she gripped the edge of her seat to refrain from ducking. His apology was good.

"I should have apologized the first time we bumped into each other, or at least in the JCC, and I don't have an excuse, other than shock. Which, when you think about it, is a weak excuse since you've lived here the whole time and seeing you is a reasonable expectation." His phone vibrated on the table, but he ignored it.

She held up her hand to stop the deluge. "I appreciate that."

She took a deep breath. Should she admit how hurt she was when he left? *Did it matter after all this time?*

"Our breakup was inevitable because our lives were going in different directions," she continued. "There's no way we could have stayed together. Don't beat yourself up any longer. You've got a lot on your plate right now. As for an apology when we bumped into each other—it wasn't the right place. We're good."

Caroline was amazed at how reasonable she was to the man who'd broken her heart years ago. When the breakup was fresh, she'd imagined all sorts of scenarios where she'd have a chance to tell him off. But now? Ten years later, she was older and wiser. Better to find out how unreliable and different from her he was then, than now.

By the look on his face and the bobbing of his Adam's apple as he swallowed multiple times, Jared was surprised, too. A glimmer of satisfaction rippled through her. She drank her coffee to keep from gloating.

"That's all?" he asked. "You're not going to say anything else?"

"What else would you like me to say?"

She waggled her fingers at Becca, whose face was a gummy mess of cracker crumbs and milk droplets. Thank goodness she sat across the table from the angelic looking but messy toddler. She didn't want the mess to get on her.

Jared shrugged. "I guess I expected I'd have to grovel a lot more."

Caroline's mouth dropped open. "Jared, it's been ten years."

He smiled, and she caught her breath. He'd grown more handsome since their relationship ended. She'd bet the women he encountered fell all over themselves.

"I'd love to hear about your job and your life—" His phone buzzed with another text, and he paused midsentence.

Caroline took advantage of his distraction and pushed away from the table. It was one thing to be cordial. It was something else to try to resume a relationship. The chair legs scraped against the rustic wooden floorboards.

"Unfortunately, I've got to return to work. I'm teaching a yoga class in twenty minutes. But it's been nice to see you and to meet Becca. And I do appreciate the apology."

She waved to them both and grabbed her cup to throw away.

"Caroline, wait!" Jared half rose from the table. "Please. I'd like to catch up on your life."

"Jared, what's the point? Our lives are different. You're in LA, I'm here. You're busy. Don't you think it's better if we leave the past in the past?"

"Come on. One dinner before Passover. Please? It's my chance to hang out with an adult. You won't deny me that pleasure, will you?"

She groaned and gripped the back of the walnut chair. "Don't give me the puppy dog eyes." He didn't think she'd fall for that, did he? As if his deep blue eyes could erase their past…and then he grinned.

How did anyone resist him?

"Ugh, all right. Fine. Dinner. But only because everyone needs to take advantage of good *treif* food before Passover."

He followed her to the trash and held open the flap while she threw away her cup. "How about I pick you up Friday night? What time do you get out of work?"

"We get out early on Fridays for Shabbat," she said. "I have a political discussion group that I run in the afternoon, and I'm finished at three." She'd planned to dig into the JCC funding with her extra time.

"I'll pick you up at six." He held out his phone. "Give me your address."

She gave him the same address she'd always had, since she'd remained in her mom's house after her death.

"See you Friday," he called after her.

Their relationship wasn't going anywhere. Why did a frisson of excitement run up her spine?

Chapter Four

"Sorry, Jennifer, but Fran is a great lawyer." Jared spoke into his phone as he dressed for his dinner with Caroline. "I'd never leave you with someone I didn't trust. I promise she can handle this movie deal as well as I could."

He scanned the shirts in his closet, phone wedged between his shoulder and jaw. Blue oxford or gray pinstripe?

"No, I'm not ending my vacation," he said. What was it with his clients? Didn't they understand the concept of vacation? Outside his bedroom door, his dad walked by, and Jared waved him inside. "I'm away through Passover. I'll be back early April."

He held up both shirts and his dad pointed to the gray. With a nod, he took it off the hanger and pulled it over his head. "We good, Jen? Okay. Thanks."

He hung up the phone and threw up his hands in disgust. "Celebrities are a pain."

His dad laughed. "Nice problem to have. Will you be out late?"

Jared shook his head, once again feeling like a teenager. "No, I'm taking Caroline to dinner."

"Have fun. Oh," he added as he was leaving the room, "you might want to be careful what you say in front of Becca. She's going to be talking and repeating what you say before you know it." His dad clapped his palm against the doorjamb and left.

Now he felt like a teenager. Except he would have gotten in trouble as a teenager for his colorful language. Now he had to censor himself for his niece. He let out a sigh. Life was weird. Putting his phone on Do Not Disturb, he jogged downstairs. His parents were in the kitchen, feeding Becca at the same scratched wooden table they'd used for his entire life.

"I'll see you guys later. Thanks again for watching her. I shouldn't be home too late."

His mother rose from the table and gave him a hug. "Whenever you get home is fine. We'll light the Shabbat candles with her and put her to bed."

He kissed Becca's head and walked to his car.

When he'd asked Caroline for her address, he hadn't considered she'd still be in the house she'd grown up in. As he drove, he remembered countless times when he'd picked her up to drive to school, brought her home afterward, or sat in her driveway, making out. He slowed his car as he searched for the address. The blue clapboard house looked the same, maybe a tiny bit shabbier but still neat. He rang the bell, his palms damp.

Her voice echoed behind the door. "I'll be right there!"

Less than a minute later, the door opened, and Caroline stepped outside. Unlike the last time he'd seen her, her light brown hair was down and waved around her face. A cream, knit scarf peeked above her red jacket, and below the jacket, about an inch or two of a black skirt showed. Tall black boots covered her long legs. She looked warm and pretty, and his nerves went into overdrive.

"You look beautiful. I always liked the bright colors you wore. I'm glad that hasn't changed." He talked too much, but he couldn't seem to stop himself.

"Thank you." She studied him.

He wondered what she thought of him.

"I like the leather jacket," she said. She reached out a hand and touched his sleeve. "It's soft."

In LA, he would have mentioned the cost of the imported

leather, or the exclusive store he purchased it from, but here, at home, it didn't seem right.

"Thanks," he said, and left it at that. "I made reservations at the Gilded Age."

Her eyes widened. "I've heard about that place. It's super fancy and expensive." She looked down at herself. "Are you sure we're dressed appropriately?"

"You look perfect."

Her cheeks reddened. He caught his breath. Her inability to hide her emotions captivated him. She was lovely. He ushered her to his car, held the door for her, and told her to pick whatever music she wanted. Pulling out of the driveway, he glanced at her in surprise when she chose a classical song from the playlist.

"Do you object?" she asked. "I listen to lyrics and loud music all day for my job. This is a nice change of pace."

"Not at all. I never knew you liked classical. You used to love techno."

She nodded. "I loved dancing to it, and the coach blasted it in the locker room. Later, I listened to it to distract myself when my mom was sick."

She looked out the window for a moment, and Jared waited. He wanted to say something to make her feel better but didn't want to intrude.

"I didn't think about how hard it was on you," he said when she didn't say anything else.

She turned to him and spoke. "It's funny how music can represent such specific times in your life."

"Whenever I hear country music, I think of my college roommate. He drove me crazy freshman year, listening to it all the time."

Caroline laughed. "I remember. How'd you get him to stop?"

"I stole his music collection one night when he was drunk

and told him I wouldn't give it back to him until he learned to listen to my music."

"You're kidding. How'd you not get in trouble?"

Jared shrugged. "He liked my music."

"Lucky for you!"

Jared pulled his car into the Gilded Age's parking lot.

Caroline exclaimed. "Wow! When you said you wanted to hang out with grown-ups, you meant it. I'm not sure I qualify for *this* grown up."

The building resembled a Gilded Age mansion, with an impressive marble facade, turreted roofline, and ornate hardware on the door. Caroline paused outside the entrance.

"Seriously, I don't think I'm dressed for this."

Jared allowed himself to take in every inch of her, from the top of her light brown hair to the tips of her black boots. "Trust me." Before she could argue, he opened the door and ushered her inside.

The interior of the restaurant was more lavish than the outside. Thick Persian rugs softened their footsteps. Crystal chandeliers cast a twinkling glow throughout the vast dining room. Waitstaff in tails and black evening gowns served customers in equally fancy clothes.

"Jared, we can't go in there." Caroline lowered her voice to a panicked whisper.

He placed a hand on her arm. "It will be okay. I would have told you if you needed to dress fancier."

The host walked up to them, dressed in a white tuxedo with tails. "May I help you?" His expression was reserved, his tone nasal.

"We're looking for Fat Suzy," Jared said.

Caroline whipped around, but he nodded to her and then focused on the host.

"Of course, sir, right this way."

Instead of leading them into the dining room, he led them

to the coat closet. Right next to it was a hidden door. Its outline could just be made out in the red-flocked wallpaper and mahogany molding. The host knocked on it three times, paused, and then again twice. The door opened, and a woman in a copper lame camisole top with huge hoop earrings and faded jeans greeted them.

Jared didn't know what entertained him more, watching the host perform his code signal or Caroline's reaction. Her mouth was open, and she'd gripped his hand. He looked at their entwined fingers. He hadn't held her hand in years. It still fit inside his own; it still felt right.

"Yes?" The host gestured to Jared.

"Jerry sent me," Jared said.

The woman stepped back and waved them into the dark corridor. Now Caroline squeezed his hand tighter. "Where are we?" she whispered.

The woman in front of them opened another door, and they stepped into a bar. The urban-style decor—exposed pipes, brick and cement walls, a scarred oak bar, and wire-lined lamps—contrasted with the elegance of the restaurant they'd walked through. Jared turned to Caroline. "A speakeasy."

Her face relaxed into a grin. "I had no idea this was here."

His happiness at her reaction was tempered with a trace of concern. "I didn't mean to freak you out," he said. "At first, I assumed you knew about it, but when it became clear you didn't, I wanted to surprise you."

The woman led them to a corner booth with leather seats and a polished cement table, handed them menus, and left them to get settled. After hanging her coat with his on a nearby hook, Jared sat across from Caroline.

"I'll admit, I was nervous about the opulence of the restaurant, but I should have realized if you were dressed as you are, we wouldn't get thrown out."

He nodded. He liked that she was a good sport about it.

"My friend, Eli, told me this place opened a few months ago," Jared said. "That's who I was with at the JCC."

Caroline nodded. "I thought he looked familiar, but I couldn't place him. Debate club, right?"

"Yeah. And now that he's in Browerville a few times a week, we're going to play racquetball while I'm home."

"And how long will that be?" Caroline asked.

Jared folded his hands on the table. *As long as it takes me to figure out my life.* "We're here until Passover ends."

"It's nice you can take three weeks off. I'm sure your parents love having the two of you around."

A shard of guilt pierced Jared's heart. His parents deserved more, but he didn't know how to give it to them. "They do. And I haven't taken vacation in a long time. I'm due."

"You must love your job. I can't wait for my vacation."

Did he love his job? He used to, but now he was less sure. That wasn't something he wanted to discuss now, though. After they placed their orders for appetizers and a drink for each of them, he turned the conversation.

"Vacation? What are your plans?"

Caroline's face lit up as she told him about her trip. Her enthusiasm was contagious, and Jared leaned toward her.

She paused. "What are you smiling at?"

"You."

Her face reddened.

"Don't be embarrassed," he said. "I love listening to you describe your trip. It's nice to see someone happy." Her happiness pulled him into her orbit, and for the first time in a long time, he was present.

His comment seemed to settle her because she leaned against the bench back and continued. "I've always wanted to travel, and for the first time, I'll be able to do so."

"I remember in high school, you talked about all the places you wanted to visit," he said.

"Yeah, I had lots of plans." Her expression turned wistful.

Images from high school flitted through Jared's mind—late-night phone calls where they discussed what they'd do when they left home; whispered conversations in the library as they consulted college brochures; interlocked hands as they lay on blankets in his backyard, staring at the stars and dreaming of their lives.

"We all did. I'm glad to see yours are coming to fruition," he said.

The waitress brought their appetizers and drinks.

"What about yours? In high school you dreamed of being a high-powered lawyer."

"My plans?" Panic ripped through him, and he stuffed a mushroom appetizer into his mouth to give himself time before answering. He didn't know what his plans were. He was supposed to go back to work when he returned to California, except he'd lost his drive several months ago and couldn't find it again. He didn't know what he wanted to do instead. But if he told Caroline that, he'd look aimless. She'd always admired his determination and goals.

She nodded, and he realized he'd waited too long to answer. "I'm part of a successful entertainment law practice out in LA. I'm up for partner later this year."

Her expression grew thoughtful. "You always said you wanted to make partner before you hit thirty."

The irony was he didn't know what his dreams were any longer. Inside, he was empty.

"It's not definite yet, but…"

She reached for one of the oysters Rockefeller. "You'll get it."

He took a drink from his gin rickey. "How can you be sure? We've all changed. I hope I'm not the same person I was then."

Swallowing, she stared at him. Something about the way she looked at him made him feel she was reaching into his soul.

Finally, she shrugged. "You've always known what you wanted and gone for it, regardless of what was in your way."

He could hear the "like me" hang in the air between them.

"Caroline, I never meant to make you feel like you were in the way." He probably hadn't cared about her enough. "Maybe I decided that your feelings were less important. God, I hope not. But whatever my reasons, I treated you badly, and I hope you'll forgive me."

She reached across the table and touched the back of his hand. A jolt of electricity traveled up his arm. He didn't know if she'd felt it, too, but she withdrew her hand and folded them both on the table.

"I wasn't trying to get you to apologize again. I meant that you've always been laser focused on what you wanted, and you have your success to prove it. You should be proud and confident that you'll get your promotion, even if you might have to juggle Becca."

He searched her face for any sign of lingering hurt. He replayed her conversation and didn't hear any bitterness. Maybe she had forgiven him.

"If we stayed together, I would have held you back." She munched on a cheese wafer.

"What do you mean?"

She sipped her sidecar before she answered. "Even if we'd managed long distance, with all I went through with my mom, we wouldn't have been able to survive, and the last thing I would have wanted was to interfere with your studies or career. So it was for the best."

Jared tightened his grip on his drink. She'd never understand his doubts now. Not if she thought breaking up allowed him to achieve his goals. He didn't know how to explain his lack of direction. And she was over him.

He'd have to keep his problems to himself. Only he was starting to fall for her. Again.

* * *

Jared's headlights illuminated the darkened road as Caroline watched from her bedroom window. Her enjoyment this evening surprised her. Whatever charm he'd possessed ten years ago had blossomed into a combination of sex appeal, sincerity, and depth, none of which she'd expected. She'd assumed he'd be arrogant about his career and his celebrity clients. Yet he hadn't mentioned them at all. He'd asked about her goals and dreams, turning the conversation back to her. Along the way, wisps of attraction stirred.

She'd hoped he'd kiss her good night.

In the driveway, engine off, there was a moment when he'd turned in his seat toward her. His eyes had darkened to midnight blue, his hand on the steering wheel clenched, and the drag of his coat against the seatback as he'd shifted focused her attention on him. The air grew charged, like the moments before lightning strikes. She'd waited, wondering if he would kiss her, wondering if she wanted him to kiss her. Before her body and brain had a chance to chat, his posture eased, he spoke of how much fun he'd had with her, and the spell was broken.

She snorted as she turned away from the window. Jared? What kind of a glutton for punishment was she? Yes, he was attractive, but plenty of men were. She'd fallen for him once and his abandonment had crushed her. They were a lot more similar then than they were now. Now she was free of any commitments—personal or financial. While he was guardian to his niece. He held a high-powered job clear across the country, and she had her job here. He'd abandoned her before when she'd needed him most. This time around, he possessed a return plane ticket to California. The abandonment might be of a different kind, but he was still leaving, and she'd be alone again. She'd gone through it once already with him, and once with her mom. She wasn't about to be left again. There was no way they could be anything more than friends.

And even friendship was questionable. She would have sworn before today that he wasn't the kind of friend she'd ever want. Yet he'd proven otherwise. It might be nice to have him for a friend. But anything more would never happen. As she finished getting ready for bed, she satisfied herself with the idea that her revived attraction to Jared was due to the unexpectedness of it all.

Her phone pinged with a text right before she was about to turn out the lights.

I had a good time tonight. Let's do it again.

Her fingers hovered over her phone keyboard. She didn't want to be rude, but what was the point?

I had fun, too.

She'd literally finished lecturing herself about him. She wasn't about to jump into anything, even another harmless dinner.

Does that mean you don't want to do it again?

Maybe he still was arrogant. Or if not arrogant, then unaccustomed to rejection. Wasn't that kind of the same thing?

I'm surprised you have the time.

Yes, she was avoiding the question, not in the mood for confrontation.

You're avoiding my question.

She jumped. What the hell? Now he was a mind reader? She preferred him when he'd been an arrogant jerk.

I don't know if it's a good idea.

You don't know if seeing me again is a good idea or if another speakeasy is a good idea? Because I was going to suggest the botanical gardens.

Do you think this makes sense? Tonight was fun, but maybe we shouldn't get too involved.

Yes, it makes sense. I want to see you again.

He was used to getting what he wanted. Now that he'd set his sights on her, Caroline wasn't sure about playing into his hands. When he was through with her, he'd leave. Again. The smart thing to do would be to end this now, while she still maintained the upper hand.

Caroline, do you spend time with your friends?

Of course, she did. And he knew that. Did she need to answer the question? She waited a minute or two, but he didn't text anything else. Clearly, he waited for her.

You know I do.

So, what's wrong with our spending time together?

The speed with which he answered her text proved her right. She didn't know whether to be flattered or annoyed. Maybe a little of both.

Because we're not friends. And you're leaving.

She winced after she hit Send. That was harsh. She rushed to send him another text.

Sorry, I didn't mean to be rude. I'm conflicted.

About what?

About the purpose of this. You're not home for long, and I've got plans to travel away from here, too.

That doesn't mean we can't enjoy each other's company while we're both around.

Her phone rang.

"Texting is stupid," he said. "Caroline, why can't we get to know each other again? I haven't had as much fun with anyone in a long time, and I'd like to see you again. Would that be bad?"

It wouldn't, and it scared her.

She sighed. "Maybe not."

"Good. Let's go to the botanical garden tomorrow. They have a special Stephen Antonakos exhibit throughout the grounds I think you'll like."

"Never heard of him."

"Look him up. A client I know collects his pieces. He's Greek, and he's known for his abstract sculptures incorporating neon. Since you're going to Greece, I think you'll enjoy it."

Caroline pulled the phone away from her ear and stared at it in shock. He must have researched this in the hour since he dropped her off.

"Wow," she said. "You move fast."

"Say yes."

His voice was low and did funny things to her insides.

"I should say that I'm busy."

"Why?"

"Because you seem too sure of getting your way."

He laughed. "Habit. Come on. It'll be nice tomorrow. We can get some fresh air."

"Fine. One o'clock?" She needed to retake control of the situation somehow.

"Good. I'll pick you up then. And Caroline? You won't re-gret this."

I already do, she whispered to herself after she hung up the phone.

Becca woke Jared at six thirty the next morning, but even the early hour couldn't put a damper on his good mood. What-ever else was going on in his life, he was seeing Caroline later. He hummed with anticipation.

"Good morning, sweetheart."

He lifted her from her playpen, changed her diaper, and got her dressed in pink sweatpants and a long-sleeved shirt with a unicorn on it. The sun filtered through the tree branches by the time they made their way downstairs for breakfast. He made her cereal as his coffee percolated. Then he checked his texts and the weather while she fed herself, keeping one eye on the mess she made. His clients drove him crazy, as usual, but this afternoon would be beautiful. A perfect day for walk-ing around the botanical gardens.

His parents entered the kitchen, his dad grumbling about his tie and his mom fidgeting with her pantyhose.

"Where are you two off to this early?" he asked.

"We've got the Schwartz Bar Mitzvah," his father said. "Harriet, do I need to wear this damn tie?"

Jared's mom gave him and Becca a quick kiss. "David don't swear in front of the baby. And you don't need me to answer that question, do you?"

His dad grumbled and opened the fridge.

"What are you doing, David? We'll be late?"

"If I have to be choked to death, I at least want to die satiated. Where's the leftover pizza from the other night?"

Jared stifled a laugh. His parents never changed.

"Absolutely not." His mom maneuvered herself between her husband and the fridge and closed the door with her hip. "You'll spill grease on yourself."

"At least then I won't have to wear this damn tie."

"Language!" His mom kissed his dad. "You'd have to change it for another one, and then I'd make you change more than just your tie. There's a light breakfast at temple before the service starts, and a kiddush lunch afterward. Trust me, you won't starve."

She grabbed her black purse. "You have the card and check?"

His dad patted his breast pocket and nodded.

She turned to Jared. "You'll be okay without us?"

"Of course," he said. "Have fun, and we'll see you later." He turned to Becca. "Wave bye-bye to *Saba* and *Safta*." His brother and sister-in-law had encouraged the Hebrew words for *grandpa* and *grandma*, and he saw no reason to change that.

She waved her pudgy hand and said, "Bye, bye!"

A moment later, the house was quiet.

Too quiet.

In LA, there was always noise—traffic, city, people, whatever. And there were always a million things to do. But here in the suburbs, it was quieter. Last night when he went to bed, the moon shone through his window and stars twinkled above the tree line. It was quiet, except for the rustling of animals in the woods behind his parents' house. And until his date with Caroline, the day stretched endlessly.

Date? As he gulped the last of his coffee and cleaned breakfast residue off Becca, he wondered. They'd made plans. It wasn't an appointment nor was it a meeting. But a date implied romance, and while he was attracted to her, he got the distinct impression *date* would scare her off. She was skittish.

Had he made her that way? His stomach burned with guilt. He'd have to be careful.

He'd also have to get out of this house if he didn't want to go crazy. In LA, he'd have handed Becca over to the nanny and gone to work. But a part of him kind of liked the idea of time alone with Becca. He just hadn't yet figured out how to navigate the slower pace.

Packing his niece into the stroller, he covered her legs with a blanket—thanks to his mom's purchase of a winter coat, he didn't have to bundle her like he had on his way here—grabbed a couple of toys and left the house. The cool air was bracing. He took a deep breath. He could already smell spring. A ten-minute walk, and he reached downtown Browerville. He paused in front of Isaacson's Deli and closed his eyes as memories assailed him. Noah had worked here after school and during the summer. His brother used to sneak him a bagel when Jared stopped by, making him feel special. Could he return to a place tied to his brother?

He thrust back his shoulders. If he could handle his childhood home, a deli shouldn't be a problem. Besides, he'd missed the bagels—bagels in LA were not the same. Clenching his jaw, he entered.

The scent of garlic, yeast, and pickles greeted him the moment he opened the door. Early on a Saturday morning, the place was packed, with long lines at the counter. He didn't see Aaron, but there were at least six people behind the counter, serving customers. After he placed his order—an everything bagel with egg, cheese, and avocado—he sat with Becca at one of the tables and watched the customers. The place had changed, adding tables and chairs along one wall and multiple display cases with breads, meats, and cheeses—separated to maintain kosher rules. His brother's shadow didn't lurk in every corner, and for the first time since he'd entered, some of the tension left his neck.

"Jared, hi. Caroline told me you were back."

He looked up. Sarah Abrams stood next to him. He rose. "Hi, Sarah. I am. In fact, I'm seeing her later today. How are you?"

She knelt next to Becca. "I'm well. Becca's adorable." She turned her face toward him, her voice gentle. "I was sorry to hear about Noah and Rachel. How are you?"

He shouldn't be out of practice with the question, since it was the first thing anyone here at home asked him. However, the accident had happened a year ago, and now most of his friends in LA were past it. He doubted he ever would be. His chest ached. He swallowed. "It's been an adjustment."

She rose. "I'll bet. I know how hard it was for me to come home, and I didn't have to deal with the memories you do."

The hair on the nape of his neck rose as images of Noah sweeping the deli floor, ribbing him when he had more money than Jared, and the smell of the bagels that Noah brought home after work flooded him. He looked away to try to get ahold of himself.

Sarah's voice brought him back to the present. His heart ached.

"I remember how your brother and Aaron competed to finish the chores around here. Noah always made Aaron laugh."

He smiled, despite the pain talking about his brother caused.

"You're a natural with Becca," Sarah said in a low voice. "I'm sorry. I didn't mean to make you feel worse than you do."

He exhaled. "It's okay. I can't avoid the memories, no matter how much I might want to. And someday, I'll be glad for them." *Just not right now.*

Sarah nodded. "Well, it's good that you're home."

She rose, and Jared spoke before she turned away.

"Aaron's not here?"

"He's catering breakfast and kiddush lunch for the Schwartz Bar Mitzvah. He's at the temple, overseeing the last details."

Of course he was. Isaacson's Deli made the best food around. "Tell him I say hello."

"Will do. Bye, sweetie!" She waved at Becca and went on her way.

He exhaled in relief. It was hard being reminded of his brother everywhere he went and listening to others talk about their memories of him. At the same time, there was something about a place where people remembered him and could talk about his brother with fondness that made Jared feel part of the community.

Becca started getting antsy. When their breakfast was ready, he took it to go and walked around town, letting Becca gnaw on the bagel and help him push the stroller to get out some of her energy.

Most people at this time of day were on their way somewhere. Since it was a weekend and the stores weren't open yet, the sidewalks were empty, except for joggers, dog walkers, and a few early birds. The open space gave him time to explore. Although he'd been home after college graduation, there were still a lot of changes to the town. He walked past Hard as Nails. It was one of the few nonfood businesses that was open this early. Women of all ages, and a few men, were inside. His mother stopped here every week for a mani-pedi. When he was in high school, he'd dropped her off and picked her up so he could use her car while she was busy. The first time, he'd gone inside to find her, but after being oohed and aahed over way more than his teenage self could handle, he'd waited for her in the car. It was his first experience with salons—the gossip, music, smells, and constant chatter. In LA, his girlfriends all had their nails, hair, and God knew what else polished, cut, and waxed. Through the window, a little girl sat with her mother getting her toes painted. He looked at Becca. Would she want to do that someday? Who would take her? There were many things a girl needed her mother for. Would he be enough for her?

He continued down the sidewalk, his pace slow to match Becca's. The Gold Bar was up ahead, the bar that Eli suggested they meet at when Jared flubbed it and suggested beer to a sober guy. He didn't know the story behind that, but plenty of his friends in LA were focused on their sobriety. And plenty of others should be. He reached for his phone to text Eli about a time to meet.

Want to get together for a meal? Doesn't have to be a bar.

He hit Send and was about to replace his phone in his pocket when it dinged with a text from Caroline.

Sorry, I have to cancel today.

His shoulders bowed with disappointment. He'd looked forward to seeing her again.

Is everything okay?

He expected her to answer right away, but she didn't. There wasn't something wrong, was there? Was she ill or hurt, or had she changed her mind for some reason? Finally, the dancing dots appeared on his screen, and he waited in the middle of the sidewalk for her answer.

Yeah. Didn't mean to worry you. I can't today.

That wasn't an answer. If she were ill or hurt, she'd have said so. And if a conflict had come up, she'd mention that as well. Which meant she'd changed her mind. He walked toward the library as he considered what to do.

Inside, quiet surrounded him. The old stone building

smelled like books, and he took a deep breath. Turning right toward the children's section, he found a toddler-safe area and let Becca wander. As he followed her around, he thought about Caroline. She'd been reluctant to go out with him in the first place, but he thought he'd changed her mind. He'd failed. Now he had two choices. He could let it go, or he could pursue her.

Letting her go would be the easiest and kindest thing to do. He wasn't here for long, and his focus should be on his family. The more time he spent with her, the less time he spent with his parents. But he enjoyed Caroline's company. She kept him from getting too deep inside his own head. And she was pretty, even prettier than when they'd dated. Would it be bad to spend time together? Unless when he left, he hurt her. He'd already done it once; he didn't want to do it again. He was older and wiser now, more aware of how his actions affected others. She'd suffered enough, and he didn't want to contribute to it. If only there was a way to spend time with her. He wasn't ready to give up yet. He needed to show her he wasn't the same guy he was in the past. But he also needed to keep her feelings in mind.

As he read books to Becca in the library, she babbled and pointed to pictures on the pages. He named the animals, and she repeated them. This was new, and his chest swelled with pride. He debated his strategy. When she got tired of the book, she walked away, and he followed her, debating his Caroline strategy. He wasn't a successful lawyer for nothing. The best thing to do was talk to her in person. He knew where she lived. It was a Saturday, and he assumed she didn't have to work. His parents were busy. He'd have to take Becca with him, but she was part of his life now.

Once again, he pulled Becca onto his lap to read her a story. She leaned against his chest and stuck her two middle fingers in her mouth as he read *Hop on Pop*. When he finished, he kissed her soft cheek and put her into the stroller.

It was time to take the battle to Caroline's home turf.

Chapter Five

"I ran into Jared today," Sarah said when Caroline answered her phone.

Caroline frowned. She'd just texted him to cancel their plans when her phone rang. For a second, she assumed it was him, calling her to argue. She'd smiled when the caller ID showed it was her best friend. The last thing she wanted to discuss was Jared.

"Well, we all live, or in his case, are visiting, the same town," she said. "It's bound to happen."

"He said he's taking you out later. I thought you said you were over him?"

Caroline brushed out her wet hair and pulled on jeans and a sweater. Her early morning run invigorated her, but despite the chilly weather, she'd sweated, and popped in the shower as soon as she returned home.

"He's not, and I am."

"Wait, what? I saw him less than an hour ago."

"I changed my mind. I *am* over him. There's no point in spending time together."

"Ouch," Sarah said. "I hope you gave him a nicer excuse than that."

"I did." Sort of. She hadn't given him any reason, because she couldn't think of a way to beg off without being rude.

"His daughter is adorable," Sarah said. "All those curls!"

"I know. But she's not his daughter, she's his niece."

"Kinda the same thing now, don't you think?"

Becca was Jared's responsibility, regardless of her relationship to him. But before Caroline could respond, a knock sounded at her door.

"Sarah, hold on. Someone's at my door. It's probably one of my neighbors." Last week, the guy who lived next door stopped by to ask if she'd seen his cat. The week before, the older woman across the street asked if she had mistakenly picked up her newspaper. But when she opened her door, it wasn't a neighbor.

It was Jared, Becca on one hip, diaper bag slung over the other shoulder, looking like a dad, but not.

His arm muscles bulged beneath Becca's diaper-clad bottom. A shock of dark hair fell over his eye and made Caroline long to brush it back. His spicy scent mingled with baby shampoo. Somehow, it appealed to her more than expensive cologne. He filled up her doorway, not only with his physical presence but with his magnetism, too.

Caroline moved her phone up to her ear without taking her eyes off him. "I'll call you back." She put her phone in the pocket of her jeans and clutched the door frame. Why the hell was he here? What made him think he could just show up?

She'd hoped he'd take the hint when she'd canceled their plans today.

"Hi," he said. "I'm sorry for dropping by like this, but I wanted to make sure you were okay."

She wrinkled her brow in confusion. "I'm fine," she said.

"Good. Because I thought something might be wrong since you canceled earlier."

Her stomach sank to her toes. Great. If he asked why she'd backed out, she'd have to tell the truth. *Nicely*, Sarah's voice reminded her.

She blinked. He looked sincere. Unlike the Jared she used to know. Her conscience twinged. No, that wasn't fair. He'd never *not* been sincere. She sighed. "Come on in."

She retreated, and he entered, looked around her foyer, and then refocused on her.

"Want to tell me why you canceled?"

Caroline shifted from one foot to the other. "I told you last night, I didn't see the point."

He nodded toward her living room sofa. It was worn leather, had seen better days, but she'd cleaned and refurbished it, and it was comfortable.

"Mind if I sit?"

"Go ahead." She needed to be polite, no matter how uncomfortable she might be. "Can I get you a drink? Or something for Becca?" What did toddlers eat or drink? She wracked her brain for ideas that she might have on hand.

"No, we're fine. And I have her snacks and drinks in my bag if she needs." With that, he took out a toy rabbit. Becca hugged it tight.

The more the two of them were together, the more Caroline marveled at his competence with the toddler. Unlike biological parents who had plenty of time to figure things out, he'd been thrust into the role, and he appeared to accept it.

"I thought we covered all your concerns when I asked you out," Jared said.

"So, it is a date. When we talked about it, you said we were friends."

"Why is it necessary to quantify our relationship? Can't we enjoy ourselves?"

Caroline bristled. "What does *that* mean?"

"To me, it means we see each other while I'm here."

"See each other?" Caroline curved her fingers into air quotes. "I'm not interested in starting something, Jared, casual or otherwise. You're a nice guy, but I don't want to live in the past." She didn't want a relationship right now, and she'd never been the type of woman interested in friends with benefits—it blurred too many lines and violated her sense of order.

"I have a break from responsibility for the first time in

years." Once again, the guilt surged because she blamed Becca, but she tamped it down. He might be able to handle life with a toddler, but she wasn't sure she could. He seemed to decide everything based on his schedule, and she bristled.

"We don't have to be more than friends. Like I said before. I'd never force you into anything, Caroline. Ever. But we had fun together. Why can't that continue?"

"Because I don't want to lead you on, and I don't want to be forced to wait around for when you're here." *Or deal with the abandonment when you leave.*

"Duly noted."

"Because I've discovered you're a nice guy." She cringed. That sounded...desperate?

Jared struggled not to smile. "Thanks."

"I don't want either of us to get hurt."

He sobered. "We agree on that."

"Do we?"

"I don't want to hurt you. I was enough of a jerk in the past. I don't want to be that guy again."

He looked hurt now, and Caroline deflated. "I'm sorry. I'm—" *Scared. Nervous.* "—concerned."

Jared nodded. "Tell you what. If I suggest something you don't want to do, for whatever reason, you tell me the truth. Don't leave it vague. Don't make up an excuse. Say no."

"I can do that."

"Good." He rose and juggled everything until the bag and Becca were settled. "I'm glad we understand each other."

The Jared from the past would never have taken his niece in, he'd never have come over to make sure she was okay. He wasn't the selfish idiot from ten years ago, and maybe it was time to give him a chance.

As he made his way to the door, Caroline rushed ahead of him. "Wait," she said.

He stopped, hand on the doorknob, one eyebrow raised.

"Do you still want to go to the botanical garden?"

"Yeah. I've read great things about the exhibit."

"Then, let's go."

"For real, this time?"

She smiled. "For real."

Jared stood with Becca and Caroline at the entrance to the botanical garden in the glorious sunshine. It was one of those clear early spring days where you could taste spring. The sky was pale blue, like Caroline's eyes, and while the air was brisk, there was an underlying warmth.

Caroline was dressed in the same red coat she'd worn the other night, with a red-and-white scarf around her neck and fluffy white mittens. The red emphasized the rosiness of her cheeks.

"You never told me how much I owe you for the tickets," she said as he handed hers over.

He hadn't thought to ask her to pay for her ticket. It went against everything he stood for—he'd suggested the activity, and he made more money than she did. But he remembered the concern marring her expression when she'd resisted him. Her independence was important to her.

"Fifteen dollars."

She stared at him a moment. He could see her mind buzz but couldn't be sure of her thoughts. So, he waited. After a moment, her mouth curved.

"Do you have Venmo?"

He nodded. His chest expanded with the knowledge he'd done the right thing.

"Ready?" he asked.

He pulled out the map of gardens and pushed the stroller in the direction of the special exhibit. Early spring flowers and shrubs dotted the stone paths as they meandered along. The scent of fresh-tilled soil greeted them as they passed gardeners preparing the beds for spring. Up ahead, a structure resembled the Parthenon.

"That must be it," Jared said.

Peach trees—clearly marked with labels otherwise he'd have barely known they were trees, much less what type—surrounded the structure, and crocuses carpeted the beds around it. Inside the structure, spotlights highlighted the modern, neon installations of the artist.

"Oh wow," Caroline said. "This is so cool!" She nodded toward the stroller. "Too bad she's asleep. She'd love to run around here."

They wandered the exhibit. The energy and movement of the display captivated Caroline. Caroline captivated Jared. Her exuberance filled him with joy as she practically danced from one piece to the next. The neon lights turned her hair hues of pink, blue, and yellow. On other people, it would have looked strange, but on Caroline, it served as a moment in time, a glimpse of her thoughts and feelings in slow motion.

She spun around to him, hair flying outward. "I love this! Thank you."

"You're welcome."

Modern art wasn't his thing, and he didn't understand what all the fuss was about. Except for the piece in the center, White Light. It was round, made of wood, paint, neon, aluminum, fur, and a light bulb. It was odd, but if he must choose, it was the piece that interested him the most.

Caroline made it worthwhile. Such a little thing, this exhibit. In comparison to her life, which involved heartache—and he cursed himself for his part in it—this exhibit was nothing. Yet she embraced it with complete abandon.

Unlike him, she wasn't lost. She forged ahead, made plans, and carried them through. He shook his head.

"What?" she asked. "Why are you shaking your head?"

He froze. "I'm in awe of your ability to find such complete enjoyment in the little things."

"This isn't little." She spread her arms. "This is the artist's creative soul on display. There's action and energy and joy right here for us to experience."

He squinted. "I've gotta be honest. All I see are a bunch of lights."

Her laughter was low and vibrated in his chest. He wanted to bottle it, to save it for when he was no longer here. Take it out and taste the joy. Instead, he joined her.

"Then, it's even nicer that you brought me here when it's something that isn't of interest to you. Thank you."

"If I get to witness your pleasure, I'm good."

She touched his arm, and through his wool coat, electricity shot up his arm and straight to his chest. He didn't know if she felt it too, or if she was aware she'd touched his arm. Knowing how uncomfortable she'd been with him before, he remained silent. Instead, he concentrated on every thought, feeling, and emotion, burning it into his memory.

She gave a small smile. "I'm finished here," she said. "We can go."

"Want to walk a little while longer?" he asked. "It's nice out, and I feel like we should take advantage of Becca's nap as long as possible."

Caroline nodded. "If you're sure. I don't want to take advantage of you."

He pushed the stroller and looked quizzically at her. "Take advantage of me?"

His mind went to places she didn't mean. A part of him wished she did. An image of how she could take advantage of him popped up, and he squashed it.

"You already took me to an exhibit you had no interest in. I don't want to force you to walk around a garden if you're not into it, either."

He stretched his arms and made a show of looking at different parts of his body. "I see no signs of suffering, nor do I see evidence you forced me to do anything. Don't forget, I'm the one who suggested it." He resumed pushing the stroller.

Her pleasure satisfied him. "All right, then. Flowers it is!"

He strolled along the paths with her and took more notice

of Caroline than the flowers. Most of those hadn't bloomed yet, although there were yellow and purple crocuses everywhere, not just around the special exhibit. In addition to those flowers, Caroline pointed out the bluebells.

"It's funny to see the difference between California and New Jersey in the spring," he said. "We have the same flowers as you do, but the desert begins to bloom, and of course, palm trees don't demonstrate as much change as the trees here."

"Spring always reminds me there's freedom in starting over," Caroline said. "All the endless possibilities."

Maybe that was why she maintained such strength despite what she'd been through. He'd have to think about that later.

The looped trail started and ended near the parking lot. As Jared and Caroline approached the end, she turned to him. "Thanks for a lovely time. I'm glad I came."

His chest filled with satisfaction, and he took measured breaths to regulate his response. The last thing he wanted was to spook her.

"Me too."

She arched an eyebrow. "What? No gloating that I admitted you were right?"

He grinned. "I thought that would be poor form since I'm trying to prove I'm not the guy I used to be."

"Noted." She touched his forearm again. "I'm glad we can be friends again."

He tried to quell his racing heart.

She walked to her car, and when he was sure she'd arrived safely, he turned toward his. Every fiber wanted to call out to her, suggest another "date." But he refrained. He'd shown her he'd changed. If he wanted any further shot with her, he still had to move slowly. He didn't want to hurt her when he left.

If you lived long enough, anything could happen, Caroline thought to herself as she entered her house afterward. That sentiment was a favorite of her mom's. If her mother were alive for Caroline to talk about her afternoon with the one man she thought she'd never want to see again, she'd nod her head with an I-told-you-so kind of glance. A twinge of melancholy gripped her. From previous experience, she knew to roll with it, rather than fight it. Around her neck, she wore her mom's Star of David necklace. The simple gold pendant dug into her palm as she squeezed it. "Miss you, Mom," she whispered. She always would.

But Jared. Jared had changed. He'd been considerate today. He'd kept his word, and their time together was easy. He hadn't checked his phone. And he'd purposely picked something to do that she liked, though he was less than interested.

Wow.

Her phone rang, and Caroline grinned. "Emily, you're back! How was your trip?"

"Exhausting but fun. How are you?"

"Oh my gosh, I have so much to tell you!"

Emily coughed. "Jeez, I leave on a vacation for a week, and the world changes. Gimme a hint, at least. There was nothing on your social media."

Emily's daily life was recorded on social media, unlike Caroline's. "You're surprised?"

"I guess not," Emily said.

"My promotion was nixed, and Jared is back in town."

"Whoa. Tell me everything. And don't leave out any detail."

Caroline blushed. Emily was a fantastic friend. Ever since grade school, they'd been close, especially now that Emily lived nearby and commuted into Manhattan. Caroline gave her a detailed update of the past few days with Jared, ending with their afternoon get-together.

"You mean date," Emily said.

"It wasn't a date. We're friends."

Emily's silence made Caroline shift in her seat. "It wasn't. I made sure of that ahead of time. There was no kissing involved. Besides, Becca was with us."

"If you say so. I say it's a lead up to a date. And you can't use Becca as an excuse. He's a single dad. She's part of his life."

"Don't make me regret today, Em. I had a good time."

"As long as you had a good time, does it matter if it was a date?"

Caroline pursed her lips. Did it matter? It didn't feel like a date. Jared kept his word. They'd spent a few hours as friends. They'd fallen into their old rhythm with ease. But occasionally, the old familiar attraction pulled her to him, its invisible thread stronger than she thought. He was as handsome, if not more, than when they were younger. And his behavior had changed for the better. The more time she spent with him, the stronger that attraction grew.

"But we said we'd be friends," Caroline said. "I'm finally free of responsibility. Ugh, I hate the way that sounds. I have my life in order. He's apologized for his behavior, and I'm not interested in a relationship right now. I'm traveling this summer!"

"Freedom doesn't disappear when you're in a relationship, Caro. Not if it's the right kind."

"I know that. But I think you're making more out of this than is necessary. We had fun together. That's it. A relationship requires sacrifice, and right now, I want to be selfish and focus on me."

Emily remained silent for a few moments. Finally, she spoke. "You deserve to be happy, and if a no-strings relationship— sorry about that word—is what you want, then enjoy the friendship and don't worry about it. But make sure that what you think you want is what you need."

"I love how you look out for me," Caroline said.

"You're my friend, of course I look out for you. Now, what about your job?"

Thankful for the change in subject, Caroline filled her in on the budget crisis.

"I can't believe your boss doesn't know about this," Emily said. "Don't you find that strange?"

"I do." It was the first time Caroline admitted this, and now she couldn't get the idea out of her mind. "Doug is wise, and he's been a mentor to me. Yet if he knew nothing about this, what else doesn't he know? Maybe I shouldn't rely on him for my career advice."

"I have a few people who guide me in my career," Emily said. "That way, I can choose who I go to for what—whether as a woman of color in advertising, how to navigate the digital age, or professional tips."

"You sound like you could teach at a conference, based on those topics," Caroline said with admiration.

"Don't laugh, but my boss wants me to consider it for our next in-house-staff retreat."

"That's awesome! You said yes, right? Can I sneak in and watch?"

"Thanks, yes, and definitely not. Besides, we're talking about you right now."

Caroline sighed. "I never thought I'd say this but that topic is getting old."

"Fine, we'll move on to me, but only after we finish with you."

"Yes, ma'am."

Emily cleared her throat. "If you can't get information out of your boss, can you find someone else who might know something?"

"I can, but I have to be careful. I don't want to appear to go over Doug's head. I'd love to be able to see a raw copy of the budget, though."

"That would be awesome, especially with your accounting minor. Maybe you could position it as how to save money?"

"I'm low woman on the org chart, though."

"Well, if there's a way you can take control, rather than accept your fate, I think you'll feel better."

Chapter Six

After dinner with Eli the night before, Jared awoke from a restless night's sleep in his childhood bedroom to four texts from his clients. They wanted to know when he'd be back to take care of their legal issues. Why the hell did they bother him on a weekend? His body jerked at the thought. Only at his parents' house did he think about the day of the week. In LA, he worked all the time.

He sighed as he scrolled through the messages, leaning against the oak headboard while covered with the blue-plaid quilt he'd had since his teens. His colleague, Fran, was filling in for him. She was talented and tenacious, and if Jared needed an entertainment lawyer, he'd hire her. Instead, his clients wanted him, not her. He'd put in endless hours and worked hard to gain their trust. He waited for pride or satisfaction to fill him. Instead, his head ached in annoyance.

When he talked to Eli about his career, the usual thrill hadn't shot through him. Eli was impressed with the caliber of his client list, but Jared shrugged. Eli's obvious love for architectural design—and how his entire demeanor changed when he spoke about it—struck Jared.

He frowned. His job had always been his life. At one time, he'd craved the attention from his clients, name-dropped at parties and watched envy creep over friends' countenances. He'd defined his success by billable hours, hefty bonuses, and coveted tickets to events the average person couldn't get into or afford. But lately, the buzz of excitement fizzled under a haze of lethargy. He hoped time with his parents would refill the well, but if his distress over four texts was any indication, he needed more than hope.

Dashing off quick responses to each of them and referring them to Fran, he made a promise to himself to stop answering texts. And then he contemplated writing a fifth one.

His fingers flew across the keyboard. Yesterday was fun. I thought all Greek sculptors were long dead.

He hit Send, hoping this message would get a reply.

When Caroline responded a few seconds later, a shiver of excitement rushed through him.

Ha! Only the very old ones. I enjoyed it, too. Even more excited for my trip now.

I'll bet. When do you leave?

May 18, aka, not soon enough.

God, he missed being excited about something.

Be here before you know it.

Hope so. You traveling at all?

He hadn't given it any thought. Besides, traveling here was about all he could manage.

Kinda hard with Becca.

Oh, yeah. Right.

But someday.

Would he travel with Becca? Or would he leave her with the nanny? The nanny—crap, he needed to find a new nanny to replace Lucinda. It was too early to call the service, so he emailed instead, describing the ideal candidate and salary. Then he checked his phone. Caroline hadn't responded.

He was disappointed. He wanted to see her again. If he asked her now, would it be too soon? He needed to exercise patience with her, and he didn't want to scare her away. But he wanted to see her.

See you soon?

She didn't answer for a long time. There could be a million reasons why—she stepped away from the phone, she was in the shower—crap, now he couldn't stop thinking of her naked.

He hadn't seen her naked since high school, but his imagination filled in the details his memory couldn't. He groaned and tried to focus on other reasons for her lack of response. Like, she didn't want to see him again.

This was ridiculous. Mooning over her like a teenager was beneath him. Must be sleeping in his old room that caused the problem. He put his phone on the scuffed night table and got ready for the day. She'd respond, or not, when she had time.

He did not drop clean black boxers on the blue carpet and lunge across the queen-size bed when his phone vibrated with another text.

Nope, not him. He'd deny it with his last breath.

I'll try.

He was a lawyer, rational and thoughtful. He wasn't about to assign significance to her response, infuse it with emotions that she might not feel. All he needed to do was take her response at face value.

She hadn't said no.

Caroline frowned as she studied the budget data Doug gave her Monday morning. It showed a large deficit, but the data was incomplete. She needed to see a clearer breakdown with more details and raw numbers. She walked over to his office.

"Hey, Doug. Is this the only information about our part of the budget you have? I was hoping to find the money we need to fund our entire department next year." She turned her laptop toward him.

He squinted, changed his glasses, and looked again.

"Those numbers are for the athletic department." He straightened in his chair. His black sweater strained across his stomach. "I might be able to get you numbers for the senior center and programming, but you'd have to talk to Al in finance for a more comprehensive set of figures."

She paused outside Doug's office door. He was her mentor. In fact, when she'd first started as an athletic instructor to make money, he'd suggested she take accounting, psychology, and social work classes at the community college. He'd taught her the ropes across all areas of the JCC, including senior programming and fundraising, and he understood her eagerness to learn everything. She could talk to him about anything. Al Shapiro was different. Two years away from retirement, he was the JCC's finance director, who worked with both the JCC and Federation higher-ups. She'd met him a couple of times, but those interactions were brief. She would never be as comfortable with Al as she was with Doug.

Caroline applied fresh lip gloss and rehearsed what she would say before she made her way to Al's office on the second floor. It was lunchtime, and the floor was quiet. *Probably should have made an appointment.* She walked to his office.

The desk outside, where his administrator sat, was empty. With a deep breath, she knocked on his door.

"Enter!"

She turned the handle. Unlike Doug's sparsely decorated office, this one was filled with photos of people and childlike drawings with To Grandpa in crayon. He was a family man.

Balding and dressed in a button-down, he looked up from his computer. "Can I help you?"

"Hi, Al, I'm Caroline Weiss. I work downstairs. Doug Erlach is my boss."

He nodded. "I've seen you around. What can I do for you?"

"Well, I understand our budget for next year is tight. I wondered if I could get more detailed numbers from you, more than what Doug has? I'm helping him with the numbers."

Al leaned back in his chair and rested his hands on his large belly. "Take a seat."

Caroline's posture relaxed as she entered. "Thanks. I appreciate your time."

He nodded. "Now, tell me what you don't understand about the budget."

She gripped the arms of the chair on the other side of Al's desk. Had she misspoken? "Oh, I understand it just fine. But the sheets Doug has don't have raw numbers."

Al smirked. "Raw numbers aren't necessary for people who don't understand accounting. It can be too confusing. You said you work downstairs. You're a fitness instructor, right?"

Annoyance heated the nape of her neck. "That's one of my duties, yes. I work at the senior center—"

He held up a hand to stop her. "You should stick to your area of expertise. If Doug gave you his budget sheets, that's all you need to have. Anything else will be confusing, and some of it isn't meant for someone at your level. We can't have just anyone know salaries and benefits of our top-tier employees and directors."

"Of course not," she said. "I never intended to look at that information. I hoped—"

"Your eagerness and initiative are appreciated." He came around his desk and motioned for Caroline to rise.

He was kicking her out.

"I'm glad we had this chat," he said. "Don't worry about the budget. This one is finalized and there will be plenty of time for those of us with the knowledge to handle the deficit. In the meantime, I'm sure you have exercise routines to plan, don't you?"

By now, he'd ushered her out his office door and shut it behind her. She stood in the middle of the empty department, shaking. Anger made her pulse pound in her ears. She clenched her teeth together hard enough to make her jaw ache.

How dare that condescending idiot treat her that way? She spun around, fist raised, ready to pound on his door and demand an apology. But something made her pause. And in that pause, a little bit of reason returned.

Al Shapiro was a prick. He'd lulled her into thinking he was willing to see her, and then turned around and told her to go back to her side of the playground and play with the other little girls and boys. Someone like that was unpredictable. She'd gone to him at Doug's suggestion. If Al said anything about her, Doug would support her. However, if she went *back* in there and continued her questions, she'd have no one to take her side if Al got angry. And that would place her job at risk.

No promotion was better than no job.

She'd have to find another way.

"Jared, can you help me, please?"

His mother's question greeted him Monday morning when he made his way downstairs. Dressed in sweats and a T-shirt, he'd hoped to go to the JCC and work out for an hour while his parents watched Becca. Maybe he'd run into Caroline, follow up yesterday's texts with something concrete.

"Sure, what do you need?"

He scanned the bright kitchen. Morning light streamed in from the bay window facing the backyard. Becca sat in her highchair, playing with, and eating, her cereal and fruit. His parents sat at the oval table. He frowned in concern.

"Don't look worried," his dad said. "We need your help with Passover cleaning."

The tightness in his chest eased. "Oh, right. Of course. What do you need?"

In his family, Passover cleaning was like spring cleaning. Not only did they have to get rid of all traces of bread products, but they used it as an opportunity to clean the house from top to bottom. His parents tackled different spaces in the weeks ahead of the holiday. By the time the seder rolled around, there was not a spot of dirt anywhere.

His mom spread out lists in front of her. "The curtains and bedspreads need to be picked up from the dry cleaner, the bedrooms need a last quick vacuum, and then no food up there until after the holiday, and I need help vacuuming behind the furniture."

Jared nodded. "Okay, Mom, why don't Dad and I do the heavy stuff? We'll move the furniture and vacuum the bedrooms. You can pick up the curtains from the dry cleaner."

"That would be great," his mom said. "I'll take Becca with me so she's out of your way. When I get home, we can rehang everything and put everything back in its place." She studied her lists again. "That should be enough for today, I think."

It was plenty. "Don't worry, Mom. It will all be taken care of."

Her worry overflowed as she bit her lip. "I know. It's such a process, and every year, it gets harder."

"But I'm here now. You have an extra set of hands." Guilt over avoiding home overwhelmed him.

She rose and pulled him into a hug. "Thank you."

With a vow to do better, he squeezed her waist. "You don't need to thank me. I'm here, and I'm part of the family." It had been a long time since he'd acknowledged that, with grief tangled through everything. But it was true. His parents needed him, and no matter how much he hurt from Noah's death, it was his duty to help them.

That duty, along with taking care of Becca, needed to be more of a focus in his life.

She held him at arm's length. "You're dressed for the gym—"

"Don't worry," he said. "I'll get as much exercise here doing what you need." He swallowed his disappointment at missing Caroline. "And I'm ready now. Let's get started."

"Did you eat?"

"No, I'll eat after—"

"Nope." She interrupted, a look of determination on her face. "Sit and have breakfast. You need your energy. Then you can work."

While lots of things changed in his life, his mother's concern for his eating habits—she *was* a Jewish mother, after all, and food was her love language—remained the same.

"Yes, Mom."

His dad patted him on the back. "Smart man. I'll join you."

"Honey, you already ate."

His dad's expression pleaded. "Come on, he shouldn't eat alone."

"He's not," his mom said. "Becca's with him." She handed Jared a floral plate with a sesame bagel already on it. "Cream cheese, etcetera, is on the table."

His dad gave a dramatic sigh, and she walked over and kissed his weathered cheek. "Besides, he doesn't have to watch his carbs like you do."

With a pout, his dad turned to Becca. "*Safta* is mean," he whispered.

"*Safta* mean," she repeated.

Jared choked on his orange juice, and his mom cried out. "David, what did you teach your granddaughter?"

He held up his hands in surrender. "I didn't know she'd repeat it!"

"Oh? You had no idea a toddler would repeat your words?" His mother fixed him with a glare.

Jared would have caved. But his dad handled his mother in ways he'd never understand. And although he remembered his dad telling him to watch his language in front of Becca, he kept his mouth shut.

"Relax, Harriet. It'll be fine."

"*Safta* mean, *Safta* mean, *Safta* mean!" Becca crowed in delight at the attention, and this time, Jared couldn't help but laugh.

"You might need to rethink that, Dad," he said. "Because this one didn't get the message."

His dad folded his arms on the table and groaned in defeat.

"You wait," his mother said. "I'll get my revenge." She looked at the two men. "Now, get out of here, both of you. Becca and I have errands to run."

She lifted Becca out of the highchair. "And when I return, I want to see progress."

Jared cleaned Becca's face before she left with his mom. He turned to his dad. "Upstairs or downstairs first?"

His father rose and cleared the table. "Let's move all the furniture away from the walls first. Then we can do all the vacuuming at once." He leaned toward Jared. "Besides, if your mom comes home, it's easier for her to see progress if the furniture is moved."

"You're the boss, Dad."

"Try telling your mom that."

Chapter Seven

"I can't believe Al spoke to you like that," Sarah said in the middle of the grocery aisle that evening. The two women had decided to shop for Passover items together, and while the Kosher for Passover aisle was crowded with other Jewish shoppers, the rest of the store was quiet at seven thirty on a weeknight. "How many boxes of matzah do you want?"

"One. I'm not hosting a seder, and I don't eat much of it anyway. I can always pick up another box if I run low."

Sarah laughed. "Yeah, matzah is the one thing they never run out of in the grocery stores."

"Nope, and they try to sell it every Jewish holiday during the year."

Sarah handed Caroline one box and took two for herself. "Like anyone wants to eat matzah in the first place." She shuddered. "Although Aaron makes the best *matzah brei*. His egg, matzah, and salt combo is delicious."

Caroline scanned the Passover aisle as Sarah pushed the cart.

"Gefilte fish for lunch, matzah crackers for snacks, Passover dressing for salads," Caroline said. "What else do I need?"

"You want to live on that for a week?"

Caroline shuddered. "No, but I can still eat regular protein, vegetables, and fruit, so I need things to take the place of bread."

"Back to Al. I'm impressed you didn't tell him off." Sarah grabbed a box of potato starch and matzah meal.

Caroline shook her head. "And risk my job? No way. However, I might have upped the speed of the exercise classes for the rest of the day to work off some of my anger." She winked.

"You're a better person than I am. Want to run tomorrow morning?"

"I run every morning, so I'd love the company. Six?"

Sarah nodded. "Refrigerator aisle?"

Caroline took a quick look down the aisle. "Um, wait, I need chocolate." She grabbed a couple of dark chocolate bars and some chocolate mints. "Now I'm ready."

"Dammit, I try to be healthy, and you tempt me!"

"Dark chocolate is healthy," Caroline said, "and we all deserve to indulge during Passover."

"You're right." Sarah chose two dark chocolate bars and pushed the cart toward the refrigerator aisle. They each took a frozen kugel, chicken, and kosher-for-Passover butter, before they turned to the checkout lanes.

"So, what's your plan now?" Sarah unloaded the groceries onto the belt and divided them into two sets of purchases.

"I don't know," Caroline said. "I can't sit and do nothing, but I also can't dig around without permission. Doug doesn't have answers, and Al won't give me any. So, unless something drops into my lap, I'm not sure there is anything left to do."

Sarah bagged her groceries and paid, then waited for Caroline to do the same. "I have a friend in the campaign department who raises money and handles some of the donations for the JCC. Let me see if she can give me any more information about the budget crisis that I can pass along to you."

Carrying her bags of groceries, Caroline followed Sarah out to the car. "You'll help me?"

Sarah looked at her after she loaded the bags into her trunk. "You're my friend, Caro. And if there's anything suspicious going on with donations, it affects all of us. Of course I will. I can't promise anything, but I can at least try."

"Thank you. If I can't figure out why those donations disappeared so quickly, I'm not sure my promotion will happen. As much as I love my job, I've worked hard to develop other programs for seniors. I want to expand my role."

Sarah pulled to a stop in front of Caroline's house. "I loved shopping together for Passover."

Caroline leaned over and gave her a hug. "I love how you're home now to do it with me. It's no fun alone."

Tuesday morning, Jared glanced over at Becca's playpen. She lay on her belly, head turned toward him, cheeks flushed, thumb in her mouth, butt up in the air, sound asleep.

She was beautiful and flourished here. Her vocabulary had increased, and she interacted with him and other people more than she did at home. Now that he'd been here a few days, he'd grown accustomed to being with her, more than when he was in LA with the nanny.

Speaking of nannies, the service promised to provide him a list of suitable candidates he could interview. When he'd hired Lucinda, he hadn't known what he was doing. This time around, after spending more time with Becca, he had a different type of nanny in mind. He grabbed his phone and searched his email, but the West Coast wasn't up and about yet. There also weren't any texts from his clients. Maybe they'd gotten the message.

He looked at Becca again. Now that he'd spent more one-on-one time with her, he relaxed in his role. Of course, he relied on his parents for a lot of the care right now, but they didn't seem to mind. Still, now that they were busy with Passover prep, he'd have to make sure not to overtax them. Letting Becca sleep, he grabbed the monitor, snuck out of the bedroom, leaving the door cracked so he could hear her stir, and jogged downstairs for coffee.

He set the pot to percolate and watched the rain through the sliding-glass doors leading out to the deck. At least it wasn't snow. That was the good thing about LA. No snow. Not much change of seasons, though. He'd forgotten the anticipation of spring, where every sunny day brought joy, and every drop in temperature brought entire debates of whether it would snow, how much, and how soon it would disappear. Stepping outside beneath the overhang, the chilly air made him shiver, but there was an underlayer of warmer temperature. Or, not quite warm but not the biting cold of winter. And it didn't smell like snow.

He reentered the kitchen as his dad came in wearing jeans and a sweatshirt.

"What are you doing?" his dad asked.

I have no idea. "Just seeing how cold it is." As the words left his mouth, he realized how lame it sounded. "We don't get this weather in LA."

His dad glanced at him sideways as he poured the two of them coffee. "Miss home?"

Home? He wasn't sure where that was anymore. He shrugged.

His dad patted him on the shoulder. "You'll figure it out."

He hoped so. Becca fussed through the monitor, and just as he was about to go back upstairs, he heard his mother talking to her. Drinking deep from the mug, he waited for the caffeine to kick in and sighed at the nutty flavor. "This is good."

"Enjoy it."

"What's the plan for today?"

His dad held up his hands in surrender. "That's a question for your mother."

Jared laughed.

"What's your question?" She entered the kitchen with Becca. "This one is fussy this morning."

She handed her off to Jared and prepared the toddler's breakfast.

"She feels a little warm to me," he said.

Becca cuddled close.

"I thought so, too," his mom said. "Don't worry, we can keep an eye on it. But what was the question?"

"I wanted to know what the plan is for today," he said.

"More of the same," she said. "But less heavy lifting. If you have your own plans, go do them."

"I don't, although I'd love to get a workout in at the JCC." Maybe he'd run into Caroline. He hadn't talked to her since the weekend, and while he didn't want to pressure her, he didn't want to ignore her, either.

"Good." His parents nodded. "Leave Becca here. She shouldn't be around other kids if she's under the weather. We'll be fine, and you can help after lunch."

"You sure you don't mind? I don't want Becca to make it harder for you."

His mother glared at him. "She's our granddaughter, and she's perfect. Now, stop arguing and go work out."

"Yes, ma'am," he mumbled under his breath. With a last glance at Becca, he went to get changed.

A half hour later, he checked into the JCC fitness center with his parents' membership card and kept an eye out for Caroline. He was determined to ask her out today. Not seeing her, he went into the weight room and started to warm up. The room was filled with men and women of all ages, some of whom he vaguely recognized. After he stretched, he moved on to the weights. He'd slacked off since arriving in Browerville, and his muscles protested after yesterday's furniture moving. But he found his rhythm and worked up a sweat. By the time he finished, his clothes were dark with perspiration and his hair was wet.

Caroline chose that moment to walk into one of the dance studios around the perimeter of the weight room.

Great, just great. A smelly gym rat was not how he wanted to present himself when he asked her out. As long as she didn't see him, he could sneak off to the locker room, shower, and be back in time to catch her at the end of her class. Through the window, several seniors kept her busy. He was safe.

Until one of them caught his eye, smiled, and grabbed Caroline's arm. Caroline looked at him. She waved. Another senior gesticulated, and two others took her by the elbows and walked her to the door. Their "go talk to him" echoed off the cinder block walls.

Seniors were loud.

"Hi." She stood at the perimeter of the weight room.

Grabbing a towel, he dried his face and neck, then walked over to her. Not too close, though, and hopefully downwind.

"I was going to stop in later, after I showered."

She nodded to the room behind her. "Yeah, well, they thought I should talk to you now."

Seniors were also nosy, since at least seven of them crowded in the doorway and tried to overhear their conversation.

"That's because they haven't smelled me."

Caroline laughed, and he ignored everyone else around them, especially the older people who elbowed each other like a swarm of elementary school students. Her laughter brought a sparkle to her eyes and made him feel like his old self, before the world shifted off-kilter with his brother's death and spun out of control.

"I didn't hear you contradict me," he said.

She shrugged. "I prefer to save it for the important stuff."

Now it was his turn to chuckle, but he kept his laughter subdued. He didn't want to make a scene at her workplace. Well, aside from the seniors, that is.

"Smart move," he said.

"How was your workout?"

"Good. Better now," he said.

"Most people find it better when they're finished."

He shook his head. "I'm not finished. I meant because of you."

She swallowed. He'd made her uncomfortable. Before her

discomfort lasted too long, he continued. "Do you ever go into New York City?"

"Sometimes I'll go in with Emily for dinner or meet up with Jessica. You remember her, right? Not often, though. It's expensive."

He'd never realized how tight things were for her. She'd sacrificed a lot.

"How about I take you in one night this week?"

"*You're* on vacation, but I'm not."

He nodded. "I know. But if we leave as soon as you're finished, we'll be in within an hour. I have the perfect idea, and we won't be home late. Promise."

She looked at him askance. "What's your perfect idea?"

"It's a surprise."

"I'm not big on surprises."

He remembered that about her. She'd always preferred knowing what lay ahead. She was a planner. And now he had to weigh his desire to see her face when he brought her to the location against his goal of making her comfortable with him.

"I want to take you someplace with a great view," he said. "If you want to know, I'll tell you, though."

"You never used to be easygoing," she said. "What changed?"

Good question. "Everything." He let his gaze bounce around before it returned to her. "I'm different than I was in ways I can't explain. I'm glad you noticed."

A noise behind them made her jump. "I'm late for class."

"So, will you go with me?"

"When?"

"Tomorrow night."

She nodded. "If I turn into a pumpkin, I blame you."

"Caroline, come into my office a minute," Doug said when she returned from the exercise class.

Crap. Did Doug hear she was late for class? The seniors

in her class were interested in her conversation with Jared. Surely, they didn't complain. If anything, they were disappointed when she'd stopped the gossip and turned on the music. There had to be a reason for his desire to spend time with her. No matter how much he'd changed, he never did anything without a goal in mind.

Pushing those thoughts aside, she entered Doug's office. He gestured for her to sit.

"I know I'd promised you the promotion, and I feel bad I can't make it happen." He scratched his cheek. "I shouldn't have made the promise, but it's not fair, regardless. Therefore, I thought you might be interested in a special project. It's a little outside of your wheelhouse, but it was given to me from Fundraising, and I thought it might be good for you to round out your skill set. You haven't had a lot of experience in this area, and it can only help you in your future career goals. You know about the Matzah Ball, right?"

Everyone knew about the Matzah Ball. It was one of the JCC's biggest fundraisers, held in the spring each year.

She nodded.

"Well, the person in charge this year had to go out on medical leave. They need someone to fill in for her, and I mentioned your name."

Caroline's stomach dropped. "But it's only a month away."

"All the more reason why we need someone eager and capable to run it. You're organized and you've excelled in every project you've taken on. You'll be perfect for this."

"I'm flattered, but isn't there someone with more experience, on the committee itself or in the campaign office?" Al's taunting her with being "only an athletic instructor" echoed in her mind.

"Yes, there are plenty of people with more experience. But I made the case for you to take over. Even though your promotion was put on hold, I thought you'd still want to expand your knowledge. This way, other people, not just me, will see your talent."

And know who to blame if the fundraiser fails.

"I thought you'd be happier about this." He frowned. "If you don't want the opportunity…"

"No, I do. I'm flattered. I was…surprised."

He beamed. "Great. Go upstairs to Fundraising and ask for Jacki. She'll give you all the information you need."

She nodded and started to leave. Doug stopped her at the doorway. "I know you'll do a great job, Caroline."

"Thank you." She jogged up the stairs to the second floor and searched the bullpen for Jacki.

She knocked on the edge of the cubicle. "Hi, I'm Caroline Weiss. Doug told me to find you regarding the Matzah Ball."

Jacki's face lit up, and her red, frizzy hair bounced with excitement. "Yes!" She spun in her chair and reached for an overstuffed manila folder. Lifting it with two hands, she swung around and held it out to Caroline.

"Here you go. This is everything I have on the Matzah Ball."

"Wait, what? I thought there was a committee…"

"Oh, there is. Everything you need is inside the folder. It just requires a little organization. Plus, you'll have to make sure nothing fell through the cracks when Olive stepped away."

Caroline's heartbeat increased. Cracks? Organization?

Suddenly, remaining an athletic instructor forever didn't sound like such a bad idea.

"Don't look scared," Jacki said. "Everything should be there, and if you have any questions, you can always ask me. If I can't answer them, I'll find someone who can. This thing practically runs itself. And you have a great committee. Believe me, no one wants this event to fail this year."

Now Caroline's stomach hurt. She plastered what she hoped was a smile on her face, thanked Jacki, and returned to her office. For the rest of the day, in between her classes, she sorted through the information in the folder and attempted to organize it in a way that made sense to her. The ball was the week after Passover, which gave her a short time to make sure everything was perfect.

Normally, she didn't bring work home with her. Her job didn't lend itself to it, other than researching political and current events for the senior discussion groups. Today, she brought the entire folder home. She'd need every spare minute to figure out how to pull this off.

With stacks of papers spread out on her living room rug, her laptop open to four different programs and six different internet tabs, and music playing in the background, Caroline was deep into her to-do list when her cell phone rang. Barely focused on anything other than the task at hand, she answered without looking at the caller ID.

"Hello?"

"Hey, it's Jared. I wanted to make sure you were okay about tomorrow night. I know you hate surprises, and if you want to know where we're going, I'll tell you. The last thing I want to do is make you uncomfortable."

Jared. Tomorrow night. Crap. Caroline sighed. "I'm sorry. I have to reschedule." There was no way she could go out tomorrow night with him.

"It was the surprise, wasn't it? Darn, I knew I pushed you too far—"

"No, that wasn't it."

Jared was silent for a few moments on the other end of the phone.

"Then, may I ask what the problem is?"

If she were smart, she'd fall back on the it's-not-a-good-idea excuse. But he'd been kind enough to check up on her and make sure she was comfortable about their date. It wasn't fair to be anything but kind. Besides, she'd agreed to be honest with him.

"I got saddled with this huge project," she said, "which I know sounds crazy to you, who has a million huge projects and manages to juggle life and work and a baby, but I'm not used to it and—"

"Caroline, take a breath." A soft chuckle sounded over the phone. "I'm glad it's not me. But you sound overwhelmed. Maybe talking about it will help?"

He should be the last person she'd confide anything to, but he'd called at the exact right time, and before she could think of all the reasons not to talk to him, she'd filled him in on the Matzah Ball.

"It's a yearly fundraiser. Only as far as I can tell, other than ridiculous ticket prices that no one, other than our older, wealthier donors will pay, I can't figure out how in three weeks they will turn this into a magical fundraiser to solve the budget crisis."

Jared inhaled. "Three weeks? That's tight."

"Right? And the worst part is, if I don't make this into a success, I'll never get a promotion. Doug said he volunteered me to take over for Olive so I could prove my worth."

"Yeah, no pressure there at all," Jared said.

"Now you know why I can't go out tomorrow night, or pretty much any day, night, or in between for the next three weeks." She hated being forced into something beyond her control.

Again, there was silence. "Tell you what," he said. "How about if I come over tomorrow with dinner, wine, and an extra set of hands or brain, and help you with whatever you need?"

She paused. His suggestion confused her. The Jared she remembered… Well, maybe it was time to stop comparing new Jared to old Jared.

"I don't know what I'll need to do, or if I'll be home," she said. "It's a lovely idea, though."

"Call me tomorrow afternoon, say, four thirty. You can tell

me where you're at and what you need. If you need me to be a delivery guy for some food so you don't have to cook, I'll do that. Whatever. I can be flexible."

"But you have Becca."

"Yes, and Becca has grandparents who love to take care of her."

"You sure you want to do this?"

"Caroline, I wanted to take you to dinner and a nice night out. You have to work. So, I can adapt. Can you?"

Chapter Eight

Jared showed up to Caroline's house the next night with a bottle of red wine, a bouquet of pink tulips, takeout from the local Thai place, and a pounding heart.

He'd spent the entire day convinced she'd cancel and tried to temper his desire to see her with that very real possibility. But Caroline called at four thirty, agreed to bring her work home, and Jared promised dinner. Although they'd left out the word *date*, it was the unacknowledged presence between them. He'd never been more nervous about a date. He cleared his throat and squeezed the parcels in his arms.

His parents added to that worry. They'd assured him Becca would be fine when they took her from him, and they were thrilled to spend time with her. But in the next breath, his mother warned him not to get involved with someone who had been through so much. "Do not hurt her," she'd said. The command rang through the house, as if that was his intention. How cruel had he been perceived, if his own mother warned him away? His father suggested the flowers and reminded him that it was never wrong to make a woman feel special.

If anyone deserved to feel special, it was Caroline. She was beautiful, but more than that, she was smart, confident, and sensitive. She cared and wasn't afraid to show it. Warmth flooded through him. He wanted to show her not only how special she was but how she made him want to do better. To be better.

So, he stood on the front porch of Caroline's Cape Cod–style home, the same one he'd visited countless times in high school, sweating like a Bar Mitzvah boy before being called to the Torah. He shifted from foot to foot, and the porch floor creaked in the same spot it did then. He glanced at the wide planks and remembered how they'd avoided that spot when he'd dropped her off after a date. If it didn't creak, they'd have a few extra seconds for a longer good-night kiss.

Would she let him kiss her this time?

His mouth moistened at the thought of taking her in his arms.

She opened the door, and he raised his gaze to meet hers. A few strands of hair framed her face, and her Star of David necklace shone against her collarbone. His hands trembled with a desire to brush the hair off her face, to feel the necklace against his palms and see if it was warm like her skin. Instead, he gripped the flowers harder. She retreated a step and he entered.

Staring at everything in his arms, she raised an eyebrow. "You know it's the two of us, right?"

Her voice interrupted his musings. "Oh? Then, I guess I'll have to give *you* the flowers." He winked, relieved that, somehow, she'd removed any potential awkwardness.

Her cheeks reddened as she took them from him. "I meant the size of the Thai takeout bag. How much did you order?"

He followed her into the kitchen and admired her butt in the black leggings she wore and the messy bun in her hair. He swallowed.

"I was hungry," he said.

"That explains it." She turned to him. "Thank you for the tulips. They're lovely."

Not nearly as lovely as you. "You're welcome." *Thanks, Dad.* He grew light-headed at her nearness. The faint scent of the tulips mixed with her perfume, and he inhaled.

She pointed to the kitchen table, already covered with her computer and spreadsheets. "If you move everything to one end, we can eat at the other. I'll get the plates."

He reminded himself he was here to help her, not jump her bones, no matter how much he might want to.

"I take it as a good sign you can eat first," he said. "I envisioned having to feed you while you stared at the computer." Not that it would be bad. He could sit as close to her as he wanted.

"I was worried about that, too. But I refuse to sacrifice meals for work." She sat next to him and unpacked the bag. "This all smells good." She inhaled.

"Good plan." He'd have to remind her of that later, and maybe see if she'd want to squeeze in other activities, too.

"Oh, you got the curry puffs!" Using her chopsticks like a pro, she took one from the package and put it on her plate, along with salmon *khing sod* and drunken noodles.

"Are they good? I asked for help with variety," Jared said. The Thai place wasn't one he was familiar with, but his parents recommended it.

"Amazing! Here, try." She put one on his plate.

He would have preferred she feed him, but that would take more time. He added *pad see ew* and red curry with chicken to his plate, before tasting the curry puffs. "You're right," he said.

They ate a few seconds in silence. He tried not to stare at her mouth. Instead, he looked at the familiar oak grain of the table. "I remember sitting here doing homework together." He smiled at the memory. "Or I should say, pretending to do homework. Most of the time, I stared at you." Kind of like now.

"I remember." She looked off into the distance, gaze unfocused. "My mom wouldn't let us in my bedroom together, which I thought was unfair."

"Well, it ensured we didn't spend all our time kissing and… other stuff." His body heated and he shifted in his seat.

Caroline grinned. "Remember how we sent email messages back and forth at the table?"

"I didn't want your mom to hear what I said to you. Too bad texting wasn't a thing then."

Caroline's eyes grew misty. "She knew, you know. She used to comment afterwards about how 'chatty' we were."

Jared smiled. "Guess we didn't fool her as well as we thought."

"Nope."

Jared wanted to pull her into his arms right this minute, but he gave her time to compose herself and took another bite of noodles. After another few seconds, he gestured to her computer. "What can I help you with?"

She turned the laptop toward him. "I think I understand where Olive left everything. The event is in pretty good shape, and I wouldn't be worried at all if it were any other year. It would be an event like any other, and that would be the end of it. But because our finances are in such bad shape, I feel like we need something to make a splash and maybe encourage those who wouldn't attend to feel like they can't afford to miss it." She rested her chin on her hand. "I know we can't make up the entire deficit, but if we could make a good chunk of money, it would help, and we might be able to track where the money disappears to, since I'll have easy access to those funds."

He frowned. "You don't think you can solve the fraud on your own, do you?" He held up a hand. "Wait. That sounded bad. I don't mean to imply you're not capable, but if someone took the money, they're good at hiding their actions." His heart quickened at the thought of her snooping and putting herself in any kind of danger.

"It's kind of a pipe dream. But it's in the back of my mind. In the meantime, what I really want to do is to attract younger people to the event and show my capabilities so I can get that promotion. From what I can tell, in the past, the ball has appealed more to our older donors. If I could somehow entice people of our generation to attend, that would add more guests. Paying guests." She expelled a breath. "I need to stop dreaming of how to make this better and just make sure it takes place. There isn't enough time to add anything to it, as much as I might want to."

Jared nodded. "Show me what you have. Maybe a second pair of eyes will help."

She clicked on different tabs. Their shoulders touched as she walked him through the plans for the dance.

"The Matzah Ball is a formal dance and auction held the Saturday night after Passover," she said. "They transform the JCC lobby into a cocktail area, a few of the meeting rooms into dinner areas, and the largest meeting room into a ballroom. They sell tickets, but just about break even, since it's never been featured as a fundraiser. The ball is entertainment and hopefully to attract new members." She paused. "Even though the plans are already in place, I wish there was a way make it better and raise the money we ought to be able to bring in for something like the Matzah Ball. But at this late date, I don't see how we can."

"Have you sold any tickets yet?"

She nodded. "Although most of them will be sold about a week before the event because people always wait until the last minute, so…" She opened the Tickets Sold folder on her computer. "We've sold about fifteen so far."

"And what about food? What arrangements have been made?"

"We cater from some kosher restaurant a few towns over."

"You don't use Isaacson's Deli?"

Caroline smiled. "I'd love to, but the caterer has already been hired."

"And the music?"

"We have a staff member who volunteers his time as a DJ."

Jared drummed his fingers on the table. He had an idea, an excellent idea if he could pull it off, but it would add a lot to Caroline's already full plate. Still, if it helped her make the event succeed…

"What if I could get you a big name? Someone who could draw a crowd and enable you to charge more for the tickets?"

Caroline frowned. "It's a great idea, but I can't imagine Doja Cat or Ben Platt wanting to come to our JCC," she said. "That's kind of like relegating Adam Sandler to the Bar Mitzvah circuit."

"Hold that thought." Jared pulled out his phone. He scrolled through his contacts and dialed. "Hey, Ben, it's Jared."

Caroline frowned.

"What are your plans—" he covered the phone and pulled the laptop over to him "—April second?"

She squeaked, and he held up a finger.

"Can you get your understudy for that night? My hometown JCC is hosting an event and I need you to headline it." He filled him in. "Great. I'll confirm with you tomorrow. Thanks."

He hung up the phone and turned to Caroline. She sat motionless and silent, mouth open. He waited. She remained in the same position. He waved a hand in front of her face. Still nothing. Gently, he stroked beneath her chin, enjoying the chance to touch her. His view of the room telescoped. She shut her mouth with a click.

"Did you just—Was that—How?"

Caroline was incoherent. Amusement mixed with pride filled his chest. It had been a long time since Caroline was impressed with him. Longer still since he'd felt anything other than the foggy sense of despair that had plagued him since his brother died. He liked the change. He liked her.

And she was adorable when she was shocked.

"He's my client. Yes, it was. And he owes me a favor."

"But we can't afford him."

"Don't worry about that. Like I said, he owes me a favor. If he charges, which I doubt he will, it will be minimal."

Caroline frowned. "Real-person minimal, or Jared-is-magic minimal?"

His neck warmed at the praise. "Real person."

"But we've already sold tickets."

"So, freeze them until we have this settled. In the meantime, prepare new posters to advertise his presence. And when you start again, create a VIP meet-and-greet for those who are willing to pay the higher price for this last-minute addition to the Matzah Ball."

"I'll have to increase the amount of food. Maybe Aaron will pitch in. Maybe we could convert those meeting rooms into photo booth areas..." Her voice was low, as if she spoke to herself. Jared loved watching her shift gears and think outside the box, a box which suddenly expanded to a crate. Most people would lament the extra work involved in a last-minute change. Caroline, however, was excited. Did the JCC realize what an amazing employee they had? Because the longer he spent with her, the more wonderful he thought she was.

She turned to him. "How sure are you that you can promise Ben will show up?"

"Positive. He'll sing, if you'd like, and can MC the auction." He reached for her and held her upper arms. Her muscles were firm from her training. Her gaze was bright and fierce. Although she'd asked a question, there was no insecurity in it. She'd make a worthy adversary in court, and a better partner outside it.

"If you want him, you've got him."

She nodded. "I need to talk to my boss and committee."

Caroline also needed him to stop looking so...lickable. Seated next to him at the table, watching the muscles in his forearms ripple as he reached for her computer made her want to do things she had no business thinking about. Like running her fingers along those muscles. Or his lips.

She shook her head to clear it. No way. There were too many reasons not to pursue the fantasy, no matter how attractive he was. She wouldn't trust him again, no matter how often he'd shown her he'd changed. She refused to get left twice.

Their timing was off, once again. He had a daughter or a niece, depending on how you looked at it, which meant he was tied down just when she was finally able to spread her wings. And even if she could get past those two reasons, she was swamped with work for the entire time he was here. It would be a bad idea.

Except when he turned his blue-eyed gaze to her, all those reasons faded into the background. Jeez, was it that long since she'd been with a guy? Were her hormones out of control?

"You don't think they'll agree?"

Her hormones? She blinked, trying to figure out what Jared had said. See, this was why she needed to focus on work instead of him.

"I'm sorry, what?" Her cheeks heated.

"You said you needed to talk with your committee, and then you shook your head."

Now she wanted a hole to open beneath her chair and swallow her, like the whale that swallowed Jonah.

"Oh." She bit her lip. "It was nothing." *Please don't ask.* "I think they'll love the idea."

Jared smacked the table with both hands, and she jumped. "Okay, that's it. You need a break."

"What? No, I just had a dinner break."

He stood up and held out his hand to her. The last thing she should do is touch him. Against her better judgment, she grasped it. A sizzle of awareness streaked through her hand and along her arm. Surprised, she stared at him to see if he felt it, too. His lips parted, and a crease formed between his eyebrows.

He'd felt it, too. He gripped her fingers, holding on after she rose from the chair.

This was bad. Her lungs constricted, and she opened her mouth to take in more oxygen. Why was it stuffy in here?

"You're much more than fine," he whispered and took a step closer.

Her heart pounded. She placed her free hand against his chest to stop him. Except now her palm touched hard muscles, and his heart beat as fast as hers.

"Jared." Saying his name did funny things to her insides.

"Caroline." He lowered his head as if to kiss her.

"No, wait!"

He stopped but didn't pull away. He moved his thumb in circles against her hand and brought his other hand up to her face. More gently than she thought possible, he pushed a stray lock of hair out of the way. The touch of his fingertips made goose bumps cascade down her neck.

"Tell me what you want, Caroline."

What did she want? That was the problem. She didn't know. She shouldn't want him. This close, inhaling his spicy clean scent and seeing his desire reflected at her made any reasons she might have had fade into the background.

"We shouldn't do this," she said.

He brushed her hair again before he trailed his hand along her neck. "Why not?"

"It didn't work last time."

"We were young and stupid then. At least I was. You, you've never been stupid." He smiled at her in a way that made her resistance crumble more. His dimples winked at her, and she couldn't help but be drawn to him.

"You've gotten better with your words," she said.

"I've gotten better at a lot of things. And you didn't answer my question. What do you want?"

"You're leaving in a few weeks." None of these things mattered. None of them addressed her main concerns. But they were the only things she could bring herself to say.

"You're right. And the last thing I want to do is hurt you. So you decide. I think you can tell how much I want you. But if you don't want me, say so." He drew her closer to him and stroked her back. "Tell me what you want."

She couldn't think, and she was tired of fighting her desires. She'd resist tomorrow. Closing her eyes, she sighed. "I want you to kiss me."

Caroline expected him to swoop in and kiss her senseless. When he didn't, she opened her eyes.

"Good." He cupped her cheeks and brought his lips to hers.

Soft and heady at the same time, the rest of Caroline's reason swirled away in the moment. His breath mixed with hers. Her eyelids fluttered closed, and she wrapped her free hand around the nape of his neck, sliding her fingertips into his hair. The other hand? He still held it, as if he'd never let go.

As if he'd never let *her* go.

He pulled away, and she whimpered, but he stroked her back as he trailed kisses from her mouth to her jawline to behind her ear. She tilted her head, to give him better access, while shivers of desire ran along her spine. All too soon, he took a step back.

She blinked at the sudden space between them.

Jared still hadn't let go of her hand. As reality returned, she looked at their intertwined fingers. In high school, his hand was paler and bonier. A teenager's hand. And now? It was tanned from the California sun. Stronger, although from what she didn't know. All she did know was it was different. Like his kiss.

When they dated, his kisses were insistent and a little

sloppy. Now? They were confident with enough pressure to command her attention, yet patient enough to drive her crazy with anticipation. They reminded her a little of a Shabbat *niggun*, the wordless melody played prior to the start of Shabbat services; its purpose was to set the mood and make you eager to pray.

She was eager, all right, but not for prayers.

A bubble of nervous laughter rumbled in her chest.

"I wondered what kissing you again would be like." Jared stared at their joined hands.

Caroline let the silence build between them.

As if he knew what she waited for, he smiled before continuing, "And it was better than I remembered. But I'm leaving, and if we have sex, I want it to be because you've had time to consider whether you really want it. I don't want to hurt you again."

She swallowed. It was hard to think when he was around. Disappointment mixed with awareness of how considerate he was. She nodded.

He ran his free hand through her hair, along her shoulder and rib cage to her waist, trailing a line of heat in his wake. "I'm glad I found you again," he said.

"I didn't know I was lost," she said. His touch made her ache for more.

His hand stilled. "I think maybe *I* was," he said.

"And now?"

The air thickened between them. "I don't know."

But Caroline thought he did. It was something in his eyes. She wanted to know more about what had happened to him and what he searched for, but she wasn't sure they had that kind of relationship. Maybe, or maybe she was getting ahead of herself. Before she finished the thought, he spoke again.

"I'd like to see you again, Caroline, and I don't mean just to discuss the Matzah Ball."

This time, she forced herself to pull away from him, to remove her hand from his grasp. She tried to ignore the space between them.

"I'll never say no to a volunteer," she said, "especially one who can get me such a big name." She softened her voice. "As for me, I don't want a relationship, Jared. There are so many dreams I deferred, and I want to explore who I am."

He nodded. "I know. I want that for you, too."

She'd never been one for flings before. Then again, maybe a fling was what she needed. Maybe that was part of her exploration. "We're both single, though. We're attracted to each other. Would it be bad to see what happens?"

Caroline gripped the seat back of her kitchen chair. She was busy. He had a child in his life. There didn't seem to be a whole lot of time for them to "see what happened," but if he were willing... She looked at his profile, one that was harder than when he was in high school, yet somehow less cocky. They'd agreed to be friends. Maybe they could take the next step. And it didn't hurt he was almost sexier than she could handle.

"Okay," he said.

"Okay."

Seated in the family room of his parents' home the next day, Jared couldn't remember when he'd last had to try as hard with a woman. He didn't know if he'd lost his touch or if Caroline was stubborn, but she'd said yes, and relief flooded through him. She grounded him and made him feel less overwhelmed by all the changes in his life. He hadn't felt that way in a long time.

Maybe it was because she was one of the few women who didn't jump to date him. In LA, a single, young, wealthy guy was like his grandmother's matzah balls—coveted by all.

He paused to remember. Her matzah balls were amazing—light and fluffy and oh so tasty. He hadn't eaten them since he was a boy, but his mouth watered even now. His mom was a good cook, but she'd never mastered his grandma's matzah balls.

His phone buzzed. Caroline.

"Hi," he said. He wanted to add how happy he was she'd called him. How much he missed her after twelve hours. How he wanted to see her again. But he'd recalibrated his thinking when it came to her, and he wanted to give her some control.

Instead, he jiggled Becca on his knee, playing horsey until he "surprised" her by straightening his leg and letting her "fall." She giggled and yelled, "More, more!" So simple and satisfying. Man, he missed being a kid.

"Hi," she answered. "Hi, Becca. I talked to the committee, and they love the idea. We froze ticket sales and are adding the VIP pricing. We're also making a big push toward younger people, now that we have a star who appeals to the younger crowd. I think the photo booth rooms will help."

She exhaled, as if she'd said all of that in one breath.

"Good," he said. "I'll text Ben and let him know."

"I'm nervous about redoing things midstream."

Jared changed his tone to soothing as he smiled at Becca. "I can't guarantee anything, other than Ben showing up. It's daring, but you need something to shake up your fundraiser."

"I agree. And maybe extra chaos will help us figure out what happened to the money."

"I don't know that I see the connection, but don't do anything to put yourself at risk. If you can pull this off, I think they'll have no choice but to give you the promotion."

"I hope so."

As much as Jared wanted to be supportive, he didn't want to talk about the Matzah Ball anymore. "I enjoyed last night."

Silence greeted his admission. "I did, too," she said.

He grinned.

"I've never had such assistance before." Her tone was teasing.

Jared burst out laughing. "I don't know. You did a pretty good job on your own." His mouth tingled, as he thought about their kiss.

"Thanks, but you upped the stakes. In several ways."

He coughed. The sarcastic woman he'd dated had returned. One of the things he loved about her was her sense of humor.

"Let's just say we make a good team," he said. "And I look forward to our next meeting."

Again, there was silence. What was she thinking?

"When will that be, do you think?"

He let Becca slide to the floor before he leaned forward. "Tonight."

"Suppose I'm busy?" she asked.

"Are you?"

"Thanks to you, I have a ton to do for this fundraiser."

"Thanks to me, you'll have a successful one. And you have a committee. And me."

"I give up," she said.

Finally. "I'll pick you up at eight," he said.

But at three that afternoon, Becca ran a fever. Jared had never had to deal with a sick child. The nanny had taken care of her, so he didn't know what to do. He called Becca's pediatrician, but all the way across the country, she wasn't much help.

"Why don't you take her to urgent care," his mom suggested. She'd tried to help him with her all afternoon, but Becca clung to Jared.

Part of him was glad she wanted him. The other part was scared witless.

"Do you think I need to?"

His mom put her lips to Becca's forehead. "She's running a fever. Toddlers do that all the time. I can't count how many you and your brother ran. But it can't hurt to get her checked, if only because it will make you feel better."

He packed the diaper bag with everything he could think of, put Becca, screaming, into her car seat, and drove to urgent care. By the time they were seen, diagnosed with strep, and prescribed medicine, it was six thirty.

"I don't suppose you prescribe for parents, too?" he asked the nurse.

"Are you ill?"

He shook his head. He was wiped out, though.

The nurse grimaced. "Good luck."

After he picked up the prescription, he drove Becca home, dosed her, and put her into bed. His stomach growled, and he looked at his watch. Seven forty-five.

Crap.

Chapter Nine

Caroline's cell phone rang as she was applying mascara and humming to herself with anticipation. She jumped and poked her eye with the wand. Tears streamed down her face. "Crap!" she yelled. "Ow, ow, ow." Great, she was going to show up to her date with a bright red, irritated eye, squinting like a madwoman.

She reached blindly for her phone. "Hello?"

"Caroline, it's Jared. I hate to do this, but I have to cancel. Becca's got strep."

She tensed. The sudden phone call out of the blue tumbled her back in time to her mom's diagnosis. Her vision tunneled. With a deep breath, she forced herself to focus on the here and now.

Jared.

Becca.

Strep. Not cancer. She brought herself back to reality.

"I'm sorry," she said. "Is she all right?"

"The doctor gave her antibiotics, so she will be, but she's miserable, and I can't leave her like this."

Of course he couldn't. She thought back to the countless times she'd had to change plans when her mom was sick. He was a dad first. He'd stay with Becca. Caroline wouldn't like him if he didn't. "No, I understand."

Funny how the tables were turned, and he was the one with the responsibility to care for someone. She gripped the phone harder and tried to ignore the remnants of anxiety she still felt when sudden sickness was sprung upon her.

He sighed. She imagined him raking his hair. "I was looking forward to our date. Can I get a rain check?"

"Sure, why don't you call me when she's okay, and we'll set it up?" Before she betrayed her regret and added to his guilt, she ended the call. She jammed the mascara wand into the tube, tightened the top and reached for her makeup remover.

Why did she let herself think a single dad had time for her? His first responsibility would always be—*should* always be—his daughter. Just as her first responsibility had always been to her ailing mother. Caroline knew from experience that Jared would have less freedom to spend time with her... and yet, here she was.

With a sigh, she looked at herself in the mirror. Her white cashmere sweater and black skinny jeans were not what she wanted to wear to hang out at home. Instead, she changed into pajamas, put her hair up in a messy bun, and slid her feet into her pink, fuzzy bunny slippers, before she plopped in front of her computer with a bowl of cereal to work on the Matzah Ball.

When her phone rang a second time, she let her dismay show in her voice.

"Hey, Jess, what's up?" Jessica was the third member of their four-girlfriend group.

"Whoa, what's wrong?"

"I got stood up," she answered.

"What? Who do I have to castrate?"

Caroline's insides warmed at her friend's immediate loyalty. "Relax, it was for a good reason." She explained what happened—Jared's reappearance and their agreement to have some fun together, as well as Becca's strep forcing them to cancel their plans.

"Did he apologize?" Jessica asked. "How sincere was it? Do you believe him? And what's he like with Becca?"

"Hello? I'm not the subject of a tell-all, Jess. What's with all the questions?" Caroline shifted in her seat. As a journalist, her friend questioned everything, but she didn't like being on the receiving end.

"Sorry, hazard of the trade," Jessica said. "I'll stop."

"The worst part is I can't be mad about it," she said when she'd finished her explanation. "He's a good dad, or uncle, or whatever he is, and someone who didn't care enough about their kid to take care of her would put me off. So, I shouldn't complain, even if there's a chance he could have passed it to me. But…"

"But you're disappointed because you came to terms with letting him into your life. And there's a bit of similarity between his responsibility to his niece and your responsibility to your mom. Sorry," Jessica said. "I hope that was okay to say."

"You're one of my best friends, and you can say anything to me. And you're right. I got over my guilt for thinking my mom was a responsibility and was looking forward to getting to all those things I'd pushed aside when she was sick. And then Jared returns, and I feel like I'm back at square one, waiting for him." She swallowed the bitter taste of guilt in her mouth.

"You're not, Caro. First, you've been through all the good and the bad, and you're smart enough to recognize the difference. Second, nothing you experience is out of your control. You still have your freedom. Jared's the one who doesn't. So, you can decide when and how to use it."

Caroline put her feet up on the chair next to her. "How the hell are you so smart, and why didn't you go into psych?"

Jessica scoffed. "Because I'm too nosy to be a good psychologist. I'd never let my patients come to their own conclusions. Instead, I'd force them to confront them before they were ready and make a mess out of things. That's why I'm a good reporter."

"True. You'd be a scary therapist. When will you come home for a visit?"

"I don't know."

"So, no Passover?"

"I think we're at my brother's this year."

"Darn." Caroline's phone buzzed. "Hold on, there's another call."

She pressed hold and answered the second call. "Hello?"

"Caroline, it's Jared. What are you wearing?"

"Excuse me?"

"Just because we can't get together tonight doesn't mean we can't have fun together. So, what are you wearing?"

She pulled the phone away from her ear. Was he serious? "Hold on a second," she said.

She switched over to Jessica. "Jess, I've got to go. I think Jared wants to have phone sex."

"You're insane, you know that?"

Jared smiled at the exasperation in Caroline's voice when she returned to the line.

"Maybe so, but not because of my attraction to you," he answered.

"I was on the phone with Jessica!"

"So?"

"So, I told her you wanted phone sex, and now I'll never hear the end of it from her."

He laughed until he couldn't breathe. "First of all," he gasped, "if you told her that, it's on you, not me. Second, who said I wanted phone sex?"

There was silence on the other end of the phone.

"Caroline? Are you still there?"

"You asked me what I was wearing. How is that not phone sex?"

"Relax, I'm teasing you."

"Which time, when you asked me what I was wearing or when you asked how I knew you wanted phone sex?"

Now it was his turn to pause. He was giving her a hard time now, just to have a little fun. And when he'd asked her what she wore, he'd done it in part to see what she'd say. But now? Was she willing? Or was she playing him? Either way, he was at her mercy.

For a lawyer who knew better than to ever ask a question without prior knowledge of the answer, he was failing.

"Jared?"

He cleared his throat. "Yes?"

"I'm teasing you, too."

Disappointment swelled within him. "That's too bad."

When he'd called her, Becca was finally asleep, her body tired out from the fever. His parents were out of the house, and he was lonely. The house was silent, stiflingly so. He'd looked forward to their date, and it bothered him he'd been forced to cancel at the last minute.

Well, Becca was still asleep. His parents were still out. The house was still silent. And Caroline turned him on. And while the idea of phone sex had been a spur-of-the-moment joke, his body took over, and all he could think of was seeing her naked, or at least imagining her that way.

Her voice interrupted his thoughts. "A white button-down shirt, like the kind you'd wear to court."

An image of Caroline in his shirt, and nothing else, landed in his brain.

His voice deepened with desire. "And what else?"

"A silk necktie. Draped around my neck, but not tied."

He bit his lip as his breath increased.

"Is that all?"

"Mmm-hmm."

He clenched his right hand into a fist while the phone in his left hand dug into his palm. He didn't care. "Take it off."

"I unbuttoned the first button."

His mouth dried. "Do another."

"Okay. I flicked open the second button. You can see my collarbone."

Jared relied on his memory from years ago, combined with what he'd seen at the gym, to picture her skin—smooth and creamy.

"Continue."

"The third button lets you peek at my cleavage and the swell of my breasts."

He swallowed. "Tell me how the fabric feels against your skin."

"Crisp and smooth as it drags across my body. My skin prickles as the cool air kisses it."

Jared hardened. His choppy breaths echoed through the phone. This was great, but it wasn't enough. He wanted Caroline in the flesh, not some voice over the phone. "Caroline, I need—"

"You're right," she whispered. "You need to undress, too."

At first, when he looked down at his T-shirt, stained with Becca's food and medicine, it pulled him out of the mood. But then he pictured Caroline standing in front of him, her hands reaching for him, unbuttoning his jeans, and he held back a moan.

"Oh, baby, I'm already undressed. Bare chest, boxer briefs—"

From the bedroom, Becca wailed.

He groaned as his skin cooled. "Ugh, I'm sorry. I've got to get her."

"Of course." Her voice, which was low and sensual, returned to a briskness he hadn't heard from her since the first time he ran into her.

He swore silently and scrambled to his feet. "Hold on, it will take a second."

"I should let you go."

As he loped toward Becca's room, he said, "No, wait. Please."

He opened Becca's door. She stood in her Pack 'n Play, face beet red, tears coursing down her cheeks. "Hey, sweets, I'm here. Shh." Phone balanced in the crook of his neck, he lifted Becca into his arms, patted her back, and sank into the nearby rocker, the same one his mother had used with him and his brother. "Easy, easy," he whispered. She settled into his arms, her breath hot against his neck.

"Caroline, I'm back," he whispered.

She scoffed. "I don't think we should continue our previous conversation."

With a rueful exclamation, he balanced the phone against his ear. "No, but that doesn't mean we can't talk." He was desperate to hear her voice, to maintain the connection between them. "Tell me more about your vacation. Or what you've done today for the Matzah Ball."

"You can't want to listen to me drone on about the same things all the time, Jared."

If she knew how much he wanted her, she'd never have said that. "You don't drone, Caroline. You engage. Occasionally, you snark. But regardless, I always want to hear you talk. Especially when we can't see each other."

She sighed, as if she were about to argue. He braced himself. But to his surprise, she continued.

"I have a walk-through of the space Saturday. Want to join me? I could use your opinion, especially since you know our guest of honor."

She hadn't asked him on a date, but she hadn't told him to take a hike, either. It was more than he expected.

"Yes. And if Becca feels better, which she should be by then, maybe we can do something. It's a weekend, after all. You can't work all day." Unlike him, who, when he returned to LA, would be expected to work whenever his clients needed him, weekend or no.

"Meet me at the JCC at eleven."

"It's a date," he said.

"Marge, how are the flyers?" Caroline asked the older woman on Saturday. The committee stood in the lobby of the JCC.

Marge, dressed in a large graphic tee with brightly striped leggings, pointed to boxes stacked next to the security desk. "They were delivered this morning, and I've got a group of volunteers scheduled to help me hang them around town."

A weight lifted off Caroline's shoulders. "Great." The woman's bright, mismatched outfit alone would draw attention to the event. "Dave, what about the food?"

He was a large guy in his forties who helmed any food needs the JCC required. Although not Jewish, he had a better knowledge of kosher versus non-kosher requirements than most of the Jews in the building. "The kosher caterer is a big fan of Ben Platt, luckily. She was thrilled to have to redo the numbers right before Passover."

Caroline, along with the rest of the committee, laughed.

"Maybe we can get him to sign a menu?" Caroline suggested.

"I'll make sure it happens."

The deep sound of Jared's voice startled her, and she spun around. She drank in the sight of him, from his wavy hair to his broad shoulders, to his long stride. And then she noticed his shirt—a white button-down, like she'd described the other night. Her face heated as she remembered how she'd flirted.

She turned to the committee, convinced they could see her blush. "Everybody, this is Jared Leiman, who got us Ben in the first place. Jared, this is my amazing committee, which not only hasn't thrown me in a ditch somewhere for being a newbie but also hasn't killed me for making them redo every-thing at the last minute." She added, "I owe them big-time."

"You do." Geraldine winked. "Luckily, we like you." The tiny woman stood on tiptoes and whispered in Caroline's ear. "And if you add cute guys to our committee, I will support you forever."

Caroline wished for a hole to open up and swallow her, es-pecially when Jared coughed. How long was it going to take her to get past their attempt at phone sex last night? Because it had been fun and flirty, but it couldn't continue.

"I've got to leave soon. Let's do our walk-through." She turned to face everyone, avoiding Jared's gaze. "This entire lobby will be the cocktail-hour location. Check-in will be at the security desk, coatroom will be in the meeting room to my right, hors d'oeuvres stations will be set up there, there, and there, and waitstaff will mingle with platters throughout. Alcohol will be set up along the wall of windows, there. The other two meeting rooms will have a photo booth in one, and auction items in the other."

Roseanne, a former interior decorator, and the most styl-ish of seniors, raised her hand. "My decorating committee has some suggested changes, based on our guest of honor. Since he's from Broadway, we thought we'd make this place look like a theater, with the box office, backstage, etcetera. And we thought we'd hang posters from famous musicals, but with a twist."

Struggling to focus on the task at hand, Caroline squinted in confusion. Roseanne pulled out her phone to show exam-ples, and Caroline burst into laughter. *The Phantom of the Deli, The Pharoah King, Les Yentas, A Chorus Whine, Oy! Calcutta!, Beauty & The Goyim, Jersey Goys, The Book of Moses.* These are hilarious."

Roseanne grinned. "We'll do things a little differently this time."

For the first time since she was handed this project, the tension in Caroline's neck eased. "I think this will work," she said, nodding.

"It's going to be more successful than ever," Marge said.

"How can I help?" Jared asked.

As much as she wanted to avoid him—it was the only way she could focus on business—she blinked and turned to him. Her palms were sweaty, and she wiped them on her leggings. This physical attraction was annoying.

"Do you think you could get Ben and his costars to donate some auction items?"

Jared nodded and entered notes in his phone.

"Thank you. Now let's look at the ballroom," Caroline said, glad to be able to focus on the rest of the group.

The committee left the lobby, walked down the hall, and entered the ballroom. Whispers of "red carpet" and "gold statues" trailed behind her. She flicked on the lights.

Dave stepped forward, the buttons on his checkered shirt straining. "The caterer has plans to transform this into a Broadway stage," he said. "Tables will be on the sides, dance floor in the middle, menus will look like playbills, and I'm assured we'll love it."

"Okay, then. Any questions? Anyone need extra help? Any problems?"

Jared raised his hand.

Her stomach fluttered. Again? How had he gotten so involved in this project of hers, and why did she keep responding to him this way? Maybe she was hungry. Struggling to hold on to that thought, she nodded.

"What else can I do?"

"You've provided us the star," Caroline said.

"I could use help with flyer distribution," Marge said.

"Great, I can do that this afternoon. Tell me where to go, and I'm on it."

Caroline studied Jared as he conferred with Marge. For someone who'd wanted to leave his hometown and everyone in it, he sure was eager to help. Part of her was grateful for the proof he wasn't the jerk he'd been then. Another part of her ached that their timing was off. They were destined to cross paths, but not meet, if the past and the present were any indication. And a small part of her resisted his interference—this was her project, and she didn't need a savior to sweep in and save the day—but she squashed it. Her committee was doing just as much to help her; she couldn't afford to be choosy this late in the game.

Her phone alarm pinged. "Okay, everyone, I have to go. Thank you all for your help, and text me if you have any questions."

She turned to go but stopped when Jared touched her arm. "Come with me? I'll treat you to lunch."

God, she wanted to, but no matter how much he might appeal to her, Becca would always come first, as she had last night. As she should. "I can't. I have work to do."

His expression creased with disappointment, matching how she felt inside.

"I'm sorry," she added. "I have so much to do to make sure this fundraiser is a success." It was true. She didn't want anyone to think she was a slacker. Not with a potential promotion riding on the success of the fundraiser. Besides, getting involved with him would only lead to heartache.

Chapter Ten

"Jared, can you come here?" Jared's mother called from the living room when he walked in the door.

"Sure, Mom. What's up?" He removed his leather jacket and hung it in the closet before he entered. "How's Becca?"

His mom smiled. "Much better. She's napping, but her fever is gone, and her mood is happier."

A weight lifted from his chest. "Thank God."

"I know how scary it can be when your child is sick. How's Caroline?"

He settled on the sofa next to his mother. "She's good. Did I tell you she's planning the Matzah Ball?"

His mother frowned. "But I thought she was an athletics instructor."

"She's much more than that." Quickly, he summarized why Caroline was given the assignment. "Hopefully, she'll get that promotion."

He'd witnessed her talent and ability even in the short amount of time he'd spent with her. She was calm despite the crunched timeline and last-minute change. She got along well with her committee. The more time he spent with her, the more he admired her.

"I'm sure she'll do well," his mother said. "Speaking of Caroline, we'd like you to invite her for the Passover seder."

He didn't know what surprised him more—that his mother

suggested it, or that he hadn't thought of it earlier. He met his mother's gaze. She looked innocent. Too innocent.

"I think that's a great idea," he said.

His mom jerked back. "You do? Good. I thought I'd have to convince you."

His mom was up to something, but instead of being upset, he was going to enjoy himself. "Why would you have to convince me? You don't think I'd force her to celebrate alone, do you?"

"A son I raised? Definitely not."

He was relieved to hear her joke again. She'd never get over Noah's death. None of them would. But her ability to joke and tease meant she was learning to deal with it.

And if she was able to, he would be, too, someday.

"I'll text her and invite her."

This time, his mom frowned. "I know you kids text all the time, but I think this deserves a phone call. You're extending an invitation to a religious celebration, not checking in to see how her day went."

Whoa, his mom was pushing him at her.

"I'll call her." His neck heated as he remembered their phone sex the last time he'd spoken to her, and he looked at the time on his phone to give himself a second. "But later. She's got a lot on her plate, especially with the Matzah Ball, and I don't want to add to it." He'd already upended her life, even if it was for a good reason.

"Tell her she doesn't need to bring anything other than herself, and that we'll start the seder at six, but she can come at any time before that."

Jared spent the rest of the afternoon considering nanny candidates. The service emailed five, but he wasn't happy with any of them. One attended the same training program as the royal nannies. She was overqualified and would probably try to change his behavior as well as Becca's. Another was a college student. The last thing he wanted was someone who wouldn't be a long-time fixture in Becca's life. The other three were fine, but he wanted more than fine. He emailed for more options. When Becca woke up, she was more cheerful than she'd been, and he played with her, read books to her and cuddled her. Would any of the suggested nannies do this?

"Dada."

Jared froze.

"Dada, Dada." She chanted it over and over, touching his cheeks.

His throat thickened. He wasn't her dad, but she was too young to understand that. He owed it to Noah and Rachel to raise Becca as they'd want, in the healthiest way possible, but also to keep their memories alive. What did that mean when it came to her calling him dada? If he corrected her, would it hurt her? And if he didn't, wasn't he betraying his brother?

She'd already moved on to something else, turning the pages of the book and babbling as if she were reading. There was nothing to say now, but he needed to be prepared for next time. Except how could he prepare for this? Usually, he'd ask his brother for advice. So, who could he talk to? If he talked to his parents, it would only hurt them more.

The only one he could think of was Caroline. But he didn't know how to explain his feelings. He pulled his phone out. He'd promised his mom he'd invite her to the seder. Maybe he'd judge how that call went and decide whether to tell her about Becca.

"Hello?"

"Caroline, it's Jared."

"Is something wrong? Your voice doesn't sound right."

She could determine that from three words. Suddenly, the idea of talking about it scared him. "It's nothing." He cleared his throat. "Do you want to join us for the seder?"

She inhaled. "I don't want to get in the way of your family."

"Please, I'm pretty sure my parents would rather have you than me at the seder." He only half joked.

"I know that's not true," she said. "Are you sure, though?"

"Caroline, my mom asked me to invite you."

"Do *you* want me there?"

"Yes." For the first time since his mother suggested the invitation, he longed for Caroline's presence at the seder.

"Okay, then I'd love to join you. What can I bring?"

"My mom said to tell you not to bring anything, just yourself. She also said the seder will start at six. You can come any time before then."

"I'll come over around five. You don't sound right, though. I don't want to pry, but is there anything I can do?"

He stared at the ceiling for a second before answering. "Becca called me dada today." He looked over at the little girl, playing with her toys and babbling to herself.

"Oh." Caroline's voice gentled. "That's…complicated."

"Yeah." He spoke over the lump in his throat. "I wasn't prepared."

"No, I imagine not. I don't think it's possible to prepare for something like that. But at least she's comfortable around you."

"She'll never remember them. I'll always be dad to her, which I guess is good, but at the same time, it's not supposed to be me. It should have been Noah."

Noah and Rachel had been together since they were in grade school. They'd talked about the family they'd have—a large one—the house they'd build, and all the holiday get-togethers they'd host. Family vacations, too. Jared was always career focused. It contributed to the way he'd treated Caroline when he left. Being a dad hadn't crossed his mind.

"Regardless of where you are on the family tree, Jared, you're her dad now. And you're right, she's too young to remember them, but you and your parents will tell her stories about them, show her photographs, and point out traits of theirs that she carries. They'll live in your memories and the stories you tell her."

"Maybe I shouldn't let her call me dad."

"Don't let your guilt ruin the relationship, Jared. She won't understand why she can't call you dad. You want her to feel safe and secure. Like she belongs."

"How do I know it's the right thing?"

"I don't think anyone does. That's part of being a parent. And whether you're a birth parent or an adoptive one, you're in the same boat. It's trial and error. As long as you love her, you're doing it right."

He gripped the phone as he watched Becca play in the swath of sunlight. Her curls bounced, and the sun gave her dark hair a reddish glow.

"Thanks for listening," he said. "I appreciate it."

"Anytime."

He took a deep breath. "By the way, I hung up a bunch of the flyers around town today and handed them out to people as they exited stores. Made a nuisance of myself, but it was for a good cause."

"I can't wait to see ticket sales," Caroline said. "I want to open the file, but I won't see a change in numbers for a few days. I have to distract myself."

"Want help?"

"Distracting myself?" Caroline laughed. "Wouldn't you like that?"

"I'm good at it."

"I think you've done enough, thank you very much."

"Damn. Oops, I mean, darn. Becca's right here with me. I have to watch my language."

He looked over at her and tousled Becca's hair. "Thanks for making me feel better, Caroline. I mean it."

"You're welcome. Tell your mom if she changes her mind, I'm happy to bring something."

"I will, but trust me, she has her seder meal planned weeks in advance and nothing deters her from it. In the meantime, can I reschedule the date I canceled?"

He held his breath.

"Becca feels better?"

"She does. Antibiotics are awesome."

"I'm busy tonight…"

"How about tomorrow afternoon?"

He waited in the silence, hoping to break through her walls.

"Yes."

"Great, I'll pick you up at two. Oh, and wear comfortable clothes."

"Comfortable clothes?" Caroline muttered to herself the next day. "I live in comfortable clothes. Where is he taking me?"

She should have asked Jared before they hung up yesterday. But she'd been trying to convince herself a date with him was okay—her version of breathing into a paper bag—and the moment slipped away.

And agreeing to a family seder? Was she crazy? Her brain screamed "Certifiable," while her heart whispered, "You've got this." She didn't know which was right, but she was tired of fighting the attraction. Maybe that's why she'd agreed to the date, she thought as she stared at her wardrobe.

Most people would be thrilled at the idea of comfortable clothes on a date. And she had to admit, it took the pressure off. But what were his plans? She sighed, resigned to wait until he showed up to find out. By the time he pulled up to her house at five minutes to two, she was jumpy and anxious.

She climbed into the car before he had a chance to come up to her door. "So, what are we doing that I need to be dressed comfortably?"

Jared refastened his seatbelt. "Hello to you, too."

"Hello." She clicked the buckle and tapped her foot. "What, no hello kiss?"

He leaned across the center console and caressed her cheek with his hand. Her anxiety fled. Or rather, her anxiety about their date fled. At his touch, her heartbeat quickened. The seat belt strap dug into her chest. She released it and bent toward him. Their lips met and their breaths mingled. All her questions fluttered away as she wrapped her hand around the nape of his neck and pressed closer to him. Their noses bumped in the cramped space, and he smiled against her mouth.

"Much better," he whispered. "Now, what did you want to know?"

Her mind was a blur. She licked her lips, still tasting him. "Um…where are we going?"

His expression suggested he knew how he affected her. She wanted to elbow him in the ribs to get rid of some of his attitude, but instead, she smiled.

"Dancing."

She frowned. "Dancing?"

"You're planning the Matzah Ball, right?"

She nodded.

"Well, we're going dancing."

Now she was more confused. She opened her mouth to ask questions, but his palm on her shoulder stopped her. Heat from his palm radiated through her sweatshirt to the skin beneath.

"Trust me," he said.

With a nod, she leaned back in her seat. Before he started the car, he took her hand. Would he hold it the entire time? She fought against how nice it felt. He pressed the button to start the car and pulled out of her driveway, all one-handed. This couldn't be safe. She tried to pull away, but he tightened his grip.

"How's Becca feel?" she asked to ignore her feelings. As they drove through her neighborhood, she stared out the window. Most of the houses had changed owners multiple times since her childhood.

"All better." His grin stretched his cheeks. "Eating, talking, and acting like her typical self."

"That's good. Your parents must enjoy their time with her." The day was cloudy, and rain threatened.

"They do, although I have no idea how they clean for Passover with a toddler around."

At the stoplight on the outskirts of town, they turned left, avoiding Main Street. She frowned, trying to figure out their destination. "You've helped, right?"

"As much as they'll let me. When I left them today, my mom was polishing the silver, and my dad was cleaning out the cars."

"Whoa, they take this seriously." As a child, she and her mom had replaced their bread products with matzah and held a seder together. Occasionally, they traveled to a cousin's house. But the kind of cleaning the Leimans did was foreign to her.

He nodded. "Of course."

"I'm surprised you're able to get away. Cleaning for Passover, the way your family observes, is backbreaking work."

Jared slowed the car. "Please, to see you? My mom pushed me out of the house."

Caroline's cheeks heated. "She's sweet."

"But formidable." He pulled his hand away to parallel park, and Caroline looked out the window at their destination. The Two-Step Saloon was a dance studio on a side street off Main Street.

"Wait a minute, dance lessons?"

He nodded. "I know you're talented and athletic and graceful, but every Matzah Ball chair should start the ball with a choreographed dance to make a splash."

Her mouth dropped open, and he laughed. "Come on. I signed us up for a dance lesson. I thought it would be fun. You don't have to commit to anything for the ball, I promise."

She climbed out of the car and took in the dance studio from the sidewalk. The sign resembled a marquee, with large lights around black letters on a white board. Through the big window, she glimpsed a dance studio, polished floors and mirrors shining.

Spinning around to face him, she smiled. "I think this will be fun."

"Really?"

For the first time, he looked worried. A wrinkle between his brows gave away his concerns, and she reached up and smoothed it with her finger. "Really," she said.

He took her by the elbow and led her inside.

A tall Asian woman in leggings and an athletic top—much like the clothes Caroline herself wore to teach her classes—greeted them.

"Are you Jared?" She smiled at both of them but addressed Jared.

"Yes, I am. And this is Caroline."

"Welcome, I'm Meredith Lee." She led them into the studio and turned on the lights. Floor-to-ceiling mirrors reflected multiple versions of the three of them around the room. The wood floor absorbed the sound of their feet as they walked to the middle of the dance floor.

"Now, Jared, you mentioned you wanted to learn a choreographed dance," Meredith said. "Are you two getting married?"

Caroline's face heated. "No. We're not."

Jared squeezed her hand. "Caroline's hosting a major fundraising ball, and I'd like our first dance together to wow the donors."

Meredith beamed. "What a great idea! Do you know what song you'd like to dance to?"

Jared turned to Caroline. "Any ideas?"

She shrugged. "The only music I know well are the songs I

use for my exercise classes, and most of those don't translate to a ball." She turned to Meredith. "How about you?"

"When is the event?"

"In about two and a half weeks," Jared said.

"Oh, not a lot of time. Hmm, the easiest dance to choreograph is a waltz. It's got three beats—*one*, two, three, *one*, two, three—so even the most rhythmically challenged can manage it. Not that either of you are…"

"Well, Caroline is great," Jared said. "I've seen her teach classes, and I remember our prom. I, however, am…less great."

Meredith demurred. "I'm sure you'll do fine. Let's get started and see what we can do."

Meredith positioned the two of them together, turned on the music, and instructed them in both posture and steps.

At first, Caroline was self-conscious. As much as she liked being in Jared's arms, being observed made her stiff, but as the music continued and Jared got the hang of it, she stopped overthinking and let herself enjoy the moment.

Jared's arms were strong, and with one arm wrapped around her waist, she had no choice but to be close to him. While he concentrated on Meredith's instructions, Caroline took the opportunity to concentrate on him. His jawline was firm and clean-shaven. His skin smelled of eucalyptus and mint. Caroline inhaled, and her insides turned to jelly. As she moved in tandem with him, she noticed how his muscles bunched and stretched, carrying them from one end of the dance floor to the other. She was used to taking charge. The few slow songs they'd danced to at prom involved her leading them around the dance floor, or the two of them swaying in place. This time, dancing with Jared allowed her to follow, to surrender. It was new, and lovely.

"You two are great together," Meredith called. "Now that you know the basic steps, let's try some variations."

She showed them a simple opening sequence of steps,

where they mirrored each other separately before they came together. Without Jared's arm around her, Caroline noticed the emptiness, and she chided herself for her silliness. When they came together, an electric current fizzed through her arm, and she blinked, curious where the source of the electricity was. Jared jerked, as if he felt it, too, and he gripped her tighter.

"That's it. Show how sexy you can be," Meredith said. "The waltz was provocative when it was first introduced, you know."

Caroline's skin heated. She looked away and stumbled but righted herself thanks to Jared's pulling her against him.

"Good catch," Meredith said. "How about we try a dip?"

Jared looked at Caroline. "You up for that?" He winked.

"As long as you're up for my revenge if you drop me."

"I don't know. I didn't peg you as a revenge type of person," he said, as they waited for Meredith to change the music.

"You want to find out?"

He laughed. "Not particularly," he whispered in her ear, "There are other things I'd like to find out first."

She didn't have a chance to respond before the music started up again, Jared led her through the routine, and added a dip at the end. Her skin sizzled each time he touched her. Her heart fluttered. And despite her fears, he didn't drop her. If anything, he held her tighter.

When the music changed, he pulled her up, and with Meredith's guidance, they continued their dance. Caroline's temperature increased. She didn't think it was from the activity. She worked up more of a sweat during the classes she taught. It must be her proximity to Jared.

They repeated the dance, and once she was confident of the steps, Caroline let her mind wander. All sorts of possibilities came to mind, none of which cooled her heated skin. His smoldering stare overwhelmed her. She shouldn't be the only one to suffer. The next time he met her gaze, she licked her lips. His pupils widened, and as he drew her close, his breath sounded harsh in her ear. Turnabout was fair play.

"Okay, you two, you will knock it out of the park at the ball in two weeks. I might have to go just to watch you."

"You should," Jared said. "Ben Platt will be our special guest star."

Meredith clapped her hands. "I love him! Now I *will* buy a ticket."

Caroline left the dance floor and gulped some water from the fountain.

"I'm not sure who will heat up the ball more, the two of you, or Ben," Meredith added.

Caroline choked on her water. Jared rushed over and pounded her back, while Meredith lifted her arms and told her to breathe.

Yeah, right.

Finally, her choking subsided.

"Oh my gosh, I'm sorry," Meredith said. "I didn't mean to do that to you."

With one last, deep breath, Caroline turned and gave the woman a smile. "It's okay. As with many things these days, it was bad timing. But thank you for the great lesson."

She followed Jared out to his car afterward. Her body had responded to Jared while they danced as if they were still together. Except, thinking about their dating years, she couldn't remember if her attraction to him was due to him or their hormones. The only thing she knew for sure was that this time, today, was way more than hormones. And it scared her.

He held open the car door for her and she slid into the passenger seat. He entered the driver's side but kept the engine off. The air between them was charged with an electric current. Her pulse pounded in her ears.

He looked at her, before reaching out and touching her shoulder. He remained silent, just ran his hand along her upper arm. Through the sweatshirt material, heat emanated from his touch. When she thought she couldn't stand it any longer, that she'd burst into flames, he spoke.

"As I see it," he said, voice gravelly. "We have three options."

He leaned toward her, and Caroline swallowed.

"One, we can go out to eat, make small talk, and see where the evening takes us."

She blinked.

"Two," he said, dragging a finger along her jaw, "we can find someplace private and explore what we started during our dance lessons."

She swallowed.

"Or three, I can take you home and leave you to figure out the timing that you mentioned to the dance instructor."

Caroline's chest tightened. Her body wanted option two. But her mind spun out of control. She needed to slow down and figure out what to do. He wouldn't like it, but she needed to be sure. "I might want something different, but I need to go with option three."

Jared froze. His gaze went blank for a split second before he blinked.

"Your choice," he said and started the engine.

Jared shopped for Passover items at the grocery store the next morning, including the items his parents forgot on their previous Passover shopping trip. Becca babbled and played with one of her toys in the cart. One of its wheels was wobbly, making a rhythmic thump as he pushed.

Ti-ming, ti-ming, ti-ming.

In his mind, that's what it sounded like, reminding him over and over of Caroline's response to his offer. Who was he kidding? He didn't need some noise to remind him. He hadn't stopped thinking about her response since she gave it, more than twelve hours ago.

The dance lesson was beyond anything he'd imagined.

From the moment the instructor—he couldn't remember her name—positioned the two of them, bodies close, gazes focused, hands held, his skin was on fire. They'd moved in sync and anticipated each other's needs. His heart pounded in time to the music, her scent overtook him, and she'd taken over his entire being. It was all he could do not to tear off her clothes in the middle of the dance floor.

Remembering it now made sweat pop on his neck. He opened the refrigerator door and grabbed four containers of kosher-for-Passover cream cheese for his mom's cheesecake, and stood there for a moment, cooling off.

Becca dropped her toy on the ground. She leaned over to look at it, and then up at Jared. "Dada, toy."

He picked it up. "Oops," he said. "Here you go."

She hugged it to herself and continued playing.

Caroline was as affected as he was. He'd seen her pupils dilate, her cheeks flush, her hands shake. He loved how she teased him, and how right she felt in his arms. And then she'd pulled away. She'd looked scared. He didn't know if it was of him or the situation or the thought of dancing in public. He'd given her choices of what to do next, and she'd picked the one she needed but he'd dreaded. And now he didn't know what to do. She was coming to the seder, and she'd be at the ball. In between?

The ball.

He paused. He hadn't asked her to accompany him. He was an idiot. But he'd make up for that during the seder.

The rest of it, though, filled him with doubt. What if she said no? She seemed to enjoy the dance lessons, but maybe it was a one-off thing. Maybe she would decide to go without him. Maybe she'd cancel on the seder.

She'd talked about bad timing. Did she mean him? Or was he reading into things?

Speaking of reading, if he didn't read this list and buy everything on it, his mother would have to go again herself. She had enough to do. Squaring his shoulders, he tried to push Caroline from his mind as he looked for the horseradish. She hadn't specified white or purple. He remembered seders past and tried to visualize the seder plate, with the variety of symbolic foods on it. Purple. It was purple. He grabbed the correct jar and he crossed the item off his list.

He grabbed three dozen eggs and looked around for Lipitor. No one maintained low cholesterol during this holiday.

As he checked out, his phone rang.

"Hi, Mom."

"Honey, you won't believe it. I forgot about the shank bone!"

"Again?"

The shank bone, or lamb bone, was a necessary symbol for the seder plate, but for some reason, his mother forgot it every year. Maybe because there were so many other symbolic foods needed for the dinner, maybe because it was a family joke, or maybe she had a mental block.

"Are you going to 'again' me, or are you going to help me?"

This close to the seder was not the time for him to give her sass. "Sorry, I'm still in the store. I'll grab it now."

"Thank you."

He made it through the checkout aisle the second time as Becca fussed. "Hey, baby girl, we'll go home now, okay?"

He zoomed the shopping cart around, trying to make her giggle. Once he'd gotten her packed into the car, along with the groceries, he drove home, prepared to help his mom clean for Passover. With the holiday less than two weeks away, she was in a mad scramble to get everything finished in time. But he still couldn't forget Caroline or her comment.

He brought Becca inside before he returned to the car to retrieve the groceries. Entering the kitchen, he wrinkled his nose. "I can't stand the smell of self-cleaning ovens." He opened another window.

His mother wore gloves and scoured the microwave. Everything used during the year had to be scrubbed before it could be used for Passover, thus, the intense cleaning for days before the holiday.

"I don't like it either," she said, "but I like doing it by hand less."

Jared nodded. "True. Where's Dad?"

"He's in the basement, setting up a non-Passover *treif* zone. If Becca needs normal food, we can prepare it for her."

"That wasn't necessary, Mom. Becca will be fine."

"I know, but it's just this extra microwave and a toaster oven. I don't want all the Passover food to give her a tummy ache."

Matzah, and all the food made with matzah flour instead of regular flour, did a number on everyone's stomachs by the end of the seven-day holiday.

He gave his mom a kiss on the cheek. "Thank you. That's considerate of you."

"*Pfft.* She's my granddaughter. Speaking of the basement, can you help your dad carry up the boxes of Passover pots and supplies? There should be two of them, maybe three. He'll know where they are. I don't want him doing all the heavy lifting by himself."

"Sure. The groceries are on the counter."

She looked over and nodded. "I'll take care of them."

Jared jogged down the basement steps and called out to his dad. "Dad?"

"Over here!"

He made his way to the storage area, where his dad pulled plastic bins out from under the eaves.

"Here, I'll grab one," Jared said.

"Thanks. Not sure what's in there. Be careful."

He brought it upstairs, placed it in the hallway, and returned to the basement. His dad pointed to a second one, and Jared repeated the process. When he came back a third time, his dad was restacking the other bins. He lent a hand.

"I hear Caroline's joining us for seder," his dad said. "I'm glad she's not alone."

"What's she done in the past?" he asked. Although his trips home were quick—in and out for the seder, Jared couldn't remember the last time Caroline was invited to their family celebrations. Not since college.

"Since her mom died, I think she joined a cousin in the city," his dad said, "or maybe friends. I'm not sure."

Guilt swamped him for not keeping up with her or checking in with her when he'd come home for visits. He should have known she was alone. He paused. His brother's death brought home how fragile relationships were. Although he still had his parents, he no longer had a sibling. Someday, it would be up to him, and him alone, to take care of his parents. The things he shared with his brother were no more.

The idea of being the sole person responsible for his parents overwhelmed him, and he was an adult. He couldn't imagine being in Caroline's shoes as a child. The more he thought about it, the more he realized how careless he'd been. He had a lot to make up for, even if she had forgiven him.

His dad turned out the light and led Jared out of the storage area. When his phone rang, Jared held up his pointer finger to his dad before he answered.

"Hello?"

"Jared, hi, it's Caroline."

He waved his dad on upstairs and sat on the bottom step. Queasiness shot through him as he wondered why she called.

"Hey, Caroline. I was thinking of you." *And hoping you're not giving me the brush off.*

"I wanted to tell you I'm sorry," she said.

His stomach dropped. "Sorry? For what?"

"For freaking out on you after the dance lesson. You planned this date, and I…"

"Got scared?"

"Yes. Was I that obvious?"

He let out a sigh of relief and shifted to make himself more comfortable. "It's okay, Caroline."

She cleared her throat. "It would be easy to get carried away."

"I don't want to force you to do something you're not ready for," he said. He tapped the stair with his foot. No matter what he wanted, if Caroline wasn't ready, he had to put his desires aside.

"That's just it, though. I thought I was ready. And now…"

"Now you're afraid."

"I don't know why."

He ran a hand through his hair. "Listen, don't put all this pressure on yourself. We said we'd have fun while I'm home. So, let's keep it fun. You'll come to the seder, still, right? I mean, I can't jump your bones in the middle of the Four Questions or anything."

Caroline laughed, and the sound filled him with joy. "Yes, I'll still come to the seder. Your parents invited me, and I wouldn't want to renege now."

"Good. Will you let me take you to the Matzah Ball?" He gripped the phone tight in his hand. *Please say yes, please say yes.*

"Yes."

He let out a whoosh of air. "Good. Great. The rest of the time, let's get rid of the pressure, okay?"

"I'd like that. Thank you. But Jared? I do enjoy spending time with you. Please don't doubt that."

He hung up and pocketed his phone, lost in thought. Somehow, he had to make her see she could trust him. The question was, how?

Chapter Eleven

Caroline snuggled into the corner of Emily's cream-colored leather couch the next evening, squishing a woolen pillow to her middle and eating chips and guac. Emily, in sweats with her hair in braids, lounged on the other end of the couch with a glass of white wine, and Sarah, in jeans and a sweatshirt, sat curled on the floor, close to the copper coffee table and within easy access of the food.

"I love our girls' nights," Emily said with a sigh.

"Me too," Sarah said. "I wish Jessica was home to join us."

"The last time she called, I had to hang up to take a call from Jared." Jessica had texted repeatedly to ask about their phone sex. Caroline should have known not to leave a reporter hanging. "How is she?" Caroline asked. "She didn't sound right." She rolled up the sleeves of her Life is Short, Eat Dessert First long-sleeved shirt.

"She's stressed and super busy," Emily said.

"Join the club," Caroline said.

Sarah huffed. "That seems to be the theme these days. But—" her eyes brightened "—I hear you've got an amazing fundraiser planned."

"Matzah Ball." Emily laughed. "That name cracks me up every time."

"Hey, I didn't create the name," Caroline said. "I'm nervous. There are so many moving pieces. Jared is responsible for our special guest. I hope the two of you will buy tickets."

Emily looked at her silver watch and caught Sarah's eye. "Three minutes, forty-six seconds."

"I've got four minutes, three seconds," Sarah said.

Emily wiggled her fingers in the air, as if adding. "So, let's go with three minutes, fifty-four seconds and call it a day."

"What are you two talking about?" Caroline gazed between her two friends like a spectator at a ping-pong match.

"Just how long it took you to incorporate Jared into the conversation." Emily grinned.

Caroline threw a chip at her. "It's related to work. And you asked."

"Mmm-hmm," Sarah said. "That's *all* it is."

Caroline dug her butt farther into the corner of the couch. "It can't be anything more than that."

"Why not?" Emily asked.

"So many reasons," Caroline said.

"Such as…" Sarah said.

"We didn't make it the first time, he's not here for long, he has a child, I'm going on vacation—"

Emily smacked the back of the sofa. "You can't use vacation as a reason not to date Jared. Or anyone, for that matter."

"It's not the vacation, it's the freedom. I have the time and the money to do what I want, to explore who I am and not worry about anyone else."

"Who says you have to worry about Jared?" Sarah asked.

"He has a child he has to take care of, who he'll have to take care of for the rest of her life."

"You're right, he does," Emily said. "That doesn't mean he can't have a relationship with you, though."

"I know that. But Becca places us at different points in our lives. And as adorable as she is, I don't know if I'm ready to be with someone with a toddler to tie them down."

"So, you want a relationship?" Sarah asked. "Because like you said, he's here for a short time. You could have a fling without having to worry about Becca, your identity, or your ability to take off on vacation whenever you want."

"I don't know what I want. But why start something that's complicated enough? If it turns out I don't want a relationship, then I hurt Jared *and* Becca."

"It sounds like you want Jared, but you're making excuses," Emily said.

"That's not fair," Caroline said. "He left me when I needed him most. Why am I the bad guy if I'm not ready to fall head over heels in love with him the first time he returns?"

Sarah leaned forward. "You're not the bad guy, Caroline, at all. And Emily and I were joking when we gave you a hard time about bringing him up. But you're doing everything possible to deny your feelings for him, which is fine, if you don't have them. I'd hate to see you lose out on something because you're scared."

Did she have a sign blinking above her—Scared, Scared, Scared? Because Jared told her the same thing yesterday. Only to him, she'd acknowledged it. Why was she fighting her best friends on this?

Maybe because they required her to dig deeper into herself than Jared did. Her mouth dried. "I don't think it's wrong to be afraid he'll leave me again when he already did it once," she said.

Emily reached for her hand. "What he did was unacceptable," she said. "I'd be afraid, too. I get it. But he was a kid. He's a man now."

He was definitely a man. If she let herself, she could go down that pathway, think about all the ways he'd grown into a man. But she didn't let herself.

"You have to remember that you were thrown into a grown-up world way earlier than you should have been," Sarah said. "He wasn't. So, it took him longer to catch up to you, maturity-wise. I'm not excusing him. Leaving you when he did was terrible. But if he's changed, and can prove that he has, then do you want to punish him, and yourself, for something he did as a kid?"

"No, of course not. I just…" Caroline didn't know what to say.

"Can I ask a question?" Emily raised her hand as if they were still in school.

Together from elementary all the way through high school, they'd had lots of talk sessions like this. Except then, things were easier. Or they were with the benefit of hindsight.

Until her mom got sick. Then everything changed.

"Of course." Caroline nodded.

"You claim you want to take advantage of your freedom and not tie yourself down, yet your concerns are the opposite. Do you realize that?"

Caroline squeezed the pillow harder. "Yes, no, I don't know." She took a deep breath. "I know my questions are more appropriate for someone I'm determined to have a relationship with, rather than a quick fling while he's in town. But the thing is, what if I let myself jump in and then I get attached? Just because I want to have fun, doesn't mean I want to get hurt, any more than I want to hurt them."

Emily scooted to Caroline's end of the sofa and gave her a hug. "Oh, honey, nobody wants to get hurt. Are you sure no responsibilities, no attachments are what you want?"

Caroline grabbed a chip and munched it. She wasn't sure what she wanted. And that's what frightened her the most.

Jared finished washing one of the glass shelves from his parents' refrigerator and handed it to his dad to dry. Cleaning the refrigerator for Passover was a family event and now that Passover was three days away, it was all hands on deck. Whenever he wasn't doing something for Becca or Caroline, he helped his parents prepare for the holiday.

He remembered as a kid with Noah, being banished from the house so his parents could clean without their interference and only being allowed to eat in certain rooms as the holiday got closer.

"We're going out to eat tonight, right?" he asked.

"Yes," his mom exclaimed with a sigh. "Other than for cleaning, and for Becca, this kitchen is closed until I start to cook for the seder. If you need to eat in the house, you've got the garage and the basement. Everything else is clean."

Jared nodded. "No worries. How about we go to that new Italian restaurant in town, my treat?"

His dad laughed. "New? Tuscan Delight has been there for, oh, two years at least."

Jared shrugged. "I know, but I haven't been there with you, and I couldn't remember the name. I was trying to distinguish it from other restaurants."

"David, shush." His mom's eyes sparkled. "Jared offered to pay. You want to argue over the name of a restaurant and how old it is?"

His father grunted.

"That's better." His mom patted Jared's shoulder. "Tuscan Delight is a great idea. Thank you."

He finished washing the last of the refrigerator shelves. After his dad dried the last one, they helped move the non-Passover items to the downstairs refrigerator, while his mom arranged the Passover items inside.

She rose and stretched. "I love a sparkling refrigerator, but ouch, my back hurts."

Jared returned to the kitchen. "Sit, Mom. I can do it."

"Do what?"

"Whatever you need. What's next on your list?"

"We need to change over the cabinets. I need the Passover dishes put within reach, and the other dishes moved out of the way."

"Okay, you direct."

From one end of the kitchen to the other, his mother pointed to cabinets and Jared rearranged them to her liking. Then his dad emptied the dishwasher and Jared put everything away where the items now belonged. He restarted the empty dishwasher so it would clean itself while his mother finished cleaning the stovetop and sink.

"Phew, I think we're done," she said a half hour later.

"Let's unpack the Passover boxes later," Jared said. "I'm starved."

Nodding in agreement, his parents went upstairs to change. He brought Becca upstairs, changed her diaper, and put her in a green-and-yellow dress with pink shoes. By the time he made it downstairs, his parents were waiting.

"Let's blow this popsicle stand." He jiggled Becca in his arms.

"Bwow, bwow, bwow!" She pursed her lips to blow air.

He laughed. She was adorable. The more time he spent with her here, as opposed to leaving the nanny to take care of most of her needs, the more he learned her personality. Was there any way for him to take care of her and still be successful at his firm? It was a crazy idea.

Becca kissed his cheek, and he froze. She did it again, and he kissed her back.

"You two are good together," his mom whispered as he buckled Becca into the car seat. "You're getting the hang of being her dad."

He rose, and shut the door, before he turned to his mom. "I'm not her dad. I'm her uncle."

His mother frowned. "You want to deny how she feels about you?"

"Of course not, but I can't take Noah's place." His chest tightened.

His dad stepped forward. "Noah would be the first to want you to."

"She'll never remember him, though." Jared clenched his fists at his sides, willing himself not to break down in the middle of the driveway.

"You're right. And therefore, it's cruel not to take that place, Jared," his mother said. "You can fill her mind with all kinds of stories about your brother. But don't be afraid to take your place in her life. That's what you're supposed to do."

Jared motioned his parents into the car. He cleared his throat as he started the car and wiped his eyes. "What kind of dad will I be?" He couldn't imagine himself in that role. Not for many years from now.

"A good one," his dad said. "One of the best."

"I wish I was more prepared for this." He pulled out of the driveway and drove to the restaurant.

His mother arched a brow. "Don't we all, Jared. You don't think fatherhood or motherhood comes with an instruction manual, do you?"

If only. "No, but it usually comes with nine months of preparation."

"You've done well so far," his mother said. "You'll sign the adoption papers, hire a new nanny, and reestablish your routine. It'll be okay. Although I do wish you didn't need the nanny. I love seeing the two of you interact."

"I do, too, Mom, but I can't take care of her and do my job without a nanny." He couldn't recall anyone in his firm working short enough hours to do both.

"I know." His mom sounded disappointed. A dull ache formed behind his eyes. He hated to disappoint his parents, but he didn't know what else to do.

At the small restaurant, decorated in a rustic Italian style, they took a table for four in the back, put Becca in a booster, and entertained her until the waiter brought her a plate of pasta and broccoli. While she ate her shells, he and his parents continued their conversation.

"How is the nanny search?" his father asked.

"The agency sent me five candidates' résumés, none of which I liked." He'd scrolled through all of them. They all sounded dry. Was he this picky the last time? He couldn't recall. But then, he'd been so numb with grief over his brother's death he didn't remember much of that time. "I asked for more, and I have interviews set up for later this week. After the seder. Hopefully, I'll like one of them and have her lined up by the time I return home." He didn't love any of those candidates, either, but he was running out of options. A sense of dread filled him. He wished he could manage to take care of her on his own.

He looked at Becca, as she ate and played with both of his parents. "She's had a lot of adjustments in her short life. I hope she doesn't have a problem with the new nanny."

Stabs of guilt plagued him, and he tried to shake them off. After spending all this time caring for her, handing her over to a stranger sounded less appealing by the day.

His mom reached for his hand. "One thing at a time, Jared. Do your best, and let things fall as they may."

Caroline stared at her schedule for the rest of the week and groaned in frustration. The Matzah Ball fast approached, and she was running out of time. She looked at her to-do list for the Matzah Ball. It was long, and unlike other lists, which got shorter the more things you checked off, for some reason, this one increased. Every time she accomplished something, another three things needed to get done.

She opened the third tab. She'd examined the JCC budget, digging as deeply as she could. She still couldn't figure out why with all the donations that came in, there was a budget shortfall. Sarah's contact in the Development Department was as stymied as everyone else.

Turning off the screen, she entered the studio for her next class. One of her favorite members, Sadie Isaacson, was already there. "Caroline dear, do you have a minute?"

"Of course." She loved Aaron's grandmother, despite the woman's scary matchmaking. She possessed a terrific sense of humor, was loyal to those she cared about, and knew everything about everyone. "How are you?"

"Eh, I can't complain," Sadie said. "I mean, I can, but what's the point?"

Caroline laughed. "Did you drink enough water?"

She rolled her eyes like a teenager. "Yes, I did. See?" As if to prove a point, she drank again in front of Caroline. After the woman's health scare several months ago, Caroline was pleased she was following instructions and staying hydrated.

"But I'm not here to talk about my health, and I don't need you to tattle to my grandson, Aaron, or Sarah," Sadie said. "You know I hear things, right?"

"You hear *everything*."

The older woman preened. "Anyway, I heard news you might want to know. Mind you, I'm not a gossip."

"Of course not." Caroline didn't want to contradict her. Besides, Sadie was a great source of information.

Sadie inched closer. Caroline bit the insides of her cheeks to prevent a smile. There was something about a tiny octogenarian trying to look stealthy that she found humorous. Sadie, however, would not be amused. When barely an inch separated the two women, Sadie tugged on Caroline's arm. She bent toward her.

"I hear that there's funny business going on here." She glanced around furtively. "With the finances."

Caroline froze. How could that be true? She inhaled a shaky breath and another, and reason returned. What could Sadie, of all people, know about the JCC finances?

"What did you hear?" she asked.

This time, Sadie pulled her arm hard. Caroline had no choice but to follow. Man, this lady was strong. She led Caroline over to a corner.

"I heard the money is deposited and then diverted somewhere else."

"Where?"

Sadie shrugged. "I don't know."

"Who told you this?"

The old woman frowned, hands on hips. "You want me to divulge my sources?" The woman's face stretched in horror, like she'd been told her grandbaby wasn't the most beautiful baby in the entire world.

"Yes." The only way to find out if this were true is to ask the source.

"I can't do that."

"Why not?"

"Because it's wrong! I was told this in confidence. If I were a journalist, I wouldn't have to divulge my sources."

"Sadie, first of all, you're not a journalist. And besides, journalists who don't divulge sources can go to jail."

Sadie's face whitened for a minute before it crumpled in disgust. "You can't send me to jail."

True. "No, but I can do worse."

"Really? What can you do?"

Caroline hated to play this card, but desperate times and all that. "I can talk to Aaron and Sarah. And don't forget, Sarah works for the Federation."

Sadie gasped. "You wouldn't dare."

Caroline pulled her phone out of the pocket in her leggings, swiped up on the screen, and tapped on her contacts. Sadie reached for the phone, but Caroline raised it above her head.

"Ugh, fine," Sadie said with a groan. She muttered something in Yiddish that sounded like "lying in the ground and baking bagels," but Caroline couldn't be sure. She waited, while Sadie paced. "Leslie's daughter-in-law, Shira, works with Al in finance. Leslie told me that Shira is worried but afraid of retaliation, but she said it in confidence, and I don't want to be responsible for anyone getting fired."

Sadie's face was pinched, and her forehead lined with worry. Caroline hugged her. "I'm sorry I forced you to betray a confidence. And I appreciate your telling me. I promise not to tell anyone the information came from you. In fact, I'll see what I can find out first before I mention anything to anybody, okay?"

After staring at her for several moments, Sadie nodded. "Okay, thank you. And I'm sorry for what I said about you in Yiddish."

"Thank you. I won't mention you to Aaron or Sarah, either."

Now Sadie smiled. "You're a good girl."

Caroline watched Sadie leave. She returned to her desk and pulled up the budget on her computer. Could she find out where the money was deposited or moved? Or better yet, who did it? She noodled around the spreadsheet, but couldn't link anything to anyone, and she didn't have the clearance to access certain files. She also doubted someone moving money around would make it easy to find.

Despite her promise to Sadie, she had to talk to Sarah. However, she wouldn't mention Sadie. Not until she had no other choice.

Chapter Twelve

Jared held Becca's hand and showed her the dining room table, all set up for Passover. It hit him for the first time that he was passing along religious traditions to her, and his chest filled with pride. His mother's heirloom white lace tablecloth covered the table, four sets of fancy Passover china were arranged, and the Lenox seder plate his parents received as a wedding gift held the position of honor in the center.

He pointed out each of the items on the plate to her, overwhelmed with his religious responsibility. "Matzah, bitter herbs, roasted egg, shank bone, parsley, *charoset*, and an orange." They'd go over the significance of everything during the seder, not that she'd understand. Not this young. But his mother placed a board book about the holiday at her high chair, and Jared intended to make her experience fun.

Becca reached her hand toward the seder plate. Interest, that's what he wanted to encourage. Just maybe not for fragile, breakable heirlooms. He retreated a step.

"You can give her the orange," his mother said from the doorway. "It's partly there for her anyway."

The orange represented the benefit to all Jews when marginalized people—especially Jewish women and LGBTQIA+ people—were allowed to be a part of, and contribute to, the Jewish community.

As he handed Becca the orange, he realized he had to figure out a way to empower Becca as a Jewish female as she grew up. He gulped. How did a man do that? He looked at his mother, one of the strongest women he knew, and determined to depend on her for help.

That would be hard to do living on opposite coasts.

He'd have to find a way.

He'd also have to find other strong women to help influence her.

Caroline popped into his mind. Another strong woman, also on the opposite coast. She'd had to be strong to overcome the odds, get a college degree, and become successful in her job. He was proud of how she'd stepped up, shouldered her responsibility, and still focused on her future. Would he be able to do that now?

As if he'd conjured her presence, the doorbell rang.

"I'll get it." He walked with Becca to the front door.

"Hi." Caroline smiled. "Hi, sweetie." She took Becca's hand and admired the toddler's orange as she entered the house. She looked up at Jared. "Her dress is adorable."

The yellow-and-white-striped confection was springy, with little pink rosebuds embroidered on the hem.

"My mom bought it for her," Jared said. "I was thinking about you." He closed the door behind her.

"Oh?" She removed her jacket and shifted the bouquet of flowers she carried. "Not sure how I feel about that."

His heart squeezed. Did she have so little confidence in him still? "I was thinking about the strong women I know."

Caroline's cheeks flamed, and she looked away.

He adjusted his position, so he confronted her and vowed to fix things. "And you look beautiful, too."

Caroline wore a burgundy dress, scrunched at the side, with a wide neck. It was effortless and classic, like her. She smiled. "Thank you." Her lungs expanded at the compliments, and some of his tension disappeared.

"Come on inside."

He led the way into the kitchen, and let Caroline come to terms with his comments.

"Mom, Caroline's here."

"Caroline!" His mom turned away from the stove where the matzah ball soup simmered and gave her a hug. "I'm glad to see you!"

"It's good to see you, too, Mrs. Leiman. These are for you. I know you said not to bring anything, but no one ever rejects flowers."

His mom took the bouquet of tulips, daffodils, and daisies, buried her face in them, and filled a vase with water. "Jared, this is one brilliant woman."

"I know."

Once again, he met Caroline's gaze, and dared her to argue. But this time, she laughed.

His dad walked into the kitchen. "I thought I heard you'd arrived." He gave Caroline a hug. "Honey, are we ready to start?"

Jared's mom turned in a slow circle, checking the oven and stove. "I believe we are. And I think I timed everything right, if you don't change the length of the seder from last year."

His dad hugged his mom. "No worries. Becca, I need your orange, please."

He took it from Becca, washed it off in the sink, and led the way into the dining room.

"Your table is beautiful," Caroline said.

"Thank you," his mother said. "Why don't you sit across from Jared, over there? Jared, you're next to Becca. We'll try to do a combination adult and kiddie seder, since Becca's with us."

"Mom, you don't have to go crazy. She won't understand what's going on."

"That may be true, but if we engage her a little bit at a time, the seder will become important to her. Trust me."

"I do," Jared said. "I don't know how long her attention will last."

"If we need to let her go play in the playpen or at our feet, we'll do so. Don't worry."

They all sat at the table, and Jared's father handed out the books they read during the seder, which told the story of the Exodus from Egypt and instructed participants through the rituals. "I remember this *Haggadah*." Jared turned the illustrated pages and remembered seders from the past.

"It's the same one we used when you and your brother were younger," his dad said. "I thought it would be nice to use with Becca here."

Jared's throat thickened, and he looked around the table. He appreciated this moment more than he ever expected. Caroline met his gaze, an expression of understanding on her face. He took a deep breath and waited for the seder to begin.

His father recited a prayer sanctifying the holiday, his mother lit the candles, and Jared poured everyone the first cup of red wine. They all completed the ritual hand washing, and Jared winced as Becca splashed her hands in the water. She would make a mess, but no one cared.

Now it was time for the "first dip." As his father read what they were supposed to do and why, Jared passed around the bowl of fresh parsley. Everyone took a branch, and he also gave a piece to Becca. They dipped the parsley into their small bowls of salt water and took a bite. Jared frowned at the bitter, salty taste. Yeah, it represented the tears of the Hebrew slaves, and he had to do it, but yuck. When Caroline laughed, he jerked back to the present. She pointed to Becca, who munched on the parsley while frowning.

"Yucky," she said.

"You're right." He took the slobbery herb from her.

She stuck her tongue out over and over to get rid of the pieces that were stuck to it, and he did his best to clean her off.

"Now I really need to wash my hands." Excusing himself, he rinsed them in the sink, and returned to the table.

"Caroline," his father said. "Can you pass the matzah?"

Jared's mother put the matzah in a painted silk bag with Hebrew letters on it, spelling *matzah*. Caroline reached for the bag. "That's beautiful," she said and handed it to Jared's father.

"Thank you, honey," his mother said. "We bought it on our last trip to Israel."

His father cleared his throat and continued with the seder. He explained the reason for the matzah, which represented the bread that hadn't had a chance to rise when the Hebrew slaves raced away from Egypt. Then he took the piece of matzah in the middle of the stack, broke it in half, and placed it in another, smaller bag.

This bag was made of felt, with childish scribbles and glitter on it.

"You're using the *afikomen* bag I made in Hebrew school?" Jared dropped his face into his hands. "Mom, really?"

She laughed. "Of course, I am! I saved lots of crafts you and your brother made, and I want to use them."

He groaned. "That's not my masterpiece."

Caroline's laughter filled him with warmth, and he gave her a wry grin.

"Well, now we know why you didn't become an artist." She winked and turned to Jared's dad. "You'll hide it for Becca, right?"

He nodded. "When the meal is over, we'll take her around and she can search for the *afikomen*. If she finds it, she gets a prize, and I finish the seder."

"And if she doesn't find it?" Jared asked.

His father gave him a look. "She's two years old, and she's my granddaughter. You think I'd let that happen?"

"Just checking."

His father held up a hand. "Save your questions for the Four Questions, coming up."

"Okay, you two," his mother said. "Stop your teasing, pour the second cup of wine. Oh, I forgot to fill Elijah's cup with wine for later, when we open the door for the prophet. Go ahead and fill it so that we can get to the good part."

"The story!" Jared shouted, smiling at Becca.

"Story, story, story!" She repeated the word at the top of her lungs.

"Yes, ma'am," his dad said. "Give her a piece of matzah to chew while I tell the story of how God saved the Hebrew slaves and instructed Moses to lead them out of Egypt."

He moved to where Becca sat, pulled up a chair, and read from Becca's board book. "Once upon a time…"

Jared had heard the story in one form or another his entire life. That was the point of the Passover seder, to retell the story every year. But this time, he let his mind wander. Becca sat entranced and listened to his father. Caroline watched the proceedings, a small smile on her face. He was grateful she'd joined them. Her presence, and catering the seder to Becca's needs, made today easier to bear without his brother here. As children, he and Noah argued over who got to ask the Four Questions, or who found the hidden *afikomen* first. As they got older, they'd argued with their parents about being allowed to drink wine though they were underage. And then as young adults, their mortification when their mother insisted on using the ritual items they'd made in Hebrew school, instead of more adult-looking ones.

Like today.

That reminded him, he needed to research a Hebrew school/preschool program for Becca when he returned to California. His neck tightened. There were many things he now had to consider. Caroline looked over at him, and their gazes locked. He didn't know if it was Caroline's presence, or her experience with her mom, but her pretty blue eyes calmed him. He resolved not to worry about it until after the holiday.

"And now it's time for the Four Questions," his mother said. "Jared, why don't you chant them in Hebrew, and then we'll explain them to Becca."

Jared sipped his water to clear his throat and chanted. *"Ma-nish-tah-nah..."*

As he chanted, Becca stilled. Her mouth opened, and she stared at him, transfixed. When he was finished, she clapped her hands.

"Dada, sing more!"

Everyone around the table clapped, and Jared's face heated.

"You have a wonderful voice," Caroline said. Her face was alight with admiration. "I don't know if I remember hearing it when we dated."

"What, I didn't serenade you?" He tried to lighten the mood. Deep inside, though, he was flattered. "I'll have to make up for it." He winked.

They explained the Four Questions to Becca, how there were four reasons that tonight was different from all other nights. Again, she was too young to understand, but Jared was pleased that she'd enjoyed listening to his chanting.

"How about you keep the book and play with it," his father suggested to Becca.

"I read."

Tousling her hair, his father rose and returned to his seat at one end of the table. Jared joined with the others in the prayers over leavened and unleavened bread, and the specific prayer for matzah. His mother passed the matzah around, and everyone broke off pieces to eat.

Then she passed around the horseradish—the bitter herb—that represented the bitterness of slavery, and everyone tasted some. Jared made a face as he took a small bite of the horseradish on the matzah. Caroline's sinuses burned.

"I did not mean to take that much." Her voice hoarse, she reached for her glass of water and drank it in large gulps.

"Yeah, it gets me every year," Jared said.

"Want some!" Becca held out her hand, and Jared's mother spoke up.

"Oh no, sweetheart. Here," she said, "eat the matzah instead." She gave her another piece and let her crumble it up and munch.

"I didn't want to tell her it was *y-u-c-k-y*," she spelled, "because I don't want her associating negative thoughts with Passover, but the poor thing will cry if she eats the horseradish."

Jared nodded. "I'd give her a tiny taste, but I don't want to make her miserable. You were great, Mom. Thank you. I didn't know how to answer her."

His mom reached over and patted his arm. "Comes with experience, honey. You'll get there."

Could he do it alone?

Caroline agreed. "You're great with her already, and it hasn't been that long."

Jared flushed at the praise. He thought he was a disaster. And luckily his mom didn't mention the diapers.

"Well, except for knowing what diapers to buy." She smiled. *So much for that idea.* "Thanks, Mom."

"What? It was funny."

"Yeah, yeah, yeah," Jared said. "Don't we need to get on with the seder?"

"I think I need to hear about this diaper thing." Caroline winked.

"Later," he said.

Jared's father interrupted. "As much as I love helping to make fun of Jared, he's right. We need to get on with the seder."

With a sigh of relief, Jared passed around the *charoset*, the mixture of apples, nuts, cinnamon, and wine, which represented the mortar and bricks with which the Hebrew slaves built the pyramids. This was his favorite part. He put several large spoonfuls on his plate. Then he placed some charoset and a tiny bit of horseradish on matzah, joined in the prayer, and ate the Hillel sandwich.

"Me some!" Becca said.

Her speech was blossoming on this visit, and Jared loved her little voice.

"Okay, hold on." He gave her a few tiny bits of apple and let her taste them. When she licked her lips, he gave her more, careful to avoid the nuts, and anything else she might choke on.

His mother pushed away from the table. "Time for dinner. Jared, can you collect the *Haggadot*? David, can you clear away the other seder things to make room for the food? We'll finish up after we eat."

"Here," Caroline said, "let me help you."

She followed Harriet into the kitchen.

As Jared and his dad got the table ready for the meal, his dad glanced into the kitchen, before he lowered his voice. "She's great," he said. "I'm glad you're back with her."

"We're not together, Dad." *As much as I want to be.*

"I know, but you're talking again. And who knows, maybe you'll get together in the future."

Caroline was nostalgic about being part of a family tradition again. And the more she observed Jared with Becca, the more attracted she was. Whoever said men with babies were sexy didn't exaggerate.

"I love celebrating Passover with all of you," she said. "It reminds me of when I was little, and we went to my grand-parents'."

Harriet gave her a hug. "I'm glad you're here. We'd love you to join us any time you want some family time." She went over to the stove and lifted the lid off the matzah ball soup. The scent filled the kitchen.

Caroline inhaled as she warmed from the welcome. "Mm, that smells good."

"I'm glad. Grab those bowls and you can help me serve."

Harriet spooned matzah ball soup, and Caroline brought them into the dining room, including a tiny bowl with part of a matzah ball and a soft carrot for Becca.

She was about to return to the kitchen, but she stopped in the doorway, turned around, and looked at Jared. He spoke to Becca while he cut up the matzah ball into small pieces. Caroline's heart swelled. This man…he'd changed. His devotion to Becca oozed from his pores. His hands were gentle. His voice was soft. And though he might not always know what he was doing—she wanted to hear about the diaper story—he tackled his role with devotion.

He was a natural with her. If anyone was meant to be a father, it was Jared. He took care of those he loved without complaint and put his entire self into the relationship. A woman would be lucky to have him.

What if that woman was her? Her heart skittered in her chest. Did she want to be that woman? The walls closed in around her and her clear path to the future no longer seemed clear. She didn't want to be tied down, yet the thought of someone else with Jared terrified her. She couldn't have it both ways, and wasn't that the crux of the problem? She shook her head to clear her thoughts and entered the kitchen.

"Do you need help with the gefilte fish?" she asked Harriet.

"No, I'm all set."

Harriet garnished small plates with lettuce, on top of which she'd placed the fish. Smelling a little like tuna, but looking more like whitefish, they were a lunchtime staple of her mom's during the seven-day holiday. She blinked away the moisture in her eyes and brought the plates of fish out to everyone.

"Becca, do you want some?" Jared asked.

She loved eating and nodded. "Me want, me want."

Caroline smiled. "You might change your mind after you taste it." Gefilte fish was one of those things you either loved or hated. Rarely was anyone ambivalent about it.

Jared cut her a piece and put it on her plate. She speared it with her baby fork and put it in her mouth. Her face crumpled and she opened her mouth, pushing the fish out with her tongue. Her eyes watered, and Caroline expected her to scream. But instead, she shook her head.

"Yucky. No more."

"Aww, *bubbeleh*, you're such a good girl," Harriet said. "Jared, give her something else to get rid of the taste."

He gave her more carrots. "Sorry, Mom. It's an acquired taste."

"I'm not offended at all. I'm proud she tried it."

Caroline finished her soup and gefilte fish, awash in memories of her mom. Though she had purchased the soup and the fish, it was still a time for them to be together. And when she'd gotten sick, that soup was one of the few things her mom had been able to eat. She looked around the table. Thanks to the Leimans, she was making new Passover memories. At least this year.

She rose once again.

"Honey, sit," Harriet said. "David will help clear. You've done enough."

She sat as Jared looked at her.

"You okay?" he asked when his parents left the table.

She nodded. "Why?"

"Family seder and all. I'm just checking."

His thoughtfulness struck her. Warmth flooded her, and a desire to talk about her memories overwhelmed her. "My mom loved gefilte fish."

His face brightened. "I remember that! There was that one time during Passover, I came over, and she was eating it for lunch. I made some comment or other to you, or maybe to her... I don't remember what I said, but she laughed at me when I turned down her offer to have some."

Caroline smiled. "That sounds like her. In fact, I think she would have had it during the year, too."

Jared shuddered. "Don't get me wrong. I eat it and I like the way my mom makes it, but the thought of consuming it more than at a seder is a little more than I can handle. Especially when it's in the jar with the jelly."

She touched his arm. "I have to agree, your mom's homemade gefilte fish is way better." Touching his arm was pretty good, too. Beneath his shirt, his forearms were strong, and warmth permeated the fabric.

His parents walked into the room, with serving platters filled with food, and she withdrew her hand.

"Uh, Mom, you know there are four of us, right? Four and a half, if you count Becca."

At the mention of her name, Becca looked up. "Food?" Her face widened in a grin, and Caroline laughed.

"Don't knock it, sonny boy," his mom said. "She's going to eat you under the table." His mom placed her platter in the center.

"Jared, haven't you learned by now, your mother thinks serving anything less than enough food for ten people is a sin," his father said as he also placed two more platters on the table.

His mom swatted him with a potholder. "I can make sure you starve, you know."

His dad gave her a hug. "Please, you'd last five minutes before you offered me something to eat."

She shrugged. "It's my love language."

His dad pecked her cheek. "I know."

"Okay, that's enough," Jared said. He winked at Caroline. "Some of us want to eat without gagging."

Caroline couldn't help the warmth that spread through her.

They all had such obvious love for each other, and she loved being part of it even for a short time.

If she and Jared were together, she'd have this all the time.

The aroma of brisket wafted from the serving plate and made Caroline's stomach grumble. "This looks, and smells, good." She held out her hand for Jared's plate, serving him and then herself.

"Do you want matzah kugel?" Harriet asked. "It's got mushrooms and onions in it."

"Yes, please," she said. "And the asparagus, too."

She tasted everything. "This is delicious." She wiped her mouth. "I love home-cooked meals. I wish I knew how to cook."

Harriet raised an eyebrow. "You never learned how?"

Caroline shook her head. "I learned enough so my mom and I didn't starve, but this?" She gestured to the table. "I wouldn't know where to start."

Harriet straightened in her chair. "Well, I can fix that. All of this is easy to make. The trick is the timing and making sure the ingredients are kosher for Passover. After we finish tonight, let's compare schedules and we'll set aside time for me to teach you."

"You'd do that?" Her face heated at the generosity of everyone here who accepted her without question.

"Of course, honey. I'd be happy to do so."

"That would be wonderful. I can tell you right now I won't have time until after the Matzah Ball."

"Jared tells us the fundraiser is coming along well," David said. "And everyone is talking about the guest of honor."

Caroline's neck heated with pleasure. "I'm glad it's generating buzz. Now we need to translate that buzz into ticket sales." Her stomach clenched. *And figure out who is mismanaging the funds.*

Jared reached over and squeezed her arm.

The gentleness and strength in his touch made her body

hum. His eyes darkened as they met each other's gaze. Her lips parted, and she looked away.

Clearing his throat, Jared reclined in his seat. "Dad, who's everyone?"

"The guys in my Romeo breakfast group discussed it the other morning. And some of their wives have more connections than Kevin Bacon. If they're talking about it, you know the word is out."

Harriet and Jared laughed, but Caroline frowned. "Wait, you have a Romeo group? As in, Romeo and Juliet?"

David smiled at her. "As in Retired Old Men Eating Out."

Caroline snorted. "That's hilarious."

"Don't knock it," Harriet said. "It gets him out of the house."

"Hey, I thought you love having me around," David said.

"Of course, I do, Dave. But I like having you *not* around sometimes." She winked at him, softening the words, and he looked at her with love.

Caroline swallowed. She wanted that kind of relationship someday, one where the love was deep, but independence was valued, too. She looked at Jared, who observed his parents with an expression of amusement on his face. He made eye contact with her and somehow communicated silently with her. Did he want that, too?

Chapter Thirteen

God, he wanted what his parents had, Jared thought to himself as he got ready to man the ticket desk at the JCC three days later. The more he thought about their relationship—how real it was and how deep—the more he recognized the rarity of it. Most of his clients, the ones who were married, that is, didn't have the kind of marriage his parents had. He witnessed their relationships during meetings and Hollywood parties and, on rare occasions, private events. The definition of a happy marriage appeared different there, and it wasn't something he wanted to emulate.

His brother and sister-in-law had had his parents' kind of relationship, as short-lived as it might have been. But they'd met in grade school and hadn't ever been apart after that. The only long relationship he'd had was in high school with Caroline. Sure, he'd dated plenty during the last two years of college and afterward, but nothing that lasted more than a year. For a long time, he hadn't looked for anything serious, and once he started, no one he'd met satisfied him.

Not the way Caroline did.

He'd spent the entire seder thinking about how well she fit with his family. She'd always fit in, and he'd berated himself once again for hurting her the way he did. It didn't matter that she'd forgiven him, he couldn't get past the wrong he'd committed against her. And he didn't know what to do about it.

What he did know was that Caroline was never far from

his thoughts, and he sought out ways to be near her. Hell, he'd volunteered for the Matzah Ball because of her. Sure, she ran it, but he offered to help in areas unrelated to her, like the ticket sales. All because she needed the event to be successful.

He sat at the desk in the lobby and arranged the Matzah Ball tickets, cash box, card reader, and signage to his liking. Facing the front of the building, he looked through the floor-to-ceiling windows out onto the parking lot, where lines of cars let out children for day care. A man entered the lobby and after he displayed ID to the security guard, walked over to Jared's table. He greeted him, answered his questions, hyped up the event, and sold two tickets. For the rest of his time there, a steady stream of people entered to buy tickets. The Ben Platt posters he'd helped hang around town grabbed people's attention.

"Will we get to meet him?" one of the ticket buyers asked.

Another woman put her hand over her heart and offered to marry the man. Jared hid a smile as he fielded those requests. He waved to Sarah and Aaron as they stepped up to the table.

"Hey, are you two coming to the ball?" he asked.

"The ball my best friend is running?" Sarah asked. "Of course, we are!"

"Excellent," Jared said. "Caroline will be pleased."

Sarah looked around at the people in line to purchase tickets. "You know, this used to be known as an event for people our parents' age or older. But with Caroline involved, and with your guest of honor, you're drawing a much younger crowd this year."

"I hope that's a good thing." He handed them their credit card and tickets.

"It's a great thing," Aaron said. "That's how you keep the event relevant, by attracting more people."

Jared nodded. "Caroline's worked her butt off, and I want this to go well for her."

Sarah studied him, and he met her gaze. "What?" he asked.

She retreated a step, as if surprised he'd confronted her. "Nothing."

He stared at her a minute. "Okay. Well, I'm glad you two will be there."

They waved and left the building. In the lull, he wondered about Sarah. What made her stare at him like that, as if she were trying to decide?

He reached for his phone to let Caroline know her best friend bought a ticket. And because he missed talking to her. But he stopped, fingers hovering over the keypad. He was falling for her all over again. And once again, the timing was terrible. She had her freedom, and he had a toddler living with him on the other side of the country. As much as he missed her, was it fair of him to encourage a relationship when he was leaving soon?

The thought of leaving made his stomach drop. He didn't want to go. Everything he had out in LA could be found here—friends, a home, childcare—and as a bonus, his family was here, too. Except his job. That required him to be in LA. If somehow there was a way for him to work from here. He huffed. The benefit of his A-list celebrity client list was making a ton of money at something he excelled at. But the disadvantage was they expected him to be always available and in close proximity to them. Look at how often they'd texted him while he was here.

"Hey, I'm here to relieve you." Marge shuffled over and dropped her oversize, overfilled purse on the table. "How many did you sell?"

Jared hadn't counted, but he opened the ticket box and showed her.

She whistled. "I don't know what your schtick is for selling tickets, but can you share?"

Jared shrugged. "I don't have a schtick. The line hasn't stopped since I got here. I think everyone is dying to meet Ben Platt."

"Oy, and here I thought I'd get knitting done. I'm making a baby blanket. Want to see?"

He had no desire to see the blanket, but he knew better than to say no. "Of course."

Before she unpacked her entire bag, someone came up to the table and asked for tickets.

"That's my cue to leave," he said. "Good luck!"

She waved him off, and Jared left before he got roped into staying longer. Climbing into his car, he got ready to drive home, but paused before starting the engine. His parents were taking Becca to the zoo today. He had a free afternoon.

And the only thing he wanted to do with the afternoon is spend it with Caroline. Every reason he should leave her alone presented itself like a list in his brain. All the same reasons he'd obsessed over for the past week. Nothing had changed. Nothing would change.

So why shouldn't he spend time with the one woman who gave him purpose in life?

Caroline's doorbell rang in the middle of the afternoon, pulling her focus away from her spreadsheet of tickets sold, money collected, anticipated revenue, and expenses. Her eyes burned from staring at her computer screen for so long and comparing her data to what the JCC recorded. She rubbed her lids as she pushed away from the kitchen table.

"Coming!" She walked in sock-clad feet through the front hall to the door and pulled it open.

Jared's body blocked the entrance. His eyes smoldered and lit her every nerve ending on fire.

"Hi." Her voice croaked. The sound dragged across her vocal cords and vibrated inside.

"I'm finished," he said.

She frowned. "Finished with what?"

"Finished worrying." He took a step forward. "Finished

thinking about the future." He took another step forward. "Finished thinking about anything other than you, and how much I want you."

With each step forward he'd taken, she'd retreated a step. Now Jared was inside her house and made the space feel tiny. He shut the door behind him, never taking his gaze off her. He cupped his hands beneath her elbows and backed her up until she was pressed against the wall.

"Really." She met his gaze. It was laser focused on her.

There was something heady and powerful knowing a man wanted you, and Caroline drank it up.

Jared made soft circles with his thumbs on her upper arms. Goose bumps rose along her skin.

He nodded. His chest expanded with each inhalation. The stripes on his shirt seemed to wave each time he breathed, and she stared in fascination. And then, of course, her mind wandered to what was under the shirt.

In high school, his chest had been nice, if not one of an ordinary teenager's. While not unathletic, he wasn't on a sports team, excelling instead on the debate team and in academic honor societies. Whatever muscles were the result of good genes. But now?

She'd seen him often enough in the past few days to assume he'd filled out, acquiring muscles from exercise at gyms whose A-list membership list ensured he received the best training.

The temperature in the hall rose several degrees. Would he remove his shirt?

"Since you haven't pushed me away, I think it's fair to warn you," he said. "I'm going to kiss you now."

She wanted to respond with a wisecrack, with a "not if I kiss you first" or a "thanks for the warning." But his proximity and her desire snapped the connection between her brain and her voice. He bent his head, drew her to him, and joined his mouth to hers, and all thoughts flew from her mind. With a cross between a mewl and a sigh, she leaned into him, parted her lips, and slipped her tongue into his mouth. He groaned, and thrust his tongue against hers, where they danced and tasted and licked away the last of either of their concerns.

She slid her hands beneath his shirt, his hot skin beneath her palms, and explored the planes and ridges of his rib cage. He wound his through her hair, tugging her scalp with delicious pressure.

He deepened the kiss, hardened against her, showed her how much he desired her. Heat flooded through her as her hands traveled around his back, over his belt and into his pockets where she cupped his butt. He groaned, released her hair, and hugged her to him, writhing with her in imitation of what they'd do if their clothes were off.

"I want you," he whispered, as he pulled his lips from hers. He trailed kisses along her jawline, all the way to her ear, nipping the lobe. "I *need* you."

Her heart raced at the raw desire in his voice. "I need you, too." She licked her way to his neck, into the hollow at his collarbone. His thigh muscles trembled against hers, and she squeezed his butt harder.

He panted against her neck. She loved her hold over him. She adjusted her stance. Their bodies lined up, and she rocked against him, absorbing the shocks of pleasure from the friction of their clothes. What would it be like when they were naked?

Because they *would* be naked.

Jared pulled away from her, just a few inches. "I want you. Now. Do you want me?"

Despite all the reasons she could say no—should say no—she nodded. "I want you."

He stared at her for a few more seconds, as if he waited for her to be sure. And then, without any further sound, he lifted her up. She wrapped her legs around his waist, and he carried her upstairs to her bedroom.

He paused in the doorway and stared at the room. "Whoa," he said. "I haven't been here since…"

She didn't need to turn around to see what he saw. It was the same white canopied bed from her childhood, the same movie posters on the walls, the same pink carpet on the floor. Paying her mom's medical expenses didn't allow her to re-decorate, and when she was able to save, the first item on her bucket list was her vacation.

She kissed him long and hard. When she pulled away for air, she asked, "Do you want to go somewhere else?"

Instead of answering, he strode into her room, bounced her onto the queen-size bed and climbed up after her. He re-minded her of a lion stalking its prey. On his knees next to her, he pulled her up to a seated position and lifted the hem of her sweatshirt over her head.

Shaved. Showered. Deodorant. Check. Check. Check.

Those were her last coherent thoughts. He flicked open the front closure of her bra and stared, before sucking first one, then the other. She arched as desire coursed through her.

He chuckled low under his breath before he trailed kisses around her rib cage.

"Are you still ticklish here?" He slid a finger against the skin between her third and fourth rib. Her skin twitched, and she jerked.

"Yes."

He covered her answer with his mouth once again. The tex-ture of his knit shirt against her bare skin sent shards of de-sire through her. As much as she liked it, she wanted to touch his skin. As he kissed her neck, she reached for the hem of his shirt and tugged.

He pulled away and the cold air against her skin made her cry out in protest.

"Shh." He pulled his shirt over his head.

She stared, finally seeing what she'd longed for. His body

had changed since she last saw it. Now his muscles were more defined, his shoulders were broader, and the light dusting of chest hair defined itself across his pecs, narrowing to a line as it traveled down his stomach.

Caroline needed to touch him to make sure he was real.

His skin was hot, with a texture that could only be described as male. She traced the lines of his ribs, splayed her hands across his chest muscles, leaned up and licked his collarbone.

He hissed and drew her close, so the front of their bodies came together. She ran her hands up the base of his skull and sank her fingers into his thick hair. Once again, he kissed her, their tongues jousting. She sucked his lower lip, and he growled.

Jared pushed her onto the bed again and rose over her, supporting his body with his hands on either side of her. His cobalt blue irises formed a deep blue outline. His nostrils flared as he sucked in air.

She trailed her hands across his chest, felt his skin quiver beneath her touch to where his belt wound through the loops of his jeans. She let the tips of her fingers slip beneath his waistband as she unbuckled his belt, reveling in the power she held over him. She moved slowly through her haze of pleasure, wanting to prolong the moment. He must have gotten frustrated because he yanked open his fly and pulled off his pants, refusing to let her finish the job.

A laugh burst from her lips, but as he dragged himself up along her body to kiss her lips, the laugh morphed into a gasp and then a moan. He centered himself and pressed their pelvises together, making her senses reel with desire. Before she realized what happened, he'd removed her leggings and underwear, as well as his, and they were naked. Together.

Her breath hitched, her inhalations like gasps, her exhalations stuttering from nerves, desire, or a combination of the two. Ten years dissolved into mere seconds, yet they were two different people. Their bodies were, too.

Textures, tastes, and sounds mingled. A kaleidoscope of memories combined with images from the here and now, made Caroline dizzy with need, desire, and nostalgia. At last, something anchored her and drove away the loneliness. She savored the moment while he kissed her until she couldn't breathe.

He started to pull away once again. This time, she gripped him tighter, wanting nothing to come between them.

"I need to get a condom," he whispered.

She shook her head. "I have some." Her face heated as she reached for her night table drawer. What would he think?

He kissed along her neck from her collarbone to her hairline before he took the packet from her. Their fingers touched, sending sparks of attraction up her arm. "I love a woman who is prepared," he whispered. His breath fanned her ear, and she shivered.

Sheathed, he returned to his position on top of her. Cocooned between his arms, she let everything but him dissolve around her.

"Are you sure?" he asked. His face was tight, the strain of wanting and waiting in the hard set of his jaw. She raised her hand and caressed it, his whiskers tickling her palms.

She nodded. "More than ready." *Always ready for you.*

He looked at her, really looked at her, like he memorized every detail of her face, before he trailed kisses from her lips, down her neck, over her chest, and back up. Not breaking eye contact for one second, he pushed himself against her opening and she moved to meet him. She nodded, and he entered.

Her breath caught, and she raised her hips a fraction. He was everything she wanted and more. She wrapped her arms around him, her heart beating against his. She buried her face in his neck, inhaling his masculine scent. She focused on the texture and taste of him as he pushed deeper. With one last thrust, he was fully inside, and she tightened her muscles around him. He paused again, his brow furrowed.

"Okay?" His voice was strained, and his concern for her touched her.

"Yes."

She breathed more than spoke the word and with that, they rocked together, chasing the well of desire that built between them. Higher and higher they reached, bodies slick with sweat, hearts pounding, breathing ragged, until he pushed her over the pinnacle, lights burst behind her eyelids, and she shattered. Immediately after, Jared shouted his release and collapsed on top of her.

Her chest heaved as she pulled in air. His weight comforted her. She clasped her arms around him and ran her fingers over his back, the texture of his skin so different from her own. She basked in the afterglow and enjoyed the weightless sensation as she returned to reality.

Jared rolled to the side, bringing her with him so they lay face-to-face. He caressed her cheek, making her feel wanted, treasured.

"You were amazing," she whispered.

His mouth quirked up at the side. "Real-person amazing or Jared-is-magic amazing?"

She raised an eyebrow. "I'm afraid to answer that."

His lips twitched. "Why?"

"I'm not sure I want to encourage your ego."

"You already said I was amazing." He sat up and puffed out his chest, before he collapsed onto the bed and cuddled her against him.

"See what that got me?"

He drew her to him and kissed her again. "Me."

His kiss, as always, ravished her, and she kissed him back, enjoying this side she'd been afraid of for so long. But then she pulled away. "Me, what?"

"It got you, me."

Her chest tightened. She had him but for how long? He was leaving, and she'd be a fool to think this was anything more than temporary, no matter how many nudges her heart might give her.

Drawing her into his embrace once again, he spooned with her in the front, pulled the covers over them both, and drifted to sleep.

Caroline remained awake, though, berating herself for ruining the moment by thinking of things she shouldn't.

Like forever.

Jared sat up with a start as he took in the lacy surroundings. It took him a moment to recognize where he was, and when he did, he sank into the pillows. The other side of the bed was empty. Caroline had left. But noise downstairs assured him she was still here.

Unless it was a burglar. He doubted it, but he didn't want to be found naked. He pulled on boxers and went to investigate. Sure enough, Caroline was there, talking on the phone.

"Sure, that weekend is good. I'll see you then." She hung up and pocketed her phone, her face flushed.

"Hey, gorgeous." He walked over to her and kissed her neck. "What was that about?"

"Your mom is teaching me to cook."

"That's great. I'm glad the two of you will spend time together."

Her flush deepened. He wasn't sure if that was a good or bad sign. She was always skittish about the two of them together, but cooking had nothing to do with him. Did it? He decided to let it go. If she wanted to talk to him about it, she would. And if not, he could always bring it up later. Swallowing, he vowed to give her the space she needed. He didn't want to dim the afterglow if he could help it.

His stomach rumbled, and he checked the time. Almost dinnertime.

"Can I get you something?" she asked. "I have plenty of Passover snacks."

"I'd love to stay." He clasped her shoulders and looked at her to be sure she understood how serious he was. "Truly, I would. But now that my parents are home with Becca, I should be there to put her to bed. Want to come with me?"

A shadow crossed her face. "I should stay here and finish my work."

"Which is?"

"Tracking the money we make from the fundraiser to see if I can dig deeper into the finances from before."

"I wish I could stay to help you," he said. "Will you let me know if you find anything?"

She nodded. "You should get dressed and go. I don't want you to miss Becca."

He turned to go upstairs but stopped. "You know I would stay with you if I could, right? Like, this isn't some excuse to leave."

"I do."

Somewhat satisfied, he jogged upstairs, dressed, and returned five minutes later. He kissed her, loving the taste of her, and hating to leave. "I'll call you later," he said.

A short drive later, he pulled into his parents' driveway, right behind their car. He entered their house and Becca's shrieks greeted him.

"Dada, dada!" She ran over to him and grabbed his legs.

His throat closed, and he looked to his parents for help. But their eyes were misty, too.

"How was the zoo?" he asked when he could get words past the lump.

"Grrr."

Turning to his parents again, he looked to them for interpretation.

"She's imitating the lions," his mom said.

"Oh! *Grrr*," he responded to her.

Her little face lit up, removing the last of the lump in his throat.

"What other animals did you see?" he asked her. "Hmm, did you see tigers?"

She nodded.

"And elephants?"

She pointed to her nose. "Tunks."

"That's right, they have trunks. What about giraffes?"

"Necks."

"Very good." He turned to his dad. "She's smart."

"You just figured this out now?"

"No, I've known it for a while." He lifted her into his arms, and she rested her head on his shoulder. The lump in his throat returned as her weight settled. Noah should be the one to cuddle with her and laugh at her animal identifiers. But somehow, he'd been given this gift.

He froze. This was the first time he considered it a gift. His heart hammered in his chest. Was he a horrible person? How could he justify his joy in Becca with the loss of his brother?

"I'm bushed," his dad said. "We had a great time with her, but I forgot how much energy a toddler has."

"Me too," his mom said. "Honey, would you mind fending for yourself and getting her to bed?"

"Of course not." He tried to make his voice sound as normal as possible, though his heart was shattering.

"Are you okay?" his mom asked.

He nodded. "Don't worry about me. I'll take care of everything."

With a last glance at him, his parents went up to bed. Becca was drowsy in his arms, but she needed at least something for dinner. He made her scrambled eggs and spinach and tried to feed her as many bites as he could before she cried out in protest. Then he brought her upstairs and put her to bed.

It was eight o'clock and the house was silent. There was no one to talk to and thoughts swirled in his brain.

What kind of a brother looked at his niece like a gift when it meant his brother was dead? What the hell was he supposed to do with his life? How could he fix a career gone stale? Was he falling for Caroline or was she a convenient diversion? And how did he keep from hurting her?

He paced the ground floor from the den to the kitchen to the dining room and back again, feeling claustrophobic from the memories woven into every inch of the house. He wanted to leave, to run away from all his problems. But he couldn't leave Becca, and his parents deserved to rest.

His problems wouldn't disappear, either. They'd either follow him or they'd wait for him when he returned. A deep desire to talk to Caroline filled him, but they'd spent the afternoon together, and he suspected she had a lot of thinking to do as well. Who else could he call? His friends in LA wouldn't understand. Although fun and important, none of them knew him enough to have a heart-to-heart conversation with, and he crossed them off his list.

His home friends? He didn't keep in touch with them. He and Eli played racquetball together, but that was the first time they'd seen each other or talked in years. The guy would think he was nuts to call him now.

God, he was lonely.

Footsteps in the hall interrupted his thoughts.

"Mom, why are you up?"

"I was worried about you." She sat on the sofa and pulled a blanket over her legs. "Tell me what's wrong."

He shrugged. "Don't worry about it. You should go to sleep."

"It's not that late, and I will, but I'm your mother. Telling me not to worry is like trying to break a piece of matzah without making any crumbs. Impossible."

"Under normal circumstances, I'd suggest a couple good vacuuming runs. With Becca around, though, oy," he said.

"Don't knock my granddaughter. She's perfect."

"I know she is." His voice wobbled, and he turned away, but not before a look of understanding passed across his mother's face.

"You're a wonderful father, Jared."

Rounding on his mother, he tried to keep his voice low while rage and despair filled him. "But I'm not her father. Noah was."

"And he's gone now." She closed her eyes for a moment and Jared felt awful.

"I'm sorry, Mom."

"Don't be." She patted the seat next to her, and he sat. "What happened to him and Rachel was awful. It will never not hurt. But Becca is still here. They made you her guardian. Not anyone else. They had confidence in your abilities, and so do I. Dad, too."

"But I have no idea what I'm doing." He raked his hands through his hair. "You saw what happened with the diapers." The weight of his responsibility threatened to suffocate him.

His mother chuckled.

Not helping.

"Sorry," she said. "You're getting better all the time. And the most important thing is that you show her love, which you do. You've seen how attached to you she is."

"And it kills me."

"Why?"

"Because she'll forget Noah and Rachel. I don't know how to get rid of the guilt."

His mother leaned forward and glared at him. "I'll tell you

one thing. If you wince every time she calls you Dada, or tells you she loves you, you'll do her far more harm than if you accept her love and thank God for what you have." She pulled him toward her and cupped his shoulder. "And I won't let anyone hurt my granddaughter, not even you."

His mother's statement gave him pause. He hadn't thought about the harm his reactions might cause. His heart raced. "You don't think I've hurt her—"

"No. You haven't. But keep it up, and you will."

He swallowed. He would always miss his brother. But presented in this light, he had a purpose. To give Becca the life and love she deserved. And he had nothing to feel guilty about when he looked at it this way.

He gave his mother a hug. "Thank you."

She patted his back and stifled a yawn. "Now I'm going to bed."

With a last good night, she went upstairs.

As some of his guilt lifted, he had more space in his mind to be able to figure out other things in his life.

He pulled out his phone and scrolled through his contacts. Ben Affleck, Lady Gaga, Lizzo. Yeah, no one he could call. He groaned out loud. It was time to do something, not think about it.

Seated on the sofa, he opened his notes app. He'd make a list. The first thing he needed to do was decide what kind of life he wanted. Ha, easier said than done. But, after the conversation with his mother, Becca's well-being was at the top of the list. Now he needed to figure out how to do what was best for her.

First was where to live. Second was how to support her. And third was how to nurture her. Broken down that way, the list seemed easier to tackle, because to help her, he needed to help himself, too.

Chapter Fourteen

Caroline hit the sidewalks the next morning when the sky was a purple gray, right before the sun rose. She loved jogging this early. The streets were quiet, the air was still, and the sound of her bright pink rubber soles hitting the pavement echoed as she ran.

She'd loved running ever since she joined the town track team in elementary school. At first, it was something to channel her energy and make friends. By the time she reached high school, it was her therapy and her ticket out of town. When her plans changed, she was forced to drop everything. But she never gave up running, even if she lost sleep so she could jog before her mom woke up and needed her.

During her five-mile daily jog she solved problems, created new class routines, relieved stress, and made mental lists. Today, her mind switched between Jared and her embezzlement theories. Neither subject presented an easy solution.

She was falling for Jared. Despite her promises to enjoy their time together and not think about the future, she couldn't keep her imagination from a chuppah in the synagogue, with a rabbi officiant, her best friends as bridesmaids as she wore a beautiful white gown and floral headband, stood next to Jared, and said, "I do."

Instead of dreams about her upcoming vacation, she dreamed about honeymoons and married life. Last night, when she'd browsed through her itinerary, she'd made note of a children's toy shops she could check out for a souvenir for Becca.

What. The. Hell. Her feet pounded out the expletive, but she didn't get the typical satisfaction. Not only was she falling for the man who'd broken her heart, but she was falling for his kid, too. She, Queen of No-Responsibility, looked forward to marriage and motherhood—never having been asked, of course—and contemplated loving the man and his child.

What would she do if Jared got sick? Or worse, Becca? Could she go through that again?

Her pulse pounded in her ears, and it wasn't from her exercise. She tried to talk her way out of thoughts of Jared and Becca and into thoughts about the Matzah Ball fundraiser. Of course, he'd maneuvered his way into that part of her life, as well. But she wouldn't think about how he'd been a lifesaver with Ben Platt, or how he'd helped sell more tickets than they'd sold the past three years, or how the thought of him in a tux on the night of the dance made her sweat.

No, she needed to think about how the money disappeared. Because somehow, despite the funds they'd raised this past year, they were in debt. She needed to figure out where the funds went. And how no one else had found out except her.

In college, she'd had an accounting professor who stressed the basics. Things like double- and triple-checking your work, making sure that what you looked at made sense. And something about the spreadsheets she'd looked at didn't make sense. But she couldn't put her finger on why they didn't or how to find the problem. She needed to reexamine everything.

She continued her route. Like she had time to reexamine all the spreadsheets. They were in the homestretch of the Matzah Ball fundraiser, she had her regular classes to teach, and she had her programs for the senior center. That left little time to do anything, never mind the brainpower necessary to uncover someone who stole money.

If they were stealing. Maybe it was an honest mistake. She couldn't point to evidence, much less motivation. She shouldn't jump to conclusions. That would be as wrong as Al assuming she was a brainless jock. His insult still stung these many weeks later.

By this time, she'd reached the end of her route, and she circled her driveway until her pulse returned to normal. When it did, she went inside, showered, and changed into clothes for work. She stuffed her laptop into her bag and brought it with her, in case she had extra time today to examine the numbers one more time.

She waved to the security guard in the front of the building. "Hi, Mac." Continuing on her way, she spotted several seniors in matching sweat suits and fancy rings congregated around the activity bulletin board in the lobby. No matter how many times they emailed program and calendar updates, the seniors always preferred paper calendars on the wall.

"Hello, ladies," she called out as she reached them.

"Caroline, can you please tell Paula that she doesn't need weights for the exercise class?" Melanie asked. "She doesn't believe me."

"Which one?" Caroline leaned forward and tried to see past the five women huddled in front of the bulletin board. There were a variety of exercise classes offered.

"Nine in the morning on Thursday," Paula said. "That's kind of late in the day, isn't it?"

She frowned at the older woman. "It's the same time it always is, and no, you don't need weights for that one."

Paula harrumphed. "Well, when you get up at five, half the day has passed."

Caroline patted the woman's shoulder. "I know. I'm sorry."

"It's okay, dear, I'll have to make coffee plans with my friends beforehand. Of course, then I'll have to pee during class…" Paula shook her head.

"So have juice instead," Melanie, her hair dyed a bright red, said. "You can go for coffee afterward."

Caroline backed away in silence. She hoped to escape before any more bickering started. Sometimes, these ladies were worse than teenagers.

Once in her office, she deposited her bag next to her desk and got ready for her day. She had three yoga classes, one mobility class, and a regular exercise class. Plus answering everyone's last-minute questions about the Matzah Ball. As usual, the day was packed. So much for examining the budget.

A sudden knock on the door made her jump. Janice, another committee member from the Youth Programming Department, stood in the doorway, vibrating with excitement. "Did you see the updated guest list?"

"Not yet," Caroline said. "I was about to go to class. Why?"

Janice rushed over and pointed a red manicured finger at the computer. "You have to check it out."

Caroline's heart pounded. "Oh God, what's wrong? Did everyone cancel or something?"

"Look."

She opened the guest list spreadsheet and scrolled. Her heart pounded the farther down the list she got.

"You're kidding," she said.

Janice shook her head, making her dangly earrings sway. "Nope. Maybe there's a mistake?"

"How can there be a mistake? Certainly not—" she paused and counted out loud before she continued "—seven different mistakes in one list."

"Could the names be the same?" Janice asked.

They stood shoulder to shoulder, staring at the famous names on the guest list. Seven names in particular. Seven A-list celebrities were coming to the Browerville JCC's Matzah Ball.

Caroline turned to Janice. "Can you tell my class I'm late,

and they should start stretching? I'll be there in two minutes. And yes, I'll give them two extra minutes at the end."

When Janice left, she picked up her cell phone and dialed Jared. "Do you happen to know why seven A-list celebrities are coming to my Matzah Ball?"

Jared chatted with Becca as he made them pancakes for breakfast. "What shape would you like?" He held out metal cookie cutters for her to choose from and waited until she pointed to the star.

"Star."

"Please?"

"Pwease."

"Star pancakes coming right up." Kosher-for-Passover pancake mix wasn't fantastic, but a toddler wouldn't know the difference, and with luck, the star shape would make up for any matzah taste she might otherwise fuss over.

He heated the pan on the stove, put the cookie cutter where he wanted it, and poured the batter. His phone rang, and he smiled as he answered. "Hey, Caroline."

"Do you happen to know why seven A-list celebrities are coming to my Matzah Ball?"

She didn't sound pleased. Most people would be ecstatic. But then again, Caroline wasn't most people.

"Hold on, I'm making Becca a pancake." He flipped it, cookie cutter and all. So far, so good.

"I've got to run to my class, Jared. Can you call me later and explain? I'll be done around noon."

"Sure, talk to you then."

He slid the pancake onto a plate, removed the cookie cutter, and place it on Becca's highchair.

"Voilà," he cried, impressed with his skill.

"Walla, walla," Becca cried.

He laughed. "Walla, walla is right, babe." He chucked her under the chin.

"Becca." She frowned at him. "No babe."

Whoa, two years old and already strong. "Good for you, Becca," he whispered. He gave her a hug. "Good for you." Kissing her nose, he ate his own breakfast with her.

"So, what should we do today?" His parents had plans, but he was free. Other than calling Caroline later and explaining the surprise guests on the invite list.

He wasn't sure if she was angry or surprised. He'd sent texts to a few of his area clients about the event, and they'd responded. For them, it was a cheap night out. For Caroline and the JCC, it was a big deal, especially if it enabled their silent auction portion to have some stellar offerings. Was she annoyed at his help or was it that he'd remained silent? He'd kept his mouth shut because he didn't want to promise something he couldn't deliver.

His phone buzzed with a text from his boss.

Can you call Brad and discuss the new movie contract?

When I get back I can.

Any chance for earlier?

What was going on?

Is there a problem with it?

Just like to get it moving.

I'll see what I can do.

He'd had several days without texts from his boss, and he'd

gotten used to the quiet. He'd enjoyed focusing on his family. Now, it jolted him into reality, and he sighed. Better take care of this now before he forgot.

He sent an email to Brad about the status of the movie contract and reminding him he was out of the office until next week but was available for questions regardless. He drummed his fingers on the table. He supposed he should be grateful his boss didn't demand his immediate return now that the seders were over, or that he wasn't bothered before this. But he had a hard time with gratitude now. He hadn't taken a vacation in ages. He was entitled to one every now and then.

He sighed.

"Uhhh," Becca said.

"Are you imitating me?" he asked. "Boo."

"Boo."

"Hello."

"Hewwo."

She was, and it made him smile. Wiping her mouth and hands, he cleaned up their breakfast and prepared to take her to the park to play.

And to watch what he did and said in front of her. Because now that she imitated him, he needed to be conscious of everything he did.

Caroline finished her back-to-back exercise classes that morning and took a break for lunch. Exercise always cleared the worries from her mind, and today was no exception. The difference was she checked her phone when each class ended on the off-chance Jared had texted her an explanation.

He hadn't.

And now that her body was still and her heart rate returned to normal, her mind filled with all her concerns. Namely, the A-list celebrities added to the guest list. Why were they there and what the heck was she going to do with them?

She knew them from headlines on the internet. They were demanding, and they expected the best of everything. Not to knock the Matzah Ball, but the Met Gala it wasn't.

Her phone rang.

"Jared, help." She collapsed onto the chair and put her feet up on her desk.

"Oh my God, what's wrong?"

Wrong? "Oh, I'm sorry. I didn't mean to scare you. I meant help with the Ball now that all these celebrities are coming. Celebrities, I might add, I didn't invite." She pulled up the seating chart on her computer.

"They're clients who know Ben Platt. When they heard about his performance here, they wanted to know more about it. He referred them to me, and I invited them."

"We need to speak about his performance. But later. First, why didn't you tell me?" She scrolled from table to table, wondering what could be rearranged.

"Does everyone tell you about the people who purchase tickets?"

"No, but they're not Hollywood divas and… What's the male version called?" Tapping her finger on the desk, she wracked her brain for the correct term.

"I don't know, but they're not divas."

She huffed. "Another example of sexism. Demanding women are called divas, demanding men are just men. Ugh."

Jared sighed. "I'm interested in fighting sexism, but can we tackle one subject at a time? Please? This jumping around makes my head hurt. First, why are they divas? We'll pretend for a minute it's the women *and* the men."

"Because I've seen the headlines and read the stories about all the demands they make on tour or on set. This is Browerville." Her nerves buzzed. She left her office and walked toward the lobby, trying to picture Hollywood stars here. It defied the imagination.

"You should know better than to believe the internet. Besides, these actors are looking forward to the Ball. They know it's a fundraiser, I've told them Browerville is small, and they know what to expect."

"Do they? Because I don't, not anymore. Where will I put them?"

"Caroline, relax. They'll mingle with the guests, sit together at one table, and dance. Afterwards, they'll make a large donation, along with some items for your auction, and they'll leave. Trust me, it will be fine."

"Oh my God, what do I wear? Never mind, that doesn't concern you. I'll figure that out later. Look, I appreciate your using your contacts to help me, I—I don't know. I wish I knew about it ahead of time." She paced the hallway, moving to the side as passersby tried to avoid her.

"I'm sorry. I didn't mean to cause you stress."

"It's fine." She leaned against the wall showcasing donors on a plaque and bit her nails.

"Is it really fine or is that your way of shutting down the conversation? Because I've been warned about women who say it's fine, and while I don't buy into that crap—oh shoot, I have to be careful what I say, Becca is with me…stuff, I meant *stuff*—I don't want you angry at me."

"It's really fine. It's not a code word." She lowered her voice, regretting she'd walked into a public area.

"Good. And besides, we'll be there together. I'll pick you up, drive you to the JCC, dance with you, sit with you, mingle with you—introduce you to the celebrities you're nervous about—and drive you home afterwards. There might be kissing involved."

"But I have to work the event." Her heart rate increased the more she thought about the Matzah Ball. This was way bigger than she'd planned. She returned to her office and shut the door.

"That's okay. I'll help."

She tapped her foot against the chair leg, nerves making her antsy. She oversaw the event. Did that mean she couldn't have a good time with him at the dance?

"Okay."

"Excellent. Are we okay now? Because Becca needs lunch. I've got to go, but I don't want to cut our conversation short."

"We're fine."

"Okay. Oh, and Caroline?"

"Yes?"

"I want to know more about what you plan to wear to the Ball. Much more."

He hung up before she had a chance to respond.

Chapter Fifteen

The night of the Matzah Ball finally arrived, and Jared adjusted his bow tie in the mirror. He'd never less minded putting on a penguin suit than he did now. He didn't even mind renting one when he owned several at home—the number of black-tie affairs he attended in LA made it essential for him to own a variety, but he hadn't thought he'd need one on vacation.

He couldn't wait to see what Caroline wore. Despite his pleas, she'd kept her outfit a secret. No matter what it was, she'd look stunning, but the dress she chose held his curiosity all week.

Date. He wished she were more than that, but he'd settle for date. He didn't want to tie her down if she wasn't ready. Hell, it was hard enough to get her to commit to going as a couple to the event. A long-distance relationship would never work, no matter how often he toyed with the idea in his mind.

Unwilling to darken his mood with what he couldn't change, he forced himself to concentrate on his bow tie. With a last glance in the mirror, he jogged downstairs, where his parents played with Becca.

His dad whistled. "Mighty spiffy there," he said.

His mom agreed. She rose and smoothed out his jacket lapels. "You look wonderful."

Becca pursed her lips and blew a raspberry. Everyone laughed, and she tried again. "Dada pwetty," she said, giving up on imitating her grandpa.

Jared kissed the top of her head. "Thank you, sweetheart. The next order of business will be to teach you how to respect men's manhood, though." He paused. "Maybe we'll add that to the list of things to do when you're older. Way older."

He rose and grabbed his keys from the hall table. "I have no idea when I'll be back. Don't wait up. And if you need me, I've got my phone." He patted his jacket pocket to make sure it was there, then waved goodbye and left to pick up Caroline.

In her driveway, he remembered the times when her mother would wait on the small front porch for them to return from a date. It made kissing Caroline goodbye difficult. They'd taken to stopping around the corner to end their date as they wanted, without an audience.

He strode to her front door and rang the bell. Caroline opened the door, and Jared staggered. Air left his lungs. She was gorgeous in a champagne beaded cocktail dress that hugged every curve. He perused every inch of her body, from her light brown hair swept into an updo, to the spaghetti straps on her bare shoulders, to the jagged hemline that ended somewhere above her knees, to her sparkly shoes that added three inches to her height.

"Wow." He reached out to touch her but stopped before his hand made contact with her, worried he'd do something to mess up the perfection she'd no doubt spent hours creating. "Wow."

Caroline smiled. "You said that already."

"I know, but…wow."

She laughed. "Okay, clearly your vocabulary needs improvement, but I'll take the compliment." She studied him, too. "You look great in a tux. Much better than at prom."

He frowned. "What was wrong with what I wore for prom?"

"Nothing, but you fill out your tux better now."

His neck heated. "Thank you. I'm glad you noticed."

Her cheeks flushed, and a warm buzz of satisfaction joined

the sparks of attraction inside him. But this was her night, and he didn't want to give her a hard time or add to her stress. Instead, he held out his arm for her to take, and walked her to the car.

When they were settled, he turned to her before he started the engine. "You ready for tonight?"

She made fists in her lap. "No, but I don't think I have a choice."

He started the car and drove to the JCC. "The place is decorated, the food has been delivered, the caterers are there, the DJ is there, and Ben called me an hour ago that he's at the hotel and ready. What else do you need?"

"Guests. For the place not to fall down. For the electricity not to go out. For no one to get food poisoning."

As he turned into the parking lot, he added, "You forgot a Noah's Ark–worthy flood."

She squinted at him. "No, I didn't. God promised not to do that again. However, I'm not sure about other natural or man-made disasters. Let's not list them and give karma ideas, please."

He parked the car, turned toward her, and drew her close for a kiss. Carefully, so as not to mess up her makeup, he brushed her lips before he massaged her neck. "Everything will be fine, I promise."

She nodded. "Let's go inside before I lose my nerve."

They walked inside the JCC and paused. The lobby was transformed into a Broadway show hall, with a marquee and a ticket booth and twinkle lights everywhere. Large posters from famous musicals hung on the walls. Velvet curtains covered the windows and created intimacy and elegance. Hors d'oeuvres stations were situated around the lobby area, with tall tables placed strategically for people to congregate and eat. Lower chairs, resembling theater seats, were also interspersed around the room for people who wanted to sit.

"This place looks great." Jared turned in a circle. "Trust me. Everyone will love it."

"You don't think it looks cheesy?" she asked. "I mean, Ben Platt is a Broadway actor…"

Jared shook his head. "No, it's great."

Before he had a chance to speak again, the front doors opened, and guests began to arrive. Broadway show tunes piped through the sound system and provided added ambiance. Waiters passed hors d'oeuvres and offered drinks. More and more people showed up, and soon, the place was packed.

Caroline nodded. "I see my boss and some colleagues who I need to greet. Want to come?"

Her invitation surprised him, but he recovered. "Sure."

"Doug, Helen, nice to see you here." She turned to Jared. "Doug is my boss. His wife, Helen, teaches at the high school." She turned to her boss. "This is my friend, Jared. He's responsible for our guest of honor."

Jared grasped Doug's outstretched hand and shook it. "Nice to meet you both."

Helen's face lit up. "I love Broadway. Caroline, you and your committee did a wonderful job."

Doug nodded. "It looks great. Hopefully, we pull in a lot of donations."

"Thank you both. Ticket sales smashed previous records. We should do well."

"Excellent," Doug said. "Jared, nice to meet you, and thanks for your assistance."

The two walked off, and Caroline reminded herself that Doug knew how much effort she'd put into this event. She pointed to another couple. "I work with her in the senior center. Come on."

For the next ten minutes, Caroline introduced Jared to several of her colleagues and their families. Unlike his colleagues, these people didn't boast about their accomplishments. They asked about his job and how he liked being home. They were warm and friendly, and he would have liked to spend more time with them. But like most such events, this wasn't the opportunity for long conversations, and after a few minutes, he turned to Caroline. "Ready for some A-listers?"

Her face blanched. "Oh God, what will I say? I'll look stupid. Or start hiccupping or something."

He grasped her by the upper arms. "Breathe." When he was sure she'd taken in enough oxygen, he continued. "They're people. Like the people you introduced to me. You'll say hello and thank them for coming. If they ask you a question, answer it. If you want to say something else, do so. If not, smile. It will be fine. Okay?"

She nodded. He assumed it was the best she could do. He brought her over to a famous comedian, figuring she would be the least intimidating. Besides, he preferred Caroline's humor anyway.

"Sarah, glad you could make it." The woman's curly black hair was pulled away from her face, showing off her collarbones in a halter-top navy dress. He kissed her cheek. "This is Caroline, the organizer of the Matzah Ball."

Caroline stepped forward. "Thank you for coming."

Sarah looked around. Her eyes shone. "I love the chance to help support the JCC, and I'm a big fan of Ben Platt. When Jared told me about it, I had to come. Thanks for having me."

They spoke for a few minutes, and Sarah's humor made Caroline laugh.

"When will you return from vacation?" Sarah asked.

"In about a week," he said. "We'll get together when I return—there's that great taco place I'll take you to, and we can discuss your upcoming shows over queso."

"Sounds great."

He made their excuses and pulled Caroline away. She grabbed a water from a waiter and drank.

"See? That wasn't bad," he said. He'd observed her as he'd engaged in conversation. Caroline held her own and fit right in.

"She's lovely," Caroline said. "And funny, which doesn't surprise me."

"You can do this." He put his arm around her. "Don't worry."

Caroline pointed her glass toward the other side of the lobby. "Sarah and Aaron walked in. I'm going to say hello. Join me?"

"I will, but I need to greet another client first." He kissed her and strode to the bar, where a bespectacled actor/comedian talked to the bartender, the overhead lights turning his client's brown hair rust colored.

"Seth, how are you? Great to see you here." He clapped the man on the back. "I wasn't sure if your schedule would allow you to come."

"My lawyer calls, I do what he says." Seth's distinctive baritone rose above the background noise of the other guests. "Keeps me out of trouble." He looked around. "Besides, it's for a good cause."

"I agree." A stab of guilt over the financial difficulties the JCC experienced pierced him. But he suppressed it. The problem would be solved, and in the meantime, the organization needed help.

Caroline needed help.

After chatting business for a few minutes, he moved on. His chest expanded with pride that he was able to help Caroline when she needed it. And maybe he could redeem himself. He'd done nothing to help her when she'd needed him most. If he could do anything right now for her, he could atone for his earlier sins. He hoped it would be enough.

"Look at this!" Sarah pointed to the guests mingling in the lobby. "You outdid the previous balls, Caro. I'm proud of you!"

Caroline hugged her best friend and Aaron, who nodded in agreement. "Thank you, but I have to give credit to my committee. I took over the last month, but they did all the groundwork."

"Maybe so, but I don't remember the lobby looking like this, or the ticket-sales rush you guys caused," Sarah continued. "They might have gotten things started, but you're the one who pushed to outdo last year and think outside of the box."

Aaron leaned toward Caroline. "Face it. You'll have to accept the praise, unless of course you want to listen to Sarah continue to gush for the rest of the evening."

Sarah punched him in the arm, while Caroline laughed at Aaron's rueful expression as he rubbed his bicep.

"Thank you both. And I can't tell you how reassuring it is to have you here."

"I'll admit, I always thought this was kind of for the older crowd," Sarah said, "but once I heard you were in charge and made such amazing changes, I didn't want to miss it."

"The food is great," Aaron said. "Even if you didn't have me cater it."

Caroline's heart thudded in shame. "I'm sorry, Aaron. I wanted to, but the JCC already hired a caterer, and we would have lost money if we changed it so close to the event date."

He gave her a hug. "It's fine, honest. Like I said, the food is good. Take it from the deli guy."

"I will," Caroline said. "I have to mingle, but I wanted to thank you for coming, and I'll see you inside."

Before she could turn to leave, Sarah grabbed her arm. "By the way, Jared looks hot in his tux," she whispered.

"I know, right? It's torture."

Sarah nodded. "Well, if I can't find the two of you later tonight, I'll know what happened."

Heat exploded beneath Caroline's skin, a combination of acute embarrassment and desire. "You're terrible," she muttered under her breath.

Sarah's laughter echoed in her wake as Caroline left her

friends. She spotted Jared on the other side of the room and tried not to stare. He chatted with one of his clients, and she stopped to observe him. From this distance, his body language oozed self-assurance. His expression was professional and polished, not arrogant, per se, but not the Jared she had come to know and like. He looked like he belonged with the "cool kids," but as adults, as he put his arm around the actor. Raising a hand, he flagged a waiter and passed drinks out to the people around him, as if he were the host. In a sea of celebrities, he owned the room. She shook off her discomfort and continued to mingle. There were still a few people she wanted to greet before they progressed into the main event room.

Jared appeared at her elbow. "Caroline, let me introduce you to Ben before he performs for everyone."

With a nod, she followed him to where the guest of honor stood with several other celebrities. Altogether, in a pack like that, they were intimidating, yet Jared's step didn't slow. Their gowns and jewelry glittered, their tuxedos fit like they were custom-made, and she suspected they talked about subjects no one else could relate to, like producing and starring in movies and comedy shows. And she suspected the other guests felt the same. Many stared at them, and Caroline's stomach dropped. She didn't want anyone to be uncomfortable, but she didn't know how to fix the problem. Before she had a chance to mention it, Jared led her over to them.

"Excuse me, I want to introduce Caroline Weiss to all of you. She planned this event. Ben, Caroline, I thought you'd want a moment to chat ahead of time."

As one, the group turned to her. She froze, but their expressions were pleasant, and if she wanted this fundraiser to be a success, she couldn't give in to her anxiety.

"It's nice of all of you to join us." She looked at each person. She'd never been this close to a celebrity before, much less this many. Her heart pounded, and she prayed she'd put on enough deodorant. She forced herself to relax. They were people, not idols.

"Oh, thank goodness, I thought I was in a fishbowl," Mila said in her trademark husky voice. "Everyone staring, but no one talking."

The actress was gorgeous, with long dark hair, a beautiful green-and-gold dress that highlighted her different-colored eyes, and she'd starred in a famous sitcom. *She* was uncomfortable?

The rest of them nodded, and Caroline couldn't help herself. She burst out laughing.

"I'm sorry, I shouldn't laugh, but I think we're all intimidated, especially with a group. You have no idea what fans we are of all of you. Yet you're feeling on display, which I regret. I guess I never looked at it from your point of view."

Mila joined in the laughter, and Caroline was able to see her as a pretty woman, not much different than she or her friends. "Yeah, I can see it from the other side. Do you think it would help if we all grabbed a random person's hand inside and danced with them?"

Caroline's jaw dropped. "Yes! Not that I'd ever ask you to do that. You're all guests, and I want to thank you for joining us. If there's anything at all I can do to make you all more comfortable, please let me know. I apologize for the stares."

Ben pulled at his collar. "Please don't worry. We are intimidating as a group, and we're used to people staring. But you know, Mila, that might not be such a bad idea."

Adam nodded, a mischievous glint in his eye. "I wonder what would happen if we did it." The group spoke all at once, and Caroline beseeched Jared.

He wrapped an arm around her waist. "Don't worry," he whispered. "They've got this."

"I think our security guards' heads would explode," Daniel said with his English accent, blue eyes sparkling.

Caroline opened her eyes wide. "Oh man, our cleanup crew…"

Daniel, as well as everyone else, looked over at her in surprise, before they elbowed each other and laughed. He turned to Jared. "She's funny."

She tipped her head in silent acknowledgment. "Thanks, but have no fear, I'm not angling for any of your jobs. Ben." She turned to the guest of honor. "Can I talk to you a minute?"

He nodded, and she led him to the side of the room. In her heels, the two of them were almost the same height. "Again, I appreciate your help. What's the best way to do this?"

"No worries. We'll let everyone dance, and then maybe a half hour in, you can get the DJ to stop, raise the lights, and I'll walk to the front and start. Does that sound okay?"

"Sounds perfect."

She returned to Jared, amazed at how easygoing Ben was. He met her gaze as she approached, put his arm around her waist, and squeezed.

"That's my cue, everyone," Jared said. "Enjoy, and I'll see you later."

The DJ started to play, and he drew her close to him to dance.

"Time to show off our moves," he said, his mouth close to her ear.

As he led her through the steps they'd learned, Caroline reveled in the solidity of his body, the warmth of his presence and the scent of his aftershave. All Caroline wanted to do was dance with him the rest of the night. But she had a job to do. Reluctantly, she pulled away as the song ended.

"I need to make sure everything is okay."

"That's why you have a committee," Jared argued.

She leaned closer to kiss him. "Five minutes."

With a groan, he released her, his hands to his heart as if she'd wounded him. She walked to the double doors and opened them, entered the lobby, and pulled her committee aside to have them direct people to the ballroom. The music did the rest. As the lobby emptied out, she thanked the waitstaff, did a quick scan to ensure she wasn't needed, and returned to the ballroom. She stood by the door and watched guests choose seats and crowd the dance floor. Despite Jared's claim that no one liked to be first on the floor, everyone danced to the popular tunes the DJ played.

The table closest to where she stood was filled with older people whom she recognized from her senior programs. She walked toward them.

"Frank, Millie, you look wonderful! I'm glad you could join us tonight."

Millie's hair was dyed onyx, as were her brows. Her makeup was perfectly done, and her purple dress was striking. The woman sparkled, along with her jewelry. "It's a wonderful party, my dear, although a little loud."

"But we don't mind, because it's for a good cause," her husband, Frank said. His purple bowtie matched his wife's dress, and his white hair was trimmed. He tapped his hand on the table in time to the music.

"And you have so many younger people here this year," Millie added. "I'm glad to see that."

Caroline nodded. "I am, too. I hope to see you both on the dance floor later. I've seen your moves in my classes, and you could put everyone to shame."

They nodded, and with a light touch on their arms, Caroline left to find Jared. After she wandered through the room, stopping at tables to greet those she still hadn't seen, she found Jared with Eli and another man.

Jared's face brightened, and he drew her next to him. It was as if he couldn't stop touching her when she was nearby. She shouldn't like it. It meant she was growing more attached and attracted to him, but she couldn't help it. Her body warmed and her heart filled each time he was near.

"Caroline, this is a great party," Eli said. "Have you met my husband, Larry?"

"Thank you," she said. "No, I haven't. Nice to meet you. How did you two meet?"

"We met in college," Larry said. "I beat him in our first debate."

Jared whistled, and Eli ran a hand down his face. "Nice, Lar. You don't know her and already you're gloating."

"I'm not gloating." He winked. "She asked, I answered."

"I'm glad I asked," Caroline said. "You'll have to tell me more about that. What do you do now?"

"I'm a contract lawyer with my own firm in Manhattan," he said.

Caroline was impressed. "That's awesome. You must get such satisfaction from your career."

"I do. And with my own firm, it's a little easier to balance family and career," he said. "Plus, we can both focus on passion projects instead of billable hours. Not that those aren't important, too."

Caroline's stomach tightened. "That sounds like a lot of responsibility."

"It is," he said. "And unlike what people tell you, it's not possible to have it all, all the time. I think it comes in waves. But I try not to feel guilty when I mess up."

"Sounds like you've got it under control." Jared glanced between Eli and Larry.

Eli shrugged. "Control is a mirage," he said. "I don't think any of us have it or know what control is. And when we think we've found it, bam, there it goes again."

"Yeah, I have to say I get you," Jared said. "Now that I've got Becca, I think I've got everything handled and then either she changes, or a movie star throws a tantrum or gets arrested, and all my supposed control is gone. It's humbling."

Caroline shivered. They confirmed all her fears—of responsibility, of being able to do what she wanted, and the ability to balance the two.

"Oh, the DJ is playing my favorite song," Larry said. "Will you excuse us? Eli, dance with me?"

He nodded at Larry, took his hand, and turned to Jared. "Never say no when a handsome guy asks you to dance." With a wink, he left.

"What do you say?" Jared asked. "Dance with me?"

She nodded. "I guess I should listen to Eli."

Jared grinned. "Aw, you think I'm handsome?"

He drew her into his arms and danced with her to the slow song the DJ played. Caroline tried to banish the worries their conversation had brought up, to enjoy the success of the evening, and the sexy man who held her in his arms.

But it was only a matter of time until she had to face them head-on.

The clock struck midnight, the guests left—all of them raving about Ben's voice and the prizes they'd won from the auction—and the committee oversaw cleanup. By the time all of Caroline's responsibilities were finished, it was two in the morning. She'd tried to get him to leave, but he'd refused. Since she wouldn't let him help, he'd schmoozed with his clients a little longer, and then settled on one of the sofas in the lobby to wait for Caroline to finish.

Finally, she emerged, looking worn-out but satisfied. He waved, and when she spotted him, her face lit up and she hurried over, heels in hand.

"Did you know Ben was going to make that plea for additional donations?" she asked.

In the middle of his ten-song set, as well as at the end, he'd reminded the audience how important the role of the JCC was in their lives and asked them to consider an additional contribution. That request alone pulled in more than $70,000 from

Jared's clients. What she still didn't know was that his firm would contribute enough to make it an even hundred thousand.

"I suspected he'd do something to enable my clients, and his friends, to donate," he said. "I didn't know the specifics."

"Well, they were generous." She leaned toward him and kissed him. "As were you."

"Thank you." Despite his fatigue, his body hummed with desire when she pressed her lips to his. "I have another surprise. Come with me."

He held out his hand, and she took it, her blue eyes cloudy with confusion.

"Jared, it's late, or early, depending on your point of view," she said. "Either way, can it wait until mor—later in the morning? Like maybe after I've slept and drunk coffee?"

"Trust me." He brought her outside to his car.

"But my car—"

"Trust me." This time, he emphasized the words, like he did with nervous clients. As with them, she closed her mouth and got into the car when he opened the door.

He turned the radio to a jazz station and made the volume low. With her hand in his, he ran his thumb over her hand as he pulled out into the deserted street and drove through town, the opposite way of her home...and his.

Three miles outside town he pulled into the parking lot of a hotel and shook Caroline awake.

"Surprise."

She squinted out the window. "A hotel?"

"Where we can sleep as late as we want, order room service for breakfast, and use the spa tomorrow to recover from your very-successful-but-very-exhausting fundraiser."

"But I don't have any clothes with me."

"You don't need any tonight, and well, I might have asked one of your colleagues to grab an extra set of exercise clothes for you." He smiled. "I figured they were more comfortable than that gorgeous and sexy-as-hell dress."

She looked from him to the hotel and back to him again, multiple times. He held his breath in hopes that she'd agree to stay here with him. He didn't want to part yet. Spending the night at his parents' house was out, and her house, well, it still reminded him of high school. He didn't want to be reminded of their past. He wanted to focus on the future with what little time together they had left.

"Thank you," she said, as he began to get light-headed from a lack of oxygen.

He let his breath out in a whoosh.

She yawned. "I'd say more, but I'm too tired to make sense or to be funny."

"Let's get you to bed, then," he said. Jogging around to his trunk, he pulled out the bag with their clothes in it, took her hand, and entered the hotel. After checking in and getting their key card, he led the way to the elevator, pushed the button for the top floor, and wrapped his arm around Caroline's waist, and drew her close.

The room he'd reserved had a king bed, a full bathroom with a Jacuzzi tub, and a sitting area near the window that overlooked a lake. He dropped his bag on the navy carpet and pulled down the silver-and-blue-striped bedspread.

"A bed has never looked so good," Caroline said.

He waggled his eyebrows. "I know."

Her eyes widened.

"Don't worry, I'm too tired for anything but sleep right now." He walked over to her and took her face in his hands. "I look forward to having you next to me."

She blinked, a small smile curving her lips. Spreading her hands across his chest, she removed his tuxedo jacket and slipped out of her heels. "Me too, but I'm not against a little enjoyment until we get there."

His gaze burned with desire as he slipped the straps of her dress off her shoulders and spun her around to unzip her. As her dress slid off her body, she turned and unknotted his tie, pulled on the ends to draw him closer for another kiss. Desire streaked along his spine, and he drew her close as his tongue plundered her mouth. He ran his hands over her bare back and cupped her butt, pressing her body against him.

With a murmur of protest, she pushed away from him, far enough to slide her hands in between their bodies to unbutton his shirt. Their kiss and their hands maintained the connection as they finished undressing each other and tumbled naked into bed.

He raised himself up so he could see all of her, admire her breasts and her skin and her curves. She bit her lip as she stroked his chest.

"You're beautiful, you know that?" he whispered.

"You're handsome," she responded.

The simple comment, spoken with sincerity, filled him with warmth. Lying next to her, he drew her body against his, spooning with her, and enjoying the closeness. This was where he wanted to be. Caroline settled him. If only there was a way for them to be together without sacrificing her dreams or disrupting his career. He didn't want to contemplate their inevitable separation. He'd face that later. For now, he wanted to spend a peaceful night—or what was left of it—with her.

The sun slanted through the space in the curtains the next morning and woke Jared from a confusing dream with Caroline, Becca, and cats. He squinted at the clock. Ten thirty. Folding his arm over his brow, he lay next to Caroline and enjoyed the warmth of her body curled against him. She'd fallen asleep as soon as she hit the pillow. He'd spent a few extra minutes listening to her breath slow. Once she slept, he'd marveled at his luck with such an amazing woman in bed with him.

Because she was amazing. She'd met every challenge thrown

at her. Instead of growing bitter, she'd grown stronger. The fundraiser was a perfect example. With less than a month to go, she'd taken her last-minute assignment and run with it. Most people would have been horrorstruck to be put in charge of something that late in the game. But instead of complaining, she'd met with her committee, figured out what needed to be done, and taken care of it all. The challenge inspired her. As a result of her efforts, it would be one of the most successful Matzah Balls in recent memory. He doubted he'd have been able to do that.

In fact, thinking about his own career, he couldn't help but draw comparisons between the two of them. He couldn't remember the last time anything inspired him. Chatting with his clients last night hadn't done it. Sure, he'd talked to them and joked around, but it was like a Purim costume that didn't quite fit. Had he always felt this way? He couldn't recall. Last night, whenever he was with his clients, he acted the way he was expected to act, like he went through the motions. But when he was with Caroline, he was himself. And analyzing even more, talking to his clients was the only time since he'd come home that he felt that way.

"It is too early for you to have that expression on your face," Caroline said, her voice hoarse from sleep.

He turned onto his side and drew her into his arms. "What expression?" He kissed her.

"Mm, I don't know. Kiss me again."

He might be confused about a lot, but there was not enough confusion in the world to prevent him from obeying a woman when she asked him to kiss her. He drew her close and touched his lips to hers, increasing the pressure as he wrapped his arms around her and played with her hair. She was warm and soft and hazy in the first awakening stages. What would it be like to wake up like this every day?

When she pulled away, he folded an arm beneath his head and drew the blanket over her shoulder.

"Morning," he said.

"What were you thinking about?"

"Last night and you and work."

"I hope I wasn't the reason for your frown," she said.

"Never. And in case you forgot, you were amazing last night." When she started to smile, he continued. "I meant the fundraiser."

"Thank you. And I know, but it was funny to hear it that way in bed with you. Speaking of which, what time is it?"

"Almost eleven."

She gasped. "I've got to get up!"

He reached for her shoulder and traced light circles on her skin. "What for?"

"Don't we have to check out?"

"I've got it taken care of. We have spa appointments at noon. If you want to order breakfast, we can do so now. But we're in no rush."

She shook her head. "I don't know what you did or how but thank you."

"I told you, I wanted to do something for you after all the time you put into the fundraiser."

"It wouldn't have been the success it was without your help," she said.

"I disagree. You redesigned the entire theme, handled ticket sales, and publicized the event. All I did was invite some people."

"Famous people, you mean."

He shrugged. "It wasn't a big deal."

"I disagree."

"You're welcome. Now, do you want to order breakfast?"

"Yes, and then do I have time for a shower?"

"You have all the time you want."

They examined the room service menu and while he placed the order, Caroline started the shower. When he hung up, he got out of bed and opened the bathroom door. The room was already warm, with traces of steam from the two-person shower and fogged beveled mirrors. He peeked around the white, gray, and silver curtain.

"Want some company?"

She nodded. Climbing in, he stood under one of the two showerheads, held her in his arms, and kissed her. Their wet, naked bodies pressed together, molded into one. His senses jumped to hyperalert—heated spray rained on his neck, cool air caressed his spine, soft skin tantalized his palms. She wrapped her arms around his neck, drawing him closer. He lifted her, leaned her against the wall. When she touched the cold tile, she gasped, and he took advantage of her open mouth to plunder it with his tongue. Desire swelled, and he groaned deep in his throat. He couldn't get close enough to her. She stroked his back, lowered her hands to his butt and up again, and sent shivers of need up and down his spine. Tilting his head toward her ear, he whispered, "I don't have a condom." He'd left it in his bag in the other room, and the thought of pulling away from her, of leaving her for mere seconds, filled him with dread.

"I'm on the pill."

"I'm clean." He was vigilant about that and tested every few months.

She nodded. "It's okay."

"Are you sure?" No matter how much he didn't want to step out of the shower, he would if it made her feel better.

"Yes."

Holding her hips steady as he entered her, slowly at first, until he could no longer stand the delay. With one last thrust, he entered fully. Her muscles squeezed around him, the pressure exhilarating. She nipped his shoulder and brought exquisite pain and pleasure at the same time. His heart pounded as their bodies found a rhythm. With one hand, he touched her, found her sensitive areas, and drove her higher and higher, until her panting matched his. She shook in his arms as she brushed her fingers through his hair, kissed him senseless as she brought him closer to the edge. But he wouldn't surrender first. He massaged her breasts, trailed kisses along her neck as he thrust with a tempo his body seemed to already know. His nerves buzzed and his control was a tenuous filament, like a shimmering mirage in the distance. His breath grew harsh, and his body shuddered with need. With jerky movements and a gasp, Caroline stiffened right before her release, and with that release came his permission to follow. His pulse pounded, his muscles quivered, and with one last push, he crested the edge. Water sluiced over his shoulders as his breathing rasped. He braced himself against the wall, supporting Caroline and himself.

As they calmed, he washed Caroline's body with a soft washcloth, sudsy with shower gel. His circular motions were firm, and she stretched like a cat. He moved on to her buttocks and then turned her around to lather her chest and stomach. Even after their lovemaking, her nipples hardened at his touch. When he finished, she rinsed off, then held out her hand.

"My turn."

Her gentle and hypnotic touch made his entire body ache with need once again. She interspersed her washing with kisses, and by the time she finished, his body was hard once again.

"I think we should have washed first," she whispered in his ear as she turned off the water.

He took her in his arms and kissed her with abandon until a knock on the door interrupted him. He tipped his forehead against hers, not wanting their lovemaking to end. "Room service. I'll get it."

He wrapped a towel around his waist and answered the door. In the background, the shower started once again. By the time he'd set up their breakfast in the room, Caroline emerged in a fluffy hotel robe and slippers, hair wrapped in a towel.

"Mm, something smells good." She lifted the domed covers of eggs, hash browns, fresh bread, yogurt, granola, muffins, and fruit. "But I don't think there's enough food."

He pouted. "Variety is good."

"You know we could feed six more of us with this, right?"

"Tell me that after you finish."

"Are you saying I eat too much?"

"Nope. I'm saying you're hungrier than you think."

She stared at him. "Nice save."

"I wasn't sure it would work."

"I'm still not sure it has."

"Great."

They continued eating and joking until Caroline pushed away from the table. "I told you there was no way I could eat all of that."

Jared looked at what was left. "True, but I'll bet you ate more than you thought you would."

She bit her lip. "I might have misjudged my hunger level."

"Might."

"That's all you get out of me."

He glanced at his watch. "We have a couple's massage and spa appointment downstairs in twenty minutes if you want to go."

Caroline's eyes widened. "When did you book that?"

"A week ago."

"Seriously?"

"I wanted to do something special for you after the fund-raiser. This seemed like something we could enjoy together."

She came around the table, sat on his lap, and kissed him. "Thank you. It sounds perfect. Let me get dressed."

His gaze tracked from the top of her towel to the toes of her slippers. "I kind of like you like this."

Shaking her head and laughing, she returned to the bathroom and emerged a few minutes later with her wet hair in a ponytail.

As he dressed, he continued to stare at Caroline, admiring her body, as well as her appreciative stares at him. No matter their differences, attraction wasn't one of them. After longer than it should have taken, they left the room and walked hand in hand to the spa.

"You'll love this, Caroline," he said as they approached the entrance to the spa. "The owner is from LA."

She turned a quizzical stare on him. "Do you know them?"

He opened the glass door for her and followed her inside. "No, but some of my clients talked about it yesterday." The lobby was decorated in shimmering pearl and ice blue. A soothing fountain covered one wall, in front of which was the front desk.

Caroline stiffened.

"What's wrong," he asked.

"Nothing. I don't want someone who's used to celebrities to intimidate me."

"Don't judge it until you try it," he said. After giving his name to the receptionist, they were led into a changing room with low lighting and instructed to remove all clothes and cover themselves with the ice blue velour robes.

Caroline stripped out of her leggings and sweatshirt. "Hmm, maybe we could have come downstairs as we were."

"I tried to tell you," Jared said.

"Yeah, while drooling," she said.

"Some girlfriends would enjoy the idea that their boyfriends were attracted to them."

She raised an eyebrow. "So, you're my boyfriend?"

Jared paused. He didn't mean to label their relationship. They'd agreed not to. He'd suspected any labels would frighten

Caroline, but he'd slipped and now would have to deal with the consequences.

He was about to respond when there was a knock on the door. "Ready?" the voice from the other side asked.

Caroline opened the door. "Yes."

Jared followed Caroline and the woman into the couples massage room, wondering when Caroline would return to their conversation. Because she wouldn't let it go. He hoped she could put aside her concerns and enjoy the massage.

He inhaled eucalyptus-tinged air. The deep gray walls would have made the room dark, but one mosaic wall was lit from within, illuminating the various shades of blue. Pinpoint lights also decorated the ceiling and provided a soft glow. They both climbed up on the massage tables and slid under blue blankets after they removed their robes. Soft tunes played from hidden speakers. He lay on his stomach, rested his face in the special massage pillow as the masseuses entered and attacked his knots. Oiled hands were strong and firm, and he couldn't help but groan in relief. He hoped Caroline felt the same.

By the time their forty-five-minute treatment was finished, his muscles were jelly. He rose and rotated his shoulders while sitting on the table, before he put on his robe. Caroline did the same. He met her gaze.

"How was it?" he asked.

"So good," she said.

The masseuse led them to the steam room, and they removed their robes once again and sat against the cedar wall.

"I'm not sure I'll be able to walk out of here," Caroline murmured.

"Listen, about before…"

She waved her hand half-heartedly. "Forget about it. Let's not ruin this moment."

"Okay, but later—"

"It's fine."

Chapter Sixteen

Caroline searched her refrigerator for something to make for dinner, her body numb, her head aching. She'd begged off an afternoon with Jared after they checked out of the hotel, explaining she had to get ready for Monday. And her excuse was true. She needed to get herself organized.

But the organization applied to more than her professional life. Jared was leaving soon, and she had to prepare. Because no matter how she'd tried to deny it, she was falling for him. It was time to cut the cord. Jared was returning to his life in LA among his A-list celebrities, his daughter, and his job that required him to work a million hours a day, while she remained here, in the house she'd grown up in, at the same job, and aimed for a promotion.

Their lives were too different. And no matter how much she enjoyed her time with him, no matter how much she cared for him and his daughter, there was no way either one of them could upend their lives to be with the other. There was no point in saying goodbye. That would lead to tears and promises that wouldn't come true. They'd already done that once. She wasn't about to repeat it. So, she planned to be unavailable for the next few days until he was in the air on his way home.

As for the tingles of anticipation that ran up and down her spine every time she thought about him? Well, those would have to disappear, along with the slippers she'd brought home from the hotel. They were supposed to be a free thank-you gift from the hotel. However, they made her remember in agonizing detail how the light played off Jared's naked skin, how his muscles flexed when he braced himself above her, how the sound of his groan when the masseuse dissolved a troublesome knot had made her toes curl. Yeah, no slippers for her.

In fact, she'd had to shower again when she got home, because the hotel's shampoo and body wash reminded her of their shower together. She might have to resort to baths in the future, because she was certain she'd never look at a shower in the same way again. She shivered. What the heck had happened?

Sure, he was always attractive, but somehow, he'd grown sexier as he'd aged. She broke out into a sweat whenever she thought about how firm his butt was, how broad his chest was. Unless it was early menopause? One could hope, but no. It was all him. It's like he'd done it to torture her. *Sure, you can have hot sex and lots of fun with him, but even if you think it's temporary, you'll never get him out of your mind.*

She needed a distraction. Vacation. Her vacation would be a great distraction. Rushing to the coffee table, she grabbed her brochures, opened her computer email for the proposed itinerary, and tried to immerse herself in the trip details. Except as she looked at the day trips, she envisioned how Jared would enjoy them with her—climbing Mount Olympus, exploring Sarajevo and its old Jewish cemetery, walking through ancient Corinth. He'd be fascinated and enthusiastic and suggest adventures she hadn't considered. He'd relish the food and re-enact the mythological stories they'd read in high school. She could picture his humor and smiled despite herself.

Nope, not working. Angry heat flared. This was *her* trip. She'd saved for it and waited for ages to be able to do as she wanted. She didn't want him popping into her dreams and tainting her enjoyment. Frustrated, she pushed the brochures aside and returned to the kitchen. Throwing a container of leftovers into the microwave, she waited for the timer to beep. When it did, she brought the now-warm chicken and veggies over to the kitchen table, opened her laptop, and scanned the budget one last time. If she couldn't find anything wrong with the budget, she'd track the money they made from the fundraiser and make sure that what they brought in was recorded. And then she'd leave it to Finance to handle. It galled her, but there was nothing left to be done.

She scanned the expenses—monthly utility payments, quarterly HVAC, monthly mortgage payments, random office expenses, biweekly salary payments—nothing looked out of the ordinary. The deposit side also gave up nothing—random donations, periodic fundraising drives. She studied how donations were recorded so she'd know what to expect from the Matzah Ball. She then looked at previous years' Matzah Ball numbers and pride surged through her. They'd raised three times as much this year. Of course, she'd been responsible for it for the last month, and Jared helped… Ugh, she needed to stop thinking about him.

With a groan, she closed her laptop and finished her dinner. She'd find a movie off a streaming service and go to bed early. Tomorrow she'd wake up refreshed from the weekend and resolute about Jared.

Her phone rang as she was about to turn on the TV. She stared at it, nervous that it was Jared, but the caller ID said Sarah.

"Hi." She smiled. "I'm glad it's you."

"Well, that's nice, I think," Sarah said. "Why?"

"I'm avoiding Jared."

"Uh-oh. You two looked great together last night. That was why I called. Well, not about Jared, but to tell you how much fun we had, and to compliment you on a fantastic job. Even my boss was impressed."

Warmth flooded through Caroline. "Thank you, I appreciate that. And I'm glad you and Aaron enjoyed the ball. I wish I could have spent more time with you, though."

"That's what these fundraisers do, they pull you in a million directions. Don't worry about it at all. But why are you avoiding Jared?"

With a sigh, Caroline told her. "He was in his element with his clients. I barely recognized him. He's meant for that life." He'd even bragged about the LA owner of the hotel, as if that automatically made it better. "It'll be hard enough when he leaves. I don't want to make it worse."

"Oh wow, you care for him, don't you?"

Caroline swallowed. "Doesn't matter how I feel. He's leaving, and I'm getting my freedom back." But her words sounded hollow and less appealing than ever.

"Of course, your feelings matter, Caro. And just because he's good at his job doesn't mean he isn't right for you."

She kicked off her slippers and stretched out on the couch. "I know that, but did you see how he was with them? He was so much like the old Jared, it gave me chills. What if that's the real him, and who he is here is a mirage?"

"Aaron and I both saw him mingling with people. But that's just it, they were people, not you. With you, he's different."

"Then, how do I know which is the real him?" And at this point, what did it matter? He was leaving.

"Ask him."

"There's no point."

"Caroline don't end it like this. At least talk to him, find out what's going on and where you two stand. Then you can decide based on actual information rather than supposition."

She was right. Without a conversation, she'd never get him out of her mind. She'd have to see him one last time.

Jared called Caroline as soon as he woke up the next day. The desire to talk to her was so strong, he dialed before he looked at the time. 6:43 a.m. Oof. He should hang up. No one wanted to receive a call that early in the morning. He was about to disconnect when she answered.

"Hello?"

Her voice sounded surprisingly awake, but her breath was choppy.

"I'm sorry," he said. "There's nothing wrong, but I shouldn't have called you this early."

"It's fine, I'm up."

"What are you doing? I hear weird noises..." It sounded like she was outside.

"Jogging, like I do most mornings."

"Right, phew. At least I didn't wake you."

"You didn't, but you're up early," she said.

He sighed. "Yeah, well, I have a toddler who wakes with the sun."

"Ah yes. Hi, Becca. Is she there or am I talking to nothing?"

"She's here in her playpen, and even if she wasn't, you're still talking to me."

"You know what I mean."

Jared lifted Becca out and changed her diaper. "I'm giving you a hard time."

"Is that why you called me?"

"No, I called to see if we could get together today. We go tomorrow." The words made his stomach drop. The longer he was here, the more he dreaded leaving.

"I have to work. Are you free tonight? Or will you be packing?"

"Regardless of what I'm doing, yes, I'm free tonight. Want to come here for dinner? I'm sure my parents would love to see you again."

There was silence on the other end. "We need to talk, Jared. I'm not sure doing so in front of your parents is the best idea."

He swallowed. It was never a good sign when someone said, "we need to talk."

"You're right," he said. "How about I come over after dinner? We should be finished by seven. Three of the four of us like to eat early."

She laughed at that, and he relaxed. Regardless of whatever issue she wanted to discuss, if she could laugh, it couldn't be terrible.

"Aw, you're outnumbered. How cute."

"Thanks."

"Come over whenever you're finished. And Jared?"

"Yeah?"

"It's not that I don't want to see your parents or Becca..."

"I know. It's okay. I'll see you later."

He hung up the phone and brought Becca downstairs, fixing her breakfast on autopilot as he thought about Caroline. What did she want to discuss? It was probably because he called her his girlfriend, and he cursed to himself. He never should have let that slip.

"Good morning!" His mother entered, smiled at Becca, and startled him out of his reverie. "You look pensive," she said.

"I've got a lot on my mind," he said.

"Want to talk about any of it?"

Did he? He'd stewed about things the entire time he was here, afraid to burden his parents with his problems when they had such a serious one of their own. But they'd both looked happier the longer he was here. Maybe it was time to talk.

"Yeah, I do."

His mom's expression relaxed. "Good. I hoped you'd say that."

He frowned as he poured coffee for the two of them. "Really?"

"You've had a lot on your mind, and your dad and I didn't

want to pressure you, but you're leaving tomorrow, and time is running out."

His parents had always been involved in his brother's and his lives. They'd always discussed things as a family. It didn't surprise him they wanted to talk. What did surprise him was they knew.

"I thought I'd gotten better at hiding my feelings."

She laughed. "Keep working on that. Or don't. Now, what's going on in that head of yours?"

He groaned as he sat with Becca. "So much. Work, life, Becca, Caroline…"

"Well, let's start at the top. How about your job?"

He splayed his hands on the table in front of him. "I haven't felt passionate about it in months. I've been going through the motions without the satisfaction I used to get. My clients' constant texting annoys me. It used to make me feel important. Now I feel like there are no boundaries."

"I've noticed your phone buzzes a lot." His mom gave a wry smile. "Part of that is because you're good at what you do."

"I'm excellent at what I do, and I've made a lot of money. But I'm thirty years old, and I'm not sure what's left for me to do. I mean, more of the same for the next thirty years? I don't know if I want that."

"Well, if it were six months ago, I'd say not to make any major decisions. But now, maybe it's time to think about what you'd like to do if there were no restraints on you. If you could do whatever you wanted, what would it be?"

"I don't know. I love being a lawyer, or at least I thought I did."

"Maybe it's time to see what other opportunities are out there. Talk to some headhunters. Open yourself up to different ideas."

He nodded. "I think I will. I don't want anything getting out to my colleagues or clients."

His dad walked in and joined the conversation. "Headhunters do this for a living. No one talks about who is looking for jobs. If they did, they'd have no business."

His dad made a good point. "I was supposed to hire a nanny for Becca by the time I got home, but I haven't liked any of the candidates."

"Maybe you don't want to," his mom said.

"Regardless of my wants, I can't work and take care of her at the same time."

"Does the service you use have a trial period for the candidates they send to you?"

He nodded.

"So, use the trial period for yourself, too. And add that piece into your job search. Maybe there's something you can do with fewer hours that would allow you to take care of Becca part-time."

He hadn't thought of that. "I should have talked to you two sooner."

His dad grinned at his mom. "I hoped this day would come," he said to her.

"Shh, don't make it too obvious or he'll take back what he said."

Jared looked at the two of them. "You do know I can hear you both, right?"

His parents reached for his hands. Squeezing them, they remained silent for a minute. "It's nice to have you with us, and to know you value our opinions," his mom said. His dad nodded.

"I always have," Jared said. "I just haven't always been great at showing you." He needed to do better. The closeness he'd experienced while here reminded him of that, and he didn't want to lose it when he left.

He looked over at Becca and then at his parents. "You know, I was scared of the responsibility."

"I know," his mom said. "But you're good with her. And she loves you."

"I love her, too." And for the first time, he believed it. He stilled. It's not that he hadn't loved her before, because he had. He'd loved her from the moment she was born. But he'd been the uncle. When the responsibility for her was thrust upon him, fear took over, making him numb. This love washing over him when he looked at her was new, and he relished it.

"So, you'll sign the adoption papers when you get home?"

He nodded. "I never considered not signing them," he said. "I... I think the idea made Noah's loss real." His throat thickened, and he swallowed.

His father gripped his shoulder. "We never thought you'd refuse to sign, and the delay has nothing to do with Becca. I'm glad you're taking care of it, though."

"I still hate that he's gone, but I want to honor his memory by raising Becca. Like, I *want* to."

"You'll make an amazing dad. You already are one," his mom said. "And I'm proud of you."

"Thank you." For the first time, he had an inkling of what Caroline had gone through, stepping up to take care of her mom. Of course, she'd sacrificed way more than he had. She'd put aside all her dreams. He'd only hired a nanny.

"What should we do for our last day together?" his dad asked. "I assume you want to see Caroline and have to pack, but maybe a trip to the merry-go-round at the mall or a walk downtown?"

"I'm going to see her tonight. The merry-go-round at the mall sounds great."

"I'm glad you two have gotten close again," his mom said. "Do you want to invite her for dinner?"

His first thought was to gloss over Caroline, but maybe they could help with her, too. "I invited her, but we have to talk, and it might be awkward over dinner." He refrained from saying "because you're there," but it was obvious. His parents were smart.

His parents glanced at each other, once again doing that wordless communication that baffled Jared. And then, they remained silent.

Jared was a lawyer. He never asked a question whose answer he didn't already know. He was logical. He was an excellent debater. And he often used silence to his advantage.

So why did he want to squirm? Maybe hide under the breakfast table? He hadn't felt this uncomfortable since he forgot to study for his Bar Mitzvah class, and the rabbi pinned him with a look before making him read from the Torah anyway.

His mom started to speak, but his dad put a hand on her thigh, and she stopped.

"What?" he asked.

With a nod to his wife, Jared's dad spoke. "You're a great son, and we are proud of the man you have become. The one time—the only—time, we've ever been ashamed of you, was when you broke up with Caroline."

Jared's body ran hot and cold. His parents were ashamed of him? "Dad—"

His dad held up his hand. "Not because you broke up with her, but how you treated her during the breakup."

His pulse pounded in his ears.

"Her mother was dying, Jared," his mom said. "And you broke up with her, ignored the death and the funeral, though I suggested you be there, and whenever I asked if you'd spoken to Caroline, you said no."

"Mom, I was nineteen." He gripped the edge of the table, his knuckles white.

"I know how old you were. But we raised you to do the right thing, and you didn't. She was all alone. She had to give up her dreams, handle everything by herself, and re-create her life. Even if you weren't together, you could have been there for her. As a friend."

Why did they bring this up now? "She wouldn't have wanted me there. We'd broken up. It would have made her feel bad."

"Did you ask her?"

"No." Did they know how many times he'd gone over this since he'd been home?

"You were young then, and inexperienced with grief. Knowing what you know now, I hope you are careful with her when you talk to her tonight."

Now he was angry. He swallowed, trying to gain control of his emotions. "What makes you sure I'm the one who doesn't want to pursue a relationship?"

"Do you?" his mom asked. "Because Caroline has been through too much for you to toy with her."

"You keep saying that, as if I don't know."

"Harriet, don't—"

"No, David, it's time I said something."

Time she said something? He lost the tenuous control he's struggled with. "Why do you think you have the right to involve yourself in this?" Jared asked. "We are adults. Anything between Caroline and me is just that, between us. I don't need you butting in."

"Jared, watch how you speak to your mother," his dad said.

Becca began to cry, and Jared picked her up. "Shh," he said. "It's okay." He took a deep breath, still angry. He wasn't a child, and they had no right to treat him like one.

"Maybe you don't need us butting in," his mother said, "but when your behavior reflects on us, I have every right to speak up. We did not raise you to treat her the way you did."

"I know that. And I've apologized to her. But we broke up, Mom. What? You'd have me stay with someone I didn't want to be with?" He paced with Becca in his arms.

"Of course not, but did you ever think about why you didn't

want to be with her? Or consider her feelings when you decided to break up? You could have handled it many ways, and instead, you abandoned her when she needed you the most."

"I was nineteen!"

"And she was eighteen."

His shoulder was damp from Becca's tears. "Mom, I know I did a terrible thing, okay? I treated her badly. I've apologized. What more do you want me to do?"

"I want you to treat her with the respect she deserves."

His body trembled with fury. "What do you think I've done since I've been here?"

His mom brushed her hand over Becca's hair. "I want to know that you'll teach Becca to be kind and considerate. To think of others and to put yourself in their shoes."

His head pounded. "Of course I'll teach her that, Mom. Jesus, you treat me like I'm a horrible child. You're being unfair."

"I'm sorry," she said.

He nodded, afraid to say anything else while he was angry. He strode to the window and looked outside. The sun shone in a crisp blue sky. Inside his parents' kitchen, the angry atmosphere oppressed him.

"Forget about the mall, I'll take Becca to the park," he said. "If you'd like to join me, you're welcome to." He didn't look at either parent as he said this. He wanted to go alone, but he wouldn't prevent his parents from spending time with their grandchild on his last day here. If his mom gave any consideration to how much he'd changed, she'd see this as yet another example. But she, and his dad, were stuck in the past.

Jared fumed.

Caroline ran errands that day in town, including stocking up on bagels. Now that Passover was over, she craved carbs. Which was ridiculous, she told herself as she entered the Isaac son's Deli and waited in line. She didn't eat carbs often—they made her morning runs harder. But somehow, being forbidden them for an entire week led to dreams about them. Now she knew how Eve felt in the Garden of Eden.

"Caroline," Aaron said from behind the counter. "What can I get you?"

"A dozen bagels, plain, sesame, and everything, please. Thanks again for coming the other night."

"Sarah and I had a great time. Here you go. Oh, the HVAC guy is here." He untied his apron and came out from behind the counter. "I've got to go deal with him."

Caroline turned to leave and spotted a guy wearing a red Worton's Heating & Cooling T-shirt. She smiled as she passed him.

"You're the same company who services the JCC," she said.

He nodded. "Yep, once a year. I've got clients all over town." He handed her a business card. "Call if you need me."

Caroline pocketed the card and left, Aaron's conversation with the service guy fading into the background. She entered the nail salon, Hard as Nails, needing a gift card for Sarah's birthday. Irma, the owner, greeted her with a smile. In her mid-fifties with rainbow-dyed hair, Irma put her creative mind to good use at the salon, offering themed sales and specials. Today it was Spring Fling. Pastel colors were on sale, flower nail art was half off, and the music was '60s flower-child themed.

"The director of the most successful Matzah Ball in years has entered my nail salon. Ladies, look who's here!"

As a group, both customers and employees turned toward the front of the small boutique salon and cheered, drowning out Joni Mitchell over the speakers. Irma leaned across the glass desk, rainbow hair swinging. "They'd clap, but then they'd ruin their manicures."

Caroline squirmed, a little uncomfortable. "I had a lot of help but thank you. I appreciate all your support."

"Modest, too. They recognize a good person when they

see one," Irma said. "Now, what can I interest you in—gel mani-pedi, nail art, French? You know about our sale, right?"

"It's not for me. I want to buy a gift card for Sarah Abrams's birthday. What does she get?"

"Oh, Sarah, she's a doll. All you girls are. She gets a gel mani-pedi."

"Great, I'll take the gift card to cover that."

Caroline chatted with Irma while the gift card was drawn up, waved to the ladies and left. She was tempted to get her nails done, too, but she'd never been a huge fan of manicures, and she wanted to save her money for her vacation. She was going alone. It's not like Jared was going with her. She stifled the twinge of…something…and continued on her way. She was no longer in debt, but the habit of thinking about luxuries versus necessities hadn't yet disappeared. She wondered if it ever would.

She stopped at the bank and the pharmacy before going home. She had a few hours to herself before Jared showed up. She heated up leftovers for dinner and cleaned the house. After she cleaned the bathrooms and the kitchen, she vacuumed. The activity made her warm, and she turned on the ceiling fan. Someday, she'd get central air conditioning installed, but for now, the ceiling fans and window air conditioners in the summer would have to do.

Air conditioners.

HVAC.

Something tickled her brain, but she wasn't sure what. Leaving the vacuum in the middle of the living room, she opened her laptop and pulled up the budget for the JCC. She scanned the expense column. *HVAC*. There it was. Quarterly inspections.

So why did the service guy in the bagel place say once a year?

Chapter Seventeen

Jared wiped his palms on his thighs before ringing Caroline's doorbell. He was out of sorts, thanks to his parents. Tension still surrounded them all, making what should have been a joyful last day uncomfortable. It was good he and Becca were leaving tomorrow. They all needed space after living together for a month. If only it didn't mean leaving Caroline, too.

He rang the doorbell and waited for her to answer. Long ago, he'd walked into the house, but that familiarity disappeared when they'd broken up, and he didn't think they were there, yet.

Caroline opened the door. "Hi." She sizzled with energy. Her blue eyes were sharp, she bounced as she moved out of the way so he could enter, and her voice carried a lilt to it he hadn't heard in a while.

"What's going on?" He draped his coat over the newel post and followed her into the living room.

"Going on? You said we would talk tonight."

"I know, you seem excited about something. I'd love to think it's me, but…"

Caroline smiled. "I think I have an idea about the JCC budget, but I have to look into it further."

"That's great! What did you find?"

She bit her lip. "I don't want to say anything until I know for certain that I'm right. Besides, we've got a limited amount of time to talk, and I don't want to waste it."

A twinge of pain formed behind his right eye. He could already feel her pull away. Before, she'd shared all the details of the budget shortage with him. But now she wanted to wait? Swallowing his hurt, he sat on the sofa, leaving space for her to sit next to him.

She sat on the chair on the other side of the coffee table. That wasn't a good sign. The energy emanating from her seemed to move into her hands, because she fiddled with her fingers, clasping and unclasping them, without making eye contact. He waited.

"Are you all packed?" she asked.

He nodded. "For the most part. A few last-minute items to add tomorrow morning."

"What time is your flight?"

"Eleven."

"That's good. You don't have to leave at the crack of dawn, and you'll get home at a reasonable hour."

"I'll call you when we land. Maybe by then you'll be able to fill me in on the budget."

She stilled. "I don't know if that's a good idea."

With a frown, he leaned forward, elbows on his knees. "Why not?"

"I want to know you landed safely. Maybe shoot me a text, but I'm not sure talking on the phone is such a good idea."

"Why not?"

She exhaled a sigh that sounded like it came from her toes. "Because we aren't a couple and it'll only make things harder."

"What things?"

She shrugged. "Everything."

"Caroline, how about you say what's on your mind?"

She brushed her hands against her thighs. "I've thought a lot about us, about you returning to LA, and about me staying here. It's been fun doing things together, but I think it's better if we make a clean break. You'll think of me and shoot me a text, and I'll do the same. But I don't think anything else is realistic."

His heart thudded. "What? Why? I thought we were close."

"We were a long time ago. But our lives are different, more so now. And thinking we're going to be anything other than old friends is postponing the inevitable. It's not good for either of us."

"We're great together," he said. "And I think you know that. You're right, our lives are different now than they were, thank goodness. We were teenagers. We're adults now. And I thought we were partners this time around. I helped you with your fundraising. You helped me with Becca."

She snorted. "You've reduced our relationship to a traditional and stereotypical set of roles right there."

He held his arms out to the side. "That's not what I meant, and you know it. We have more responsibility now and—"

"I've always had more responsibility, Jared, and I want less, not more. You never understood my responsibility then. And now? I can't figure out if you want to be with me because of who I am or because you've got all this responsibility thrown at you and you're afraid to do it alone."

He reared back as if she'd slapped him. For a moment, she looked as surprised as he was, as if maybe she hadn't meant to say it, but she pressed her lips together and remained quiet.

So, she *did* mean it.

Her words stung.

"I can't believe you said that." His voice was low and his tone deliberate. But inside, every muscle trembled in anger. "I've been supportive of you this entire time. Do you think I have some ulterior motive? Why can't anyone believe I've changed?"

"It's not that I don't believe you've changed. I know you have. I've seen it. It's that I've changed, too, Jared. I'm free now, not only to go where I want to go but to evaluate what I want. And I don't want what you do."

"How do you know?"

"Because I saw you with your clients, Jared. I saw how you fit into their world. I don't want that world."

"Just because I know how to deal with my clients, doesn't mean that's my world, Caroline. And who said I'd force you into that world?"

"You're good at what you do, and your talent? It shone from your eyes when you talked to Mila and everyone. I admire that about you. I'd never stop you from doing what you love and what you're good at. But I'm now getting the chance to figure out where I want to be, and what I'm good at. I have no ties, nothing to limit me. And I want to take advantage of that."

"I want you to do that, too." He got up and strode toward Caroline. "I don't want to hold you back from what you love, either."

She rose. "And that's why we can't be together, Jared. We're too different. We don't want the same things. And putting added pressure on each other to mold to what we think the other one wants or needs isn't fair."

He gripped his hair. "I can't believe this."

"Please, Jared, I don't want to fight with you. I want us to part on good terms."

"Good terms? You think we can be on good terms after this?"

"I hope so." She gripped his upper arms and stared at him.

He wanted to look away as much as he wanted to kiss her silly, so she'd change her mind. He couldn't do either, and his anger intensified.

"You're delusional," he said.

She retreated a step, and the space between them crackled. "Maybe I am. I thought we could part as friends, that we meant enough to each other to understand the other person's point of view. But I guess I was wrong. Because when it comes right down to it, Jared, you're too selfish to understand anyone else's point of view."

"That's it. I'm done." He turned away from her. "If I'd known how little you think of me, I wouldn't have wasted my time. You're wrong, though. And maybe someday, you'll recognize it."

He strode to the door, needing to leave before his anger erupted, and he said something he'd regret. Before he left, he turned once more to her. Her face was pale, her eyes flinty, and her hands were clenched at her sides. She looked lost in the small living room. Still, a small part of him wanted to take her in his arms and pretend this argument had never happened.

"I wish you luck," he said, and returned to his car.

The moon was bright, and the streets were deserted. It was nine at night, and he didn't want to return home yet. He drove to a nearby park, turned off his car, and got out. Leaning against the hood, he inhaled the crisp spring air with a trace of the warmer weather to come. This time tomorrow, he'd be on the West Coast. He'd return to his old life, but with a new perspective. He was angry at his parents and Caroline, none of whom could see the new man he tried to become. If the people he cared about most couldn't see it, what hope did he have?

He wished Noah were here to help him figure out where he'd gone wrong. He blinked away the moisture that formed and tried to clear his mind before he returned to his parents' house. Maybe that was the problem. Home was great but brought out a lot of unresolved issues. And while there was a path to figure out his life, it wasn't yet clear which way to go. He needed to return to his apartment and take care of everything he'd avoided for so long. And then, maybe he could show his parents and Caroline why they were wrong.

Not that Caroline cared.

Caroline shut the door behind Jared, her entire body aching. The one thing she'd vowed—to never get left behind again—had happened. If they were to end things, she'd wanted to be the one to leave. Her head pounded. She'd tried to explain to Jared why they couldn't be together, and instead of understanding, he'd lashed out, leaving her once again to pick up the pieces.

The walls around her closed in and she gasped for air. Just like when her mom died and when Jared left her the first time, she was helpless. All she wanted to do was curl up in a ball. Her throat closed. But as swiftly as the grief descended, rage replaced it, sharpening the pain in her chest from dull to piercing.

Dammit. She didn't want to cry over him again, lose countless nights of sleep thinking about what could have been, or face the fog that suffocated her last time. She wasn't the same young girl as she'd been then. She was strong and independent, like she'd striven to be for the last ten years.

She took deep breaths, willing herself to look past the immediate sadness and regret and focus on the bigger picture. There was strength in solitude, in not settling for the wrong relationship. As much as Jared had changed, the two of them couldn't be together. Not with his job and her life. And asking either of them to sacrifice wasn't fair.

Tears leaked as she reminded herself that she was smart and capable. She'd stepped in and pulled off a successful fundraiser. Images of Jared's eagerness to assist her with whatever she needed, his pride in her, forced their way in, but she shook her head. She couldn't go there. It was time to wall off her personal life and focus instead on her professional life. She would figure out what happened to the budget, and when she did, her career would be secure.

And if she needed something to look forward to, to dissolve the bleakness of her future, her vacation was fast approaching. The time would pass. Her dream trip would give her the opportunity to see things she'd never seen, do things she'd never done, and meet people she didn't know. She could do this. Alone.

Except when she pushed away from the door, all her sadness returned. Her pulse pounded in her ears, her hands shook, and her breath came in gasps. She couldn't do this alone, and with her maturity came the knowledge she didn't have to. Grabbing her phone, she texted Sarah.

Help, I need you.

She curled on the bottom step and waited for her friend to arrive. When the doorbell rang, she jumped. Embarrassment flooded through her.

"Caroline, are you in there?" Sarah pounded on the door.

Caroline shook herself, fear of waking her neighbors supplanting her own embarrassment. She opened the door.

"Honey, what's wrong?"

Despite her best intentions, she burst into tears. She hated people like her. But she couldn't stop. Sarah grabbed her and held on, and her tears subsided.

"God, I hate weepy people," she said in between hiccups.

"I won't tell anyone." Sarah handed her a tissue and walked her into the kitchen. "Want me to heat up a pot of tea?"

Caroline nodded and sat at the table while Sarah heated water and rummaged in the weathered cabinets for tea bags, mugs, and honey. She shredded her tissue into a pile in front of her, unsure what to do or say. It was one thing to know she needed her friend. It was a different thing to talk about her relationship with Jared. When the whistle blew, Sarah fixed their tea, handed her a cup, and sat at the table with her.

"Now, tell me what happened."

"Jared walked out. Again." Staring at the table, she forced her voice not to shake. When she thought she could remain steady, she relayed what happened, how she'd felt, and what she'd tried to make him understand. "And in the end, he left me."

Sarah grasped her arm. "No, he didn't. You ended things by telling him why you couldn't be together. He didn't like it, and he responded in a different way than you hoped, but this is not abandonment."

"Then, why does it feel that way?"

"Maybe because deep down you hoped he'd say he'd change and stay with you?"

Caroline gave a watery nod. "Yeah, I did."

Sarah nodded.

"How stupid does that make me?" She squeezed the shredded tissues into a ball. But like her heart, the tears couldn't be mended.

"Why do you think you're stupid?"

"Because people don't change."

"But Jared did. You said he's changed from what he was as a teenager."

She had. He was different in many ways. "Just maybe not enough."

"Maybe not. But that doesn't make *you* stupid."

Caroline sighed. "I guess not. I wish he'd wanted to stay." *With me.*

"Why?"

"I don't know. That's my problem. We're not right for each other, but when he swept out the door, I panicked." No matter how independent she was, all she wanted was to call out to him and ask him not to leave her.

"Maybe you care for him more than you thought."

You love him. "I can't."

"Why not?"

"Like I said earlier, we're too different." *You still love him.*

"Being different doesn't stop you from caring about him."

Caroline glared at her friend. "Are you trying to help me?"

Sarah reached for Caroline's hand and squeezed it. "I'm trying to explain that analyzing this rationally won't help you. Instead, accept you care for him, know you're the one who stood strong, and don't feel guilty about anything. And know that I'm here for you, no matter what."

"Thank you. I love that you are."

Sarah finished her tea. "Are you okay, now? I can stay over if you'd like."

Caroline took a shaky breath, despite her desire to sweep her friend upstairs with her. "That's not necessary. I'll push forward. I'll get up and run early tomorrow, which will help. It always does. And I think I'm close to figuring out the problem with the budget."

Sarah's mouth widened. "Can you tell me?"

"Let me check on something tomorrow before I say anything. Because if I'm right, this is big."

"Big, how?"

Caroline met Sarah's gaze. "Big." Her voice was soft.

Sarah squeezed her hands around her mug. "I hate the idea of a 'big' problem, even if I don't know what that means. But if it had to happen, I guess the timing is fortunate, so it keeps you occupied."

Occupied. How long until the things she did excited her again, rather than kept her busy? Caroline shrugged. "I wish there was something else—anything else—to occupy my time. And I'm not sure anyone else will find a bright side to this."

Sarah's face whitened. "Oh boy. Listen, I trust you, but I have to remind you to make sure you have done everything you can to avoid an error. If your 'big' is what I suspect it means, you need to tread carefully. And again, if you need to run something by me, I promise to be discreet. I'd rather help you verify than have you get into trouble with a mistake."

"I appreciate it. And I will let you know. I don't want to make a mistake, either."

* * *

Jared buckled Becca into her car seat on the plane, noticing how much easier of a time he had with her. He'd needed the flight attendant to help him on the plane ride east. This time, he'd managed on his own before the flight finished boarding. He scrolled through the kid videos until he found one appropriate for a toddler and turned it on once the plane took off. For the first hour of the flight, he scrolled through his emails on autopilot, organizing them for when he returned to the office the next day, deleting junk, and putting together a to-do list. And he finalized the trial nanny.

For the rest of the flight, as he entertained Becca, he thought about his parents and Caroline. He'd screwed up big-time and let his anger get the better of him. His parents' interference pissed him off. Even now, he objected to it. But he shouldn't have yelled at them the way he had. It was wrong, and it made the last hours of his visit tense and uncomfortable. He'd have to apologize when he landed.

As for Caroline? He'd been blindsided. Rage washed over him every time he thought about their conversation. How could she have missed how much he'd changed? He wasn't the same person any longer. For that matter, neither was she. But instead of giving him the benefit of the doubt, she'd insisted they weren't right for each other. He had no idea how to change her mind. He banged his head against the back of his seat.

"Bang, bang, Dada." Becca imitated him in her car seat.

He laughed, though he didn't find anything funny. "That's right, Becs." When she did it again, though, he frowned. "No more, Becs, you'll hurt yourself. Ouch." He patted the back of his head.

"Ouch." She blew him a kiss, and he blew one back.

"She's adorable." The flight attendant handed him two bags of pretzels. "How old is she?"

"Two," Jared said. "And thanks."

The man continued down the aisle.

After the plane landed, Jared collected their luggage and pushed the stroller to his car. He wished Caroline was with him. Had she ever been to California? He loaded the bags into the car, strapped Becca into her seat—he was a pro at this—and drove the forty minutes to his apartment, all the while trying to imagine what Caroline would think. Would the traffic horrify her? What would she think of the ocean and the palm trees? They were one of the few green things in LA, and the contrast between here and home jarred him. Just like returning to this old life, the life he was determined to fix.

He dialed his parents as he pulled into the parking garage.

"I'm home, and I'm sorry I left the way I did," he said when his mom answered the phone.

"I'm sorry we interfered," she said. "It's only because we love you."

"I know, and I appreciate it."

"Good flight?"

"Uneventful."

"Those are the best kind. Love you!"

He hung up the phone, still dissatisfied. If only solving things with Caroline was this easy. Making his way into his apartment, he unloaded from the trip. Becca ran to the door and yelled, "Outside!" But this wasn't like at his parents' home, where they could hang out in the yard and play. And Jared didn't have time to trek to the playground right now. Between all the traveling, the time change, and normal toddler behavior, Becca was cranky. When the doorbell rang, he groaned with relief.

"Hi, Susan? I'm Jared and this is Becca."

The new nanny shook his hand, then tried to entertain Becca as he got to know her. If they got along well this week, he'd hire her.

Becca was clingy to Jared, but Susan handled it well. As a

caregiver, she was fine. But he had a lot more questions this time around.

"How do you handle tantrums?" he asked. "What do you do about mealtimes? What kind of play do you initiate?"

He listened to her answers and nodded. There was nothing wrong with her. Becca would adjust and their routine would return to normal. But still, something was off. Attributing his malaise to weariness from travel, he finalized things with Susan, got Becca ready for bed, and prepped for work the next day.

His mind drifted to evenings with Caroline. God, he missed her. He pulled out his phone and huffed. What was the point of calling her? She'd told him not to. Frustrated, he stuffed his phone in his pocket and went to bed.

The next morning, he let Susan in to get Becca up and dressed and left for his office.

"Welcome back," his administrative assistant said. "I've got a list of items to discuss when you get settled. How was vacation?"

Images of outings with Caroline filtered through his mind. "Thanks, okay, and it was good. Did I miss anything important while I was gone?"

"Brad has a new movie contract he wants you to review, Jennifer and Fran butted heads, but I smoothed things over, and Tom is debating whether to do a commercial. When Howard gets back later, he'll fill you in on the Fran situation."

Howard, his boss and managing partner, was always in the office. "Where is he?"

"His mother's funeral."

Jared reared back. He'd asked if he'd missed anything important. A parent's funeral was important. "How come I wasn't told?"

Marie shrugged. "He kept it quiet. There was no formal announcement."

"And he's coming in today?" He couldn't imagine being in any frame of mind to work. When Noah died, he'd taken a week, and that wasn't enough.

"Later this afternoon."

Jared exhaled. "Give me an hour to get situated, then we can go through your list."

Marie left, and Jared stared off into space. What kind of place was this, and had it always been this way? Although the days around his brother's accident were a blur, he remembered a fruit basket from the firm. They didn't give him a hard time when he took a week off, but they were glad to see him when he returned. And they didn't encourage him to take longer. Kind of like now. No more wasting time.

The rest of the morning passed in a blur as he fielded calls from clients, met with Marie, and reviewed Fran's notes. By the time lunch rolled around, it felt like he hadn't had a vacation. Refusing to eat at his desk, he walked down the block to one of his favorite cafés and ordered a sandwich to go. While he waited, he checked up on the nanny via the nanny cam. Susan and Becca played in the bedroom. Everything looked fine. His heart squeezed. He missed her.

He missed Caroline, too. The sandwich, which tasted good moments ago, lost its flavor as he remembered meals with Caroline, filled with warmth and conversation. Tossing the rest of it into a trash can, he returned to his office, walking slowly to take advantage of the fresh air. Warmer here than at his parents' house, he longed to take the day, grab Becca, and go to the beach. He'd never longed for a day off. He used to work endlessly, never caring to come up for air. But now he had to force himself back to the office.

He met Howard in the elevator on the way up to their floor.

"I was sorry to hear about your mom."

"Thanks. She'd been sick, so it wasn't a surprise. But it's still a blow."

"I'm sure it is."

Howard looked at him. "How was your vacation? I hope we can count on your presence in the office for good now, right? The old Jared is back?"

The old Jared. The one no one, other than Howard, seemed to appreciate.

"I have no vacations scheduled for the foreseeable future."

Howard patted him on the shoulder. "Good, good. There's no one like you who can appease our clients yet keep them in line."

It was one thing to know everyone was expendable. It was another thing for the managing partner of your law firm to tell you that you were not. If he were negotiating for a raise or a title, he'd be thrilled. And maybe he should be, since when he left, he'd hoped to make partner. But as the elevator doors opened and he and Howard parted ways, Jared's shoulders slumped. The weight of the world—at least the LA entertainment world—had been thrust onto him. And he wasn't sure he wanted it.

Chapter Eighteen

Caroline returned to the JCC the day after Jared left. Her emotions rolled through her like a burbling pot of chicken soup, but she was more determined than ever to focus on her career and to put Jared out of her mind. Of course, that was easier said than done. He popped in at the most inconvenient times. Like when she was in the weight room and a man exercised shirtless. It was against the rules, but of course, once she'd seen his chest muscles, rather than tell him to put his shirt on, she compared his muscles to Jared's. Jared's were far superior. She remembered their strength when he held her, how safe and right she felt in his arms, and groaned.

She checked in at the senior center and double-checked attendance for her next low-impact balance class. Jared's mom had signed up. She sighed. Fan-damn-tastic. The woman was a doll, but the last thing she needed was her presence in the class. She returned to her desk and fanned herself. Why was she sweating? Mrs. Leiman wasn't that scary. She looked at the thermostat. Someone had turned up the heat past where it had been set. She readjusted it and paused, her finger poised over the control box.

Heat. Thermostat. HVAC. That's what she wanted to check.

Too preoccupied with Jared, she'd almost forgotten her intentions. Making sure no one was around to see her activity, she logged on to her computer and pulled up the official budget documents. Searching through the expenses, she found the appropriate section, dug deeper, and pulled up the details.

HVAC. There were four payments within one year. But the guy had said he performed routine maintenance once a year.

Frowning, she opened last year's budget. Same thing. In fact, there were four payments per year for HVAC maintenance going back six years. If that discrepancy existed, what others did? She went through the budget again line by line, and looked for similar maintenance or scheduled payments, and made note of them.

She was about to close out and get ready for her next class when Miriam Schwartz from Donor Relations came over.

"Hey, Caroline, we want to list the donors from your fundraiser in our next newsletter, and we want to thank them with a personal letter. Do you have time to confirm that I'm not missing anyone?"

"Sure. I'd be glad to." She scanned the list of names. "Wait, these are the ones who gave an extra donation during the evening, right?"

Miriam nodded. "Yeah."

Caroline pulled out her list and compared it to Miriam's. The names matched.

"They're all there," she said. "Do you mind if I see the letter?"

Miriam smiled. "I thought you might want to since your name is on it, too."

Caroline's pulse increased. "Then, I definitely want to see it." She read the letter, nodding as she finished. "It's great. I like the wording. Are we not listing the exact amount of their donation?"

"We will in their end-of-year tax letter. But this is a thank-you letter."

"Their donations are entered into the computer, though, right?" Caroline said.

"Here, let me show you." Miriam leaned over Caroline's shoulder and clicked her way into the Donors file. "See, names, amounts, dates, function."

"Gotcha." She frowned. "Wait, I thought Mila gave $7200."

"How would you remember that?" Miriam asked.

"I remember I thought it was a weird number, but then realized it was a multiple of the lucky number eighteen."

"Hmm." She looked at the list. "Someone must have made a typo." She made a note. "Don't worry, I'll fix it. Great catch."

Caroline bit her lip. Was it an innocent error, or was Miriam involved, too? And was Mila's the only donation affected? Doubts filled her. She kept her thoughts to herself, though, and waved to Miriam as she returned to her office. Now that she possessed a clearer picture of what was happening, she needed to figure out the next steps. And that meant figuring out who to trust. Her chest tightened as she thought of Jared. She missed the time they'd spent together. With a sigh, she picked up her phone and called Sarah.

"I need to talk to you tonight."

"Sure. Want me to stop by your house?"

That was the best place to have a confidential discussion. "Yeah, thanks."

"No problem, see you then."

For the rest of the day, in between her exercise classes and senior programming, Caroline copied as many examples of problems as she could onto a flash drive. Every time she downloaded a file, she was convinced someone—anyone—would see her and accuse her of something awful. Her heart pounded in her chest. It was ridiculous. She wasn't doing anything she wasn't supposed to do. She had access to all these files. And she often copied a file to take home with her. Of course, those files were exercise information, or programs she had developed. Not numbers. And not evidence of a potential crime. It's nerves, she told herself.

By the time she left, she was wound tighter than the leather tefillin straps Orthodox men wrapped around their arms when they prayed. She arrived at home about a minute before Sarah did.

"I'm glad you're here." She hugged her friend before she let her inside her house.

"Oh no, is this about Jared? Are you okay? I told Aaron not to expect me home for a while, but—"

Regret enfolded her. "No, it's not about him. In fact, for a few hours, he didn't cross my mind."

"Until I brought him up." Sarah covered her face. "Sorry."

Caroline squared her shoulders. "Right now, I have to focus on the budget. I think I figured out what's going on, but I need your help to determine what I do next."

For the next twenty minutes, she explained her run-in with the HVAC repairman and her conversation with Miriam about the large donations from the fundraiser. Then she pulled out her flash drive and showed Sarah the files.

Sarah scraped the chair legs against the wood floor as she edged closer to the table. She scrolled through the information Caroline had found, shaking her head as Caroline provided more examples of how the numbers were manipulated.

"You have to take this to the board of directors," Sarah said. "I'll get you the name of someone. Show them what you've found. They'll take the next steps."

"Is it necessary to get them involved?" Caroline chewed a fingernail. "What if I'm wrong?"

"You're not. We all know there's a problem. You've found evidence. If you keep it internal, you run the risk of alerting whoever is doing this, which you don't want to do. And you risk it not being fixed. Plus, they need to know." Sarah turned the laptop toward Caroline.

"But we don't want it getting out to the general public."

Sarah put her hand on Caroline's arm, comforting her. "Trust me. It will be handled discreetly, okay?"

Caroline nodded. "I can't believe I have to do this. I hate this."

"I know. Me too. But you're doing a mitzvah. You're helping us figure out what happened with the money and enabling us to continue to help those who need it. Plus, if someone is breaking the law, you have to stop it."

Caroline stared out the window. Floodlights illuminated her backyard. "I know. I hate that it makes all of us look bad."

"Me too."

Caroline gave her friend a hug. "Thank you for this." She pointed at the computer.

"Let me get home and figure out who you should contact. I'll text you later tonight, okay?"

Caroline nodded and walked Sarah to the door. She paused. "Don't text," she said. "Call me instead."

"Becca!" Jared called as he walked into his apartment. The high ceilings and large glass panels made his voice bounce and echo.

She toddled over to him, arms outstretched. "Dada home, Dada home, Dada home!"

Lifting her over his head, he planted kisses on her belly as she squealed in delight.

"Hey, Susan, how did it go today?" With the number of times he'd checked the nanny cam, he knew no major problems had occurred, but he wanted to hear from her.

She followed Becca out of the playroom, formerly Jared's home office. "She's a doll, and we had great fun. She wasn't thrilled about napping, but we managed. Right, pumpkin?"

"No *punkin*. Becca," the toddler declared.

"That's right, I forgot!" Susan exaggerated her facial features into a look of horror.

Becca giggled, and something inside Jared settled. No matter how off his days were, Becca and the nanny got along. If he had to hire a nanny, at least he was doing something right.

"If you don't need me, I'll go," Susan said. "See you tomorrow. Bye, Becca!"

"Bye-bye!" Becca waved and hugged Jared.

"Bye, Susan."

He carried Becca into his chrome-and-black functional kitchen.

"Down, down now." She squirmed in his arms.

"Okay, Becs, take it easy." He put her down and rummaged through the fridge for dinner. His mind flashed to meals with Caroline. He missed them. Susan had prepared roast chicken, vegetables, and rice. There was something to be said for not having to cook after a long day at the office. He heated everything up and prepared plates for himself and Becca, wishing he could put out a third setting for Caroline.

As they ate, he talked to her about what she did that day and told her what he did, too. It was a ridiculous conversation, since she didn't understand three quarters of what he said, but he refused to pop her in front of the television, and he figured one day she'd learn that meals were for conversations as well as eating.

He remembered mealtime when he grew up with his brother and parents and hoped to emulate the experience with Becca, even if right at this moment, he felt silly. What would Caroline think?

"Gah!" He needed to stop thinking of that woman every second of the day.

"Gah," Becca repeated, and he smiled.

His phone buzzed, but he ignored it. Now that she mimicked everything he said and did, it was important to him not to do anything to disturb family mealtime. When they'd both finished—he finished way faster than she did, but she ate more food than she played with—he cleaned her up, cleared the table, and went into the living room to play for a bit with her until it was time for her to go to bed.

A half hour later, she began to yawn, so he got her ready for bed and read her a book about mice.

"Good night, Becca." He turned out the light and returned to the living room to relax.

Exhaustion made his lids heavy. He checked his phone. Several clients had messaged him. With a sigh, he answered them, spending the next two hours revising wording on contracts. When the words blurred on the screen, he shut down for the evening. It was ten o'clock. He knew where his child was, and as much as he'd love to watch TV, he needed sleep. Still, Caroline haunted his dreams, and his sleep was fitful.

In the morning, he awoke groggy to four more texts, which he ignored until he got to the office, choosing instead to jog with Becca.

"Where have you been?" his boss, Howard, asked.

Jared looked at his watch. It was eight in the morning, the time he always arrived at the office. "I walked in now, why?"

"You didn't answer your texts, and there are several emails waiting for you."

"Nothing is an emergency. I'll get to them as soon as I settle in for the day."

Howard frowned. "You don't act like an attorney who wants to make partner." When Jared remained silent, he continued, "Don't let me get any angry calls from your clients."

He threw his briefcase onto the leather couch in his office, loosened his silk tie, and turned on his computer. While it warmed up, he answered the text messages from his boss. None of his clients were awake yet, and his boss wanted updates on the contract negotiations regarding one client's concert tour and another's movie deal. If he bothered to look in the file, he would see everything he needed, but Howard liked things handed to him on a silver platter.

Jared clenched his jaw. When had he gotten so frustrated? Home.

It had changed his attitude toward life and what was important. If he wanted to keep this job and the lifestyle he led, he had to return to his old work habits.

His parents' advice echoed in his mind. Before he contacted a headhunter, or responded favorably to one, he needed to figure out what he wanted in a job. He pulled out a legal pad and jotted notes.

Work-life balance.

Ha! Like that was possible. He started to cross it out but stopped. If it wasn't on the list, he couldn't hope to approach it. Might as well leave it there. He added a few more items before he shoved the pad in his drawer. He pulled out the folder with the adoption papers in them. There was no need to think or delay. He loved Becca and couldn't imagine his life without her. He grabbed a pen, signed the documents, and mailed them to his attorney. Then, to make sure, he emailed her to let her know they were on the way.

His chest swelled. His love for Becca, something he hadn't been sure of when she'd been thrust upon him, had grown so he couldn't do anything other than adopt her. She called him dada, and while he'd always remember Noah's importance in that role, he valued his own place as well. Being responsible for all parts of her care didn't scare him any longer. If anything, it grounded him. She gave him the base he'd missed. A purpose.

Checking something off his list was good, too. Whoever had recommended making them to get quantifiable satisfaction was brilliant. They might help him figure out his direction, too. Determined, he settled down. When six o'clock rolled around, he pushed away from his desk and gathered his things together, proud he'd managed to avoid thoughts of Caroline for small chunks of time.

"Leaving early?" Howard popped his head in. "I hoped to discuss Brad's contract with you."

Jared straightened. "Can it wait until morning?" They still had plenty of time before the studio needed it. Howard just needed to sign off on it.

"First thing. I'm surprised you're leaving now, though, considering you just had a vacation."

Bile burned in his throat. Was his boss always like this?

"My nanny's new, and I want to see Becca before she goes to bed."

With a nod, Howard left. Jared fumed as he walked to the elevator. He'd put in long hours since day one, trying to succeed and rise in the law firm. As a single guy without any competing commitments, it wasn't difficult. When Becca first came to him, he'd still put in long hours, determined to show he was committed to his job. But now? Something had changed. The doors of the elevator closed, but not before he read the names of the partners on the firm's directory. They were all men. Was it a coincidence? Suddenly he had another thing to consider.

Caroline went for a jog the next morning before the sun came up. Between missing Jared and worrying about work, she'd gotten little sleep. Sarah called her late last night with the contact information of a board member, and Caroline planned to talk to her this morning before she left for the JCC. This was not the kind of conversation she wanted to have on-site. Right now, in the peaceful time before the sun rose, she formulated her talking points. No matter how receptive Sarah promised Audrey would be, no one wanted to get a call from a stranger informing them that someone at the JCC was cooking the books.

The sky faded from coal gray to dove as Caroline approached the high school track. Memories of early morning workouts flooded through her. She and her teammates had bonded and cheered each other on at meets, but she'd loved the solitary parts as well, relying on her own speed to reach the end. Shattering records was a huge confidence boost. As she circled the track, the remembered cheers of fans in the bleachers filled her ears. Jared had watched her compete. Why did he still consume her thoughts?

She missed his silent support, the glow in his eyes when he smiled at her, his touch. She'd begun to depend on him as a sounding board, as a partner. And for a short period of time, she'd allowed herself to consider a future with him. Her heart ached as the dream slipped away from her. She missed his smell, the sound of his voice, the feel of his skin beneath her lips. But most of all, she missed the support he gave her, the encouragement, the unwavering confidence he displayed.

What if she couldn't be successful without him? She tried to squash the thought, but it had been on her mind since Jared arranged for Ben Platt to appear at the Matzah Ball. The fundraiser was a huge success, but was it due to her hard work or his guest star? Ugh, she was a successful woman, and regardless of his help, she deserved the pride she felt at the fundraiser's success.

Her feet pounded the synthetic rubber track, and she fell into the rhythm she'd run as a teen. Slower now, but still respectable. She forced herself to concentrate on her planned conversation. Introduction, concerns, methodology, HVAC guy, evidence. That should do it. All she had to do was present the information she'd found, and Audrey would take care of the rest.

She rounded the far end of the track, and the high school came into view. Her breath caught, though she'd seen this building thousands of times. But for some reason, today,

Jared and the building intertwined. Her rhythm faltered, and her lungs constricted. She stopped, bowed at the waist, and gasped.

Dammit, she missed him. How was she supposed to manage this? Running was always a solace to all her problems. If she couldn't outrun them, if thoughts of Jared kept up with her, she wouldn't survive.

So much for independence. She straightened, looked up at the sky, and yelled out her frustration until her throat was sore and her voice hoarse. Then she paced. Soon, she'd be on vacation, living her dream, crossing off bucket-list items, and appreciating her life. That was what she needed to focus on.

Leaving the track, she returned home, showered, and forced herself to prepare for her meeting with Audrey. She entered the Caffeine Drip, cringing at the memories the place held of her first coffee with Jared and Becca. She had to do this. Ordering a latte at the counter, she sat in a corner far away from the table she'd shared with him, faced the door, and waited for Audrey to arrive. Five minutes later, the older woman entered and joined her.

"That looks good." The frosted blonde, middle-aged woman unwrapped a stylish purple scarf from her neck and arranged her olive-green wool coat on the back of her chair. "Let me order myself one, and then we can talk."

Caroline tried not to fidget, keeping her hands still and flat on the folder in front of her. *Introduction, concerns, methodology, HVAC guy, evidence. I can do this.* She repeated the mantra to herself until Audrey returned.

"Now I can concentrate," Audrey said. "Hello!"

Caroline smiled. "Hello. Thank you for agreeing to meet with me. I know you're busy."

"You are, too. And as you said, this is important. So, tell me what's going on."

Caroline took a deep breath. Once she gave this information to Audrey, she couldn't turn back. "I think I've discovered what happened to the money the JCC raised and why there's a budget shortfall."

Audrey leaned forward, and Caroline opened her folder. Step by step, she filled the older woman in on what she'd found, who she'd spoken with, and how she'd come to her conclusion. Audrey nodded along, until Caroline concluded her entire presentation. When she was finished, silence descended.

"Well," Audrey said after a few moments, "I can see why you wanted to meet in person and off-site. You've done an extraordinarily thorough job. Frankly, in addition to your concerns, I have my own about why no one else bothered to investigate this. I mean, please don't take this the wrong way, because I think you're terrific, but someone should have bothered to do this months ago." She sighed.

"I agree. And I appreciate your taking me seriously. I was afraid…"

"Afraid of what?"

"Well, when I first mentioned my concerns to Al in finance, he told me to stay in my lane. Which, now that I know his involvement, I understand, but there was a small part of my brain that wondered if I should do this."

Audrey's expression sharpened. "Do not ever doubt whether you should bring something like this to people's attention. 'Staying in your lane' is a ridiculous thing to say, especially because we are all stronger together than we are apart. If everyone stayed in their lane, life—both personal and professional—would not succeed."

Relief flooded through Caroline.

"Now, I'll go over your information again, and then I'll dig deeper," Audrey stated. "I'll have to get other board members involved. But I'll keep you updated and let you know if we need anything further from you. In the meantime, keep this to yourself, okay?"

Caroline nodded. "I will. And thank you for taking me seriously."

"I'm the board treasurer. I have to take this seriously. Thank *you* for pursuing the problem."

With that, the older woman rose, shrugged into her coat, wrapped her scarf around her neck, and picked up her coffee cup. "I'll call you soon."

As the woman left, Caroline continued to nurse her drink, stared at the businesspeople and young parents who entered and exited, and considered Audrey's response. The idea of being stronger together wasn't something she'd considered before. She'd always valued independence. Her mom had been a big believer of that as a single mother, and intentionally or not, molded her daughter with the same value. But she thought about how she and her mom had been a team. At times it was them against the world, and instead of weak, she'd felt strong when her mom had her back. So, what happened to make her think she had to do everything herself? And was that how she wanted to live the rest of her life? Her watch buzzed. She needed to return before anyone asked where she was, and her clients waited for her to teach their classes.

There was nothing left for her to do until Audrey let her know what happened. And in the meantime, she'd think about what the woman had said. Because the woman was smart, and Caroline didn't want to dismiss her advice. She wasn't sure how much of it to take.

Chapter Nineteen

Caroline wiped her palms on her thighs before she rang the doorbell of the Leiman house Saturday afternoon. Why she was nervous about a cooking lesson was beyond her, but her dreams were filled with utensils taking on a life of their own and chasing her around a kitchen filled with marshmallow fluff.

She didn't like marshmallows.

"Caroline, come on in." Harriet opened her front door wide and pulled her into a hug. "I sent David away for the afternoon so we can cook without interruption."

Caroline followed the older woman into the bright kitchen, those nerves that plagued her moments ago gone.

"Since you liked my brisket so much, I thought I'd walk you through it. You can take it home with you tonight, and it freezes well, too. Plus, it's one of those recipes that can be made at any time of year."

For the next few hours, Harriet instructed Caroline in the finer parts of making a brisket. Despite her nerves, Caroline had no trouble following Harriet's simple, step-by-step instructions.

"Wait until Sarah hears about this," she said as she browned the meat on the stove top.

Harriet watched. "Aaron's mother makes the best brisket anywhere but won't share the recipe with anyone. You might have to give your friend lessons."

"One step at a time," Caroline said. "I don't think I'm ready to give lessons yet."

Harriet put her arm around her. "Honey, you're a natural. Like everything else you've done, you excel. I don't think there's anything you won't succeed at."

Caroline's throat closed at the unexpected praise. "Thank you. I wish I was as sure of myself as you are."

Pausing their conversation to put the brisket in the oven, Harriet asked Caroline to set the timer and patted the seat at the kitchen table. "You have faced more adversity in your short life than most people do in a lifetime. Yet you've stepped up and handled it with grace. I wish..."

Caroline frowned. "What do you wish?"

"I wish my son treated you better when you two were younger. He's a wonderful boy—well, man now—but he's had to grow up a lot."

How was she supposed to answer this? Caroline swallowed. "He was a teenager. As hurt as I was then, I can see he's changed. He's not the same person."

Harriet sighed. "No, he's not. He's matured." She looked up at Caroline. "You must think I'm a terrible mother for complaining about my son. But I've lived with the embarrassment of what he did to you for so long. I needed to say something to you. You deserved much better, and I'm sorry for how he left you."

Grasping the older woman's hands, Caroline squeezed. "You have nothing to apologize for."

They hugged, and when they parted, Harriet wiped her eyes. "Thank you."

Caroline nodded toward the oven. "Thank you for showing me how to make the brisket. I hope it's half as good as yours."

As she left later that afternoon with her sliced brisket apportioned and ready to be frozen, she considered her words of comfort that she'd given to Harriet. Jared had changed. Maybe she needed to change as well.

* * *

Jared scrolled through his emails the next week, organized them into priority and secondary on his to-do list, as well as deleted the junk. He laughed to himself as he contemplated the size of his electronic mailbox. His clients would like to think everything was an emergency. He knew better. Opening an email from a client, he frowned at the tone. The guy was a B-list actor with an A-list delusion and a terrible personality. As much as he wanted to ignore the message, it would be easier in the long run to deal with his ridiculous request now. Ten frustrating minutes later, he hit Send.

"Bastard," He muttered to himself as he continued to scroll through his emails. He was about to delete one from an unknown address, when he paused. It was a headhunter. Figuring it would improve his mood, so he didn't take his frustrations out on his admin or his clients, he opened it.

To: Jared Leiman
Fr: Wooster LLC

We are a legal client talent firm, specializing in entertainment law. We'd like to discuss some employment opportunities we think might fit your unique qualifications. If interested, please contact us by responding to this email. Thank you for your time, and we look forward to hearing from you.

Joel Forten, Director

The email was generic, one that Jared would guarantee was sent out to a mass list. Normally, he'd delete it. He'd have deleted it without reading it, but he'd been in a mood since he'd returned to LA. And having taken his parents' advice and made a list of what he wanted in his professional life, it might be time to explore his options. Responding to this email required the least amount of effort and might spur him on to investigate other options. He pulled out his personal laptop and sent an email response to the headhunter.

He squeezed the laptop. He'd always believed he'd stay here for the foreseeable future. There was room to grow and get ahead, he was handling dream clients—if not based on personality than by caliber—and he'd assumed his professional life would continue down this well-trodden path. Reaching out to make a change was scary. His heart rate quickened. He contemplated every partner and associate who passed his office and wondered if they somehow knew his thoughts. And after another few moments, he sighed with relief. Nothing was different. All he'd done was send an email. People made career moves all the time. Hell, half the people in his office were probably doing the same thing right now. There was nothing to worry about.

A few hours later when he came up for air, he took a break and walked to the nearby coffee shop. It wasn't like the cute one where he'd met Caroline at home. This was a chain with little personality. There was nothing about it that made him want to spend any more time than necessary inside, which was good since he needed to get back to the office. While he waited in line, he wondered how she was before he checked his personal email on his phone in the half-hearted hope she'd sent him a message. Instead, the headhunter had responded. He opened it and read the reply.

To: Jared Leiman
Fr: Wooster LLC

Send me your résumé and let's set up a time to chat on the phone. What's your availability?

Joel Forten, Director

He took his coffee from the barista and checked his calendar. Now that he left a little earlier, or on time, he could have a conversation in the evenings. And it was just a conversation. Hitting Reply before he could change his mind, he suggested a couple of dates and times, attached a copy of his résumé, and returned to his office.

That night, after he spent time with Becca, ate dinner, and put her to bed, he researched the headhunting firm. They were well respected in the industry with a solid track record in entertainment law. He checked his email. Once again, the headhunter responded, and they were scheduled to talk tomorrow evening. He didn't need to check to see if he was free. He didn't have to worry about his boss finding out. And it wasn't a sketchy firm. There was no reason to put it off.

The next day he was fidgety. It had been years since he'd job hunted. His mind was filled with so many what-ifs, he couldn't keep track of them all. He was short with his admin and put a reminder in his phone to send her flowers as an apology later. He had no patience for his clients. And he found silent fault with everything his bosses did, deserved or otherwise. By the time the evening rolled around, and his phone rang, he was ready to forget all about it.

"Hey, Jared, it's Joel. I'm glad we could talk. Let me tell you a little about my firm."

As Jared listened to Joel, his nerves quieted a little. The only way a headhunter could exist was with discretion. And after Joel finished his spiel, Jared decided to give it a try.

"That sounds pretty good, Joel. Let me tell you what I do, and what I'm looking for."

He ran through his wish list—quality clients, manageable hours, positive work environment, room to grow. He talked about Becca, and how important it was for him to be with her. By the time he finished, he was positive the ideal job didn't exist. There was no way anyone would be able to meet all his qualifications. Getting nervous was no longer necessary.

"How do you feel about relocating?" Joel asked.

"I'm an entertainment attorney. You mean like relocate to Santa Barbara?"

Joel laughed. "I have a client in New York. Small, boutique firm. Looking for another attorney. High level. Mid-six-figure salary range. Interested?"

Jared gulped. He'd convinced himself it would be a while before he had to go through with anything. And here was an opportunity right now.

"I don't suppose I can think about it?"

"Well, it's not an on-the-spot job offer. But I can get you an interview easy. And with your client list, they'll want to talk to you. So, if you're at the feeler stage, fine, but if you think you might want it, you should jump on it now."

Jared drummed his fingers on the table. It was now or never. "Let's do it."

"Great. I'll email you when I have information, and I'll keep you in mind for other opportunities as they come up."

Jared hung up the phone and paced in front of his living room windows, hands laced behind his head. He was doing this.

Caroline exited her class with some of the older women, listened to their conversation with half an ear, and planned in her mind the schedule for the rest of her day.

"Bye, Caroline," Ginny said. She was an older woman who'd recently joined the JCC and was enthusiastic about everything.

"Bye, ladies!" She returned to her desk and answered her phone. "Hello?"

"Caro, it's Jess."

"Hey, how are you? Is everything okay?" Her friend had sounded off, though she swore she was fine. Caroline didn't buy it.

"Work stuff. Did you solve your budget problem?"

Caroline looked around to make sure she was alone. "It's being checked out now. I can't talk about it here, though."

A message from her boss shot across her computer screen.

Come see me when you get a chance.

"And now my boss wants to see me, so it's not a good time," she added. "But I'd love to find out about you and your job. I'm worried about you."

"Thanks, that's sweet. I'll be okay. And don't forget to let me know what happens with you. You can't leave me hanging."

"You are meant to be an investigative reporter," Caroline said. "You never let anything go."

"You're my friend. It's my job. We have to look out for each other."

Caroline hung up the phone and thought about Jessica's comment as she jogged upstairs to Doug's office. Friendship was a responsibility; one she'd never thought about before. But that didn't make it less important. It also didn't freak her out. Would a platonic friendship with Jared satisfy her? She barely recognized the thought before her heart cried no, and she had no time to analyze the meaning because she was about to enter Doug's office.

Great.

"Hi, you wanted to see me?"

He nodded. "Close the door, please. Take a seat."

She studied her boss's face. It was more serious than normal, and there were several disposable coffee cups scattered on his desk.

"I need you to put together all your financial information for the Matzah Ball—expense sheets, receipts, donations, etcetera. Anything with a number on it. Print it out, put it in a folder, and give it to me. Keep a copy for yourself. And if anyone on the board asks you for information, give it to them. Be honest and forthright."

"I'd never be anything other than that."

He nodded and exhaled a little, as if he were relieved. "I

know, but I needed to say it. The board is looking into the finances on the suspicion of fraud. You're not being investigated. Don't worry, but they may need you to provide information."

So, Audrey had taken the next step. Relief flooded through her. It was out of her hands. But should she say anything to Doug about her part in alerting the board? Audrey said to keep silent.

"That won't be a problem. I'll get you everything you need by the end of the day."

"Thank you. And Caroline? Don't discuss this with anybody. Keep your head down."

"That's my plan." She returned to her desk and compiled the information for Doug. This time, when she went upstairs, she noticed a silence in the outer bullpen that usually wasn't there. The office was always a friendly, chatty area. But now, everyone was bent over their desks, and no one spoke. Her phone buzzed as she returned downstairs.

You okay? Sarah's text said.

Yes, you?

Yes. Talk tonight?

Definitely.

She hated how they had to be circumspect, though they were innocent. Would the chemistry in the office change? Was anyone else involved? Would everyone be suspicious now that the fraud was identified? A part of her wished she'd minded her own business, but Audrey's words played in her brain. *Stronger together than apart.* When this was all over, she had to thank the woman for her advice. For now, she'd have to plow through and hope for the best.

Chapter Twenty

Jared scanned the headhunter's email in shock the next day. The firm looking for an entertainment lawyer was Fox LLC. As in Larry and Eli Jacobs. What were the odds his old friend's husband was hiring when he needed a job? His jaw dropped in amazement, but then he paused. Would it be awkward if he didn't get the job? Worse, what if he didn't want the job? No, he'd submitted through a headhunter. It wasn't as if he'd asked Eli if his husband would hire him. He'd keep it professional.

He returned his attention to the email, opened tabs to research the firm, jotted questions he wanted to ask, and compiled the information Joel requested. He sent everything to Joel and debated texting Eli. Not if he wanted to keep this professional and avoid any awkwardness that might occur.

What he wanted to do was call Caroline and tell her about it. She'd laugh at the coincidence and, knowing her, would boost his confidence. He missed her, and he had no one to blame for it but himself. He'd ignored her wishes and her concerns by assuming they could continue as is, regardless of where he was. In essence, he'd suggested leaving her hanging. His face heated. What a crappy thing to do.

Hope stirred in his chest. If he got this new job, could he suggest they try again? He was taking a big leap here, thinking about a job he hadn't interviewed for yet, but once his brain got ahold of the idea, it wouldn't let go. Or maybe it was his heart. He didn't know. He thought about how living in New

York would allow him to see her more often, but then his heart sank. Would she think he put his job first, coming to her after his professional life was set? His thoughts circled.

Becca toddled over to him with her rolling pin. She and the new nanny had baked cookies, and for some reason, she liked the rolling pin. It was a child-sized version, and as long as she didn't try to hit anyone or anything with it, it was okay. Weird, but okay.

"Dada, woll." She squatted on the floor, fell onto her tush, and rolled the pin on the rug before she handed it to him.

He joined her, glad for a reprieve, and he rolled it over her leg to make her giggle. She did.

There was nothing better than a toddler's belly laugh. He repeated the motion before he returned it to her. Enthralled with this new activity, she rolled the pin up and down his leg and his arm.

"I am not a cookie," he growled.

"Dada cookie." She nodded.

"You're a cookie." He scooped her up and planted a kiss on her cheek. "And the cookie has to go to sleep."

After getting her ready for bed and reading her a Cookie Monster story, he tucked her into her crib and stood in the doorway as she fell asleep. She'd changed so much in the time they'd been home. If he lived in New York, his parents could see her more easily as well. As it stood now, they had video chats on the weekends, but it wasn't the same.

Before, he'd been overwhelmed with all the changes in his life. He hadn't considered how both his parents and his daughter benefitted from seeing each other. He'd focused on trying to figure out how to be a parent while keeping his life on track and he'd barely noticed the changes in Becca. But now he couldn't help it. Nothing stayed the same for long, and he didn't want his parents to miss out on their only granddaughter.

Though there wasn't enough time for Larry's firm to get

back to Joel, and then for Joel to contact him, he refreshed his email, looking for a response. As expected, there wasn't one. But the prospect of changing jobs—or coming up with an alternate plan—took an unexpected urgency.

Caroline sat in the small break room upstairs two weeks later, her view of the executive suite unobstructed, and watched security and the police escort Al from his office. Audrey moved fast, and while there was still an official investigation to go through, she and the board had found evidence of financial fraud. Al had skimmed for several years. Not only was he fired, but the Federation overhauled its internal structure. Instead of one person in Al's position, there would be two going forward, with an entire committee working with them in the hopes that more oversight would make it harder for someone to steal money.

Donor outreach was contacting everyone and assuring them their donations were safe. Although Al had stolen the money, it would be recovered. While the theft was a PR nightmare, it was fixable. And now that her part was over, she wanted to watch him leave the building.

"Stay in your lane, my ass," she whispered.

Doug stuck his head in the break room. "There you are. Can I see you a minute?"

Her face heated. He hadn't heard her, had he?

"Sure." She followed him downstairs to his office and wondered if he'd been watching too.

"Congratulations," he said before she sat across from his desk.

She paused, halfway between standing and sitting. "For what?"

"Your promotion to assistant programming director in the senior center."

Her hand flew to her chest. "Really?"

He nodded. "It will come with a raise, of course, although the timing may be a little delayed due to the, uh, legal issues upstairs." He pointed toward the ceiling. "But you'll get the promotion and the raise, and it will all be adjusted so you don't lose out on anything."

Her heartbeat fluttered. "I didn't think it was in the budget."

"Which we've now fixed or will as soon as all of that is sorted out. And none of it would have happened without you, so it's a partial thank-you and a partial 'you deserve this.' Okay?"

Warmth spread throughout her body. "More than okay. Thank you."

He rose from his desk and held out his hand. "Congratulations again. Why don't you take the rest of the day off to celebrate?"

She raised an eyebrow. "You wouldn't be trying to get rid of me, would you?"

"Ha! If I've learned anything after this debacle—" he swept his arms out "—it's that you don't give up. Even if I tried to get rid of you, which I'm not, I don't think you'd listen."

She smiled. "True." Caroline turned serious. "I am sorry, though, about all of this."

"Me too. I'll see you tomorrow."

When she was out of the building, she called Sarah. "Meet me at the deli? I've got lots of news."

"Good, because I need answers. See you in ten."

Fifteen minutes later, Caroline and Sarah sat at a corner table in Isaacson's deli. The early morning crowd had left, and the lunchtime crowd hadn't yet arrived. There was a momentary lull, perfect for talking about sensitive subjects. The scent of yeast and garlic permeated the air and made Caroline's stomach rumble. She kept her voice low as she filled Sarah in on what had happened.

"That explains the whispers in my office," Sarah said. "They haven't made any official announcements yet, but people have heard enough to start rumors."

"I'm sure. You should see how many of us found 'reasons' to go upstairs and check things out."

"I'd feel sorry for him if he hadn't done such an awful thing.

Stealing money from an organization that helps others is horrible. Plus it makes us all look bad."

"I know. And with all you did to help combat anti-Semitism in the community, and then this happens."

"Don't forget your fundraising efforts. We've all worked hard, and a few bad apples shouldn't destroy what we've done. Now that he's been caught, well, we'll have some explaining to do, and some revising of our business practices, but I hope we'll be okay."

Caroline took a sip of coffee. "Doug gave me the promotion. I'm the new assistant programming director in the senior center."

Sarah's face broke into a grin. "That's well deserved! I'm thrilled for you, and thrilled they promoted from within."

Caroline exhaled, and the pride she'd been too shocked to express, filled her. "I am too. I didn't think it would happen this fiscal year after the warning Doug gave me. And he said the raise might be delayed, but if I know it's coming, and will be retroactive, I can wait on that piece."

"Don't wait too long, though. They need to pay you what you're worth."

Caroline reached for Sarah's hand and squeezed. "Don't worry. I'm aware of my value. I feel like I'm reaching my goals, you know?"

Sarah nodded. "I do. It's funny, because it wasn't until I moved here that I believed I was meeting the goals that pleased me. In DC, I always thought I was doing good work, but I looked through previous boyfriend's perspective. Now that he and I are no longer together, and Aaron is here, well, I've carved out my own space. Do you know what I mean?"

Caroline nodded. "Do you feel like your accomplishments are separate from him? Like, if he moved somewhere else, would you still be satisfied?" She'd wrestled with this problem since Jared appeared, more now that he was gone.

"Yes. Caro, I know you're afraid of growing dependent on

someone, but when you're with the right person, it's easier to avoid that mistake. Would I feel complete personally? No, because I love that man to pieces. But professionally? Yes. Have you talked to Jared at all?"

Caroline swallowed. The mention of his name still filled her with regret, and longing in the middle of the night. "There's nothing left to say. He left. I stayed. As usual. I miss him more than I would have thought possible, and I wish I could talk to him about all this, but there's no point. No matter how much he's changed—and I recognize he has—he won't change his life and goals for me. And I don't know that it's fair of me to want him to. We're on different trajectories. At least I'm the one who ended it this time."

"I wish there was something I could do. You deserve happiness."

Caroline sighed. "I have a job I love. I made a huge difference in the JCC world. I've got a great future with them. My personal life, well, that needs a lot of improvement. But I've always said I didn't want to give up my dreams because of a man. And if I plan to stay true to that, I have to make sacrifices. At least this time, those sacrifices are on my own terms."

Three weeks later, Jared packed up the last of the items on his desk and fielded one more call from a former client.

"No, Brad, I don't," he said. "Look, Fran will take over for me, and the noncompete clause I signed is ironclad. You're in good hands, I promise."

He nodded a few times, balancing the phone between his cheek and his shoulder and tried not to disconnect the call with his face. "I appreciate it, I do. And hey, if you're ever out East, look me up."

Hanging up, he turned in a slow circle, studying his office for the last time. He'd started as a brand-new lawyer and grown professionally here, earning this office in less than five years, which at the time, was unheard of. But he'd sacrificed a lot to get here. Was it worth it? He hoped so. This next step in his professional journey would determine how much.

He turned off the lights and carried the box of his personal items out. He'd already said his goodbyes to his boss, admin, and friends. There was nothing left to do but to go home to Becca. With a grin, he left.

A week later, the movers arrived. Most of his furniture and belongings were in storage until he found a suitable place to live. He shook his head at Becca's stuff. No matter where they lived, temporary or otherwise, she still needed most of her things. One of the biggest shocks of fatherhood was the amount of stuff one tiny human required. He didn't think he'd ever get used to it, but he looked forward to the adventure.

And what an adventure this would be.

"Are you ready to go see *Saba* and *Safta*?" They'd decided on the Hebrew words for *grandma* and *grandpa*. Becca clapped her hands and ran between the movers yelling, "*Saba, Safta!*"

He grabbed her and raised her into the air, kissed her belly, and turned to the movers. "Sorry about that."

They waved off his concern with a chuckle, while Jared concentrated on doing a better job containing Becca. With the apartment emptied, he took a last look around, locked the door, and drove to the airport. His car had already been shipped east, so he dropped off his rental and boarded the flight to New York. This time around, it was easier, so much so that he thought about traveling on a regular basis with Becca. Where would they go, and how old would she be when they first went somewhere? He'd have to consult his parents. Whether they traveled to Disneyworld or Israel or somewhere he hadn't thought of yet, he suspected his parents would want to join them. And he looked forward to making memories with them.

The closer he got to home, the more his mind filled with thoughts of Caroline. He was afraid of jumping to conclusions. He'd done that last time, even if he hadn't intended to do so.

This time would be different. And to ensure that, he needed to keep his expectations—his hopes and his dreams—under tight control.

When the plane landed, he collected a sleepy Becca and their luggage, hailed a rideshare, and rode to his parents' house, happy to have a home base for as long as he needed. He looked at his watch. Plenty of time to visit with his parents, get settled, and get a good night's sleep. He had a big day tomorrow, and he didn't want anything to mess it up.

"Jared, Becca, you're back!" His mother kissed him, took Becca from him, and swayed while she gave her a hug. His father clapped him on the back and brushed his hand over Becca's hair.

"Sorry about the job," his father said.

Jared shrugged. "I'm not. Not getting an offer at Larry's firm was the best thing to happen to me."

"Really?" his mom asked. "Why?"

"Because it made me realize that my job is not my entire life. Getting ready for the interview with them was the first time I was excited about something in a long time. And when they decided I wasn't right for their firm, I was disappointed. But more than anything, I dreaded having to stay at my firm. So, I looked at my finances and realized I don't have to be miserable. I can afford to come out here, figure out what I want to do, and take my time doing it."

His mother hugged him again. "I'm glad to hear you say that."

"The only thing pressing on my time is tomorrow. You can take care of Becca for me, right?"

She grinned. "You're sure about everything?"

"I am. Finally."

"Good. We've got her."

The next day, Caroline woke up giddy with excitement. Not even her morning jog burned off the energy fizzing through her. Her plane left for Greece in eight hours. Eight hours until her years-long dream was realized. Her suitcase was packed, her itinerary set, and all she had to do was add a few last-minute items. Then wait until her rideshare picked her up in four hours.

Four hours of anticipation.

After getting ready for the day, she opened the photo app on her phone to get ready for the plethora of photos she planned to take. Swiping through, she stopped at one from the botanical garden she'd gone to with Jared, and regret filled her. The only thing that would make this trip better was if he went with her. It wasn't that she wanted company on the trip. She was eager to go alone. But she wanted him. After weeks without him, she'd admitted to herself that she missed him. Missed talking to him about work, dreaming with him about her trip, laughing with him over Becca's antics. Yes, even Becca.

There was no point dwelling on him. Because bottom line, no matter how much she might miss him, they couldn't be together.

Her doorbell rang, and she frowned. She peeked through the peephole and gasped.

Her throat closed. She opened the door. "Jared." Her voice came out as more of a squeak than anything else and she wondered if he noticed.

Her heartbeat sped up and her breath caught in her throat.

"What are you doing here?" she asked.

"I needed to see you."

Needed? That was rich. "I'm leaving for Greece today."

"I know."

He remembered.

His presence overwhelmed her. Not only was he here, but he was close. She stepped away to gain a semblance of balance, but he stepped forward, over the threshold and into her foyer. He sucked all the oxygen from the room, his gaze laser focused on her.

She'd thought about him, and he'd appeared. He hadn't read her mind but having him show up now threw her off-kilter. She didn't know what to do with him, and she hated being caught off guard.

If only he'd leave, but that was too much to hope for. She retreated another step, and he took a step forward. She needed space to think, and he was too close. "Would you like a seat?"

Her manners hid her inner turmoil. She hoped they'd also provide her a chance to breathe.

He walked into her living room, and lowered himself onto her couch, as he'd done many times in the past. But unlike all those times she'd sat next to him, this time, she needed to be as far from him as possible. That left the chair opposite for her.

"I love you," he said.

His words were English, but they made no sense. Love. Right. Not her. She laughed without meaning to, and once she started, she couldn't stop. The hysteria took over. When she calmed, she looked at him, and he was still there. Still looking at her and seemingly unoffended by her reaction.

"Why are you here?" She couldn't acknowledge his declaration of love. It didn't change anything. It kind of made things worse. They clearly had different definitions of the word.

"I'm done running. All I've done is run away when things get tough. I ran from you when you were dealing with your mom—"

"Jared, you were a kid," she said. As much as she didn't want to defend him, didn't want to let him off the hook, she could admit the past was in the past. "I don't think you were running away so much as running toward your future." *I just didn't happen to be the future you wanted.*

"That's a generous way of looking at things," he said. "And maybe you're right. But I was afraid of what you needed from me, and I didn't think I could do it. Same with my parents."

His parents? While she'd dreamed at one time of his declaration of love for her, it didn't include a discussion of his family at the same time. "What are you talking about?"

"They challenged me—my behavior toward you, my ability to be the person others can depend on, and I left. We spent our last day together angry at each other because I wouldn't admit they were right and wouldn't talk it out." He shook his head. "I'm a thirty-year-old man, and I gave my parents the silent treatment."

She didn't want to sympathize, but somehow, she started to warm toward him. "Do we ever act like adults around our parents?" Caroline asked.

"You did. You took care of your mom."

"I didn't have a choice. And there were plenty of times I railed against the injustice of it all. I would have loved to have a hissy fit at the unfairness of it all." And she'd done so many times, always in the privacy of her room, or with her friends if she managed to get away. Never in front of her mom. And still she lived with guilt.

"The important thing is you didn't. It's taken me too long to grow up. I almost lost Becca in the process."

Caroline frowned. Had his parents threatened to sue for custody?

"Do you know how long her adoption papers have sat on my desk, waiting for me to sign them?"

She exhaled. "Jared, being afraid of signing them because it solidifies the death of your brother is different from shirking responsibility."

A stunned look crossed his face. "How am I the last to understand that?"

She shrugged. She'd always understood him, except when it came to his actions with her.

He continued. "I'm tired of being the guy who runs whenever things get tough. I want to be the guy who stays, who others depend on. Who you can depend on."

She paled. "I'm able to stand on my own two feet. I don't

want to have to depend on you or anyone." She clenched her hands together.

He leaned forward. "I admire your independence more than anything," he said. "I'd never take that from you. But *if* you need someone, *I* want to be the one you lean on. I want to support you, cheer you on, and console you. I want us. I want you."

"I don't understand."

"I don't want to lose you. I want us to try again, to go all-in."

His words were nice, but what about what she wanted? Or when his wants changed? She wasn't about to leap. Not yet. "Your job is in LA. I don't want a long-distance relationship, Jared."

"Not anymore, it isn't."

Her pulse pounded in her ears. "What do you mean?" She put out her hand, as if fending him and his plans off simultaneously. "I can't believe you changed jobs and made plans without knowing how I'd feel—"

Jared jumped up and came around to her chair. He knelt at her feet and took her hands in his. "No, wait. That's not it at all. I quit my job because I realized I hate it. Before I get a new one, I wanted you to know that I'm coming out here because I'm choosing you. I'm not going to run, and I'm not asking you to follow me, and I'm not making plans and expecting you to get in line."

He squeezed her hands. The devotion in his gaze was fierce. Her heart pounded.

"I love you, Caroline, and I want to be with you, wherever you want that to be. I'm fortunate that I don't need to work right away. I've got enough saved that I can take my time finding the right job that allows me to have a work-life balance. But I can't take my time with you. I won't, because I don't want to let you get away again. I've thought about it nonstop since I left, and I was wrong. I choose you if you'll have me."

Her vision blurred, and she blinked. She couldn't let him

see her cry. There was so much she wanted to say, and all the words stuck in her throat. "I'm going to Greece today." Her inner voice mocked her, but she was too shocked to say anything else.

"I know, and I think that's wonderful. You'll have an amazing time, and you deserve it. I'll be here when you return, and if you haven't met someone on the trip, I'd like us to try again when you return."

"I—"

He held up a hand to interrupt her. "You don't have to decide now. I know you don't want responsibility, and I know that Becca makes it tough. So, think about it. I don't want to force you into anything, and I don't want to prevent you from your dreams—"

There was a difference between responsibility and obligation, and she'd figured it out. She'd also figured out if she didn't stop him, he would talk forever.

She leaned forward and kissed him on the lips, stifling his conversation. God, she'd missed those lips. They were warm and supple and did funny things to her insides. For a second, he didn't respond, but when he did, he went all-in. Their tongues tangled, their bodies pressed together, and for the first time in weeks, Caroline was happy.

"I love you, too," she said when they parted. "But you've got it all wrong. It's not the responsibility I mind, it's the lack of choice. I love you, and I love Becca. And I love how you've given me the space to make the choice. I choose you, too."

* * * * *